Mary Reese and Deborah Burke, writing under the pen name Deborah Reese, are both grandmothers with Southern roots. Their time is divided between their families, their church activities and community service. They both enjoy reading and historical research. It has always been their dream to write a book which is fun to read, while painlessly teaching history.

They reside in Concord, North Carolina.

In addition to Stephen Burke and the late Buck Reese, we would like to dedicate this book to our extended families.

Deborah Reese

LOW COUNTRY BOIL

AUSTIN MACAULEY PUBLISHERS™

LONDON * CAMBRIDGE * NEW YORK * SHARJAH

Ordering Information
Quantity sales: Special discounts are available on quantity purchases by corporations, associations, and others. For details, contact the publisher at the address below.

Publisher's Cataloging-in-Publication data
Reese, Deborah
Low Country Boil

ISBN 9781638298267 (Paperback)
ISBN 9781638298274 (ePub e-book)

Library of Congress Control Number: 2022919718

www.austinmacauley.com/us

First Published 2023
Austin Macauley Publishers LLC
40 Wall Street,33rd Floor, Suite 3302
New York, NY 10005
USA

mail-usa@austinmacauley.com
+1 (646) 5125767

We acknowledge our Lord and Savior, who makes all things possible.

Chapter 1

"Never again," Annabelle vowed aloud as she stared across the horizon from the deck of a Barque crossing the Atlantic. "I refuse to place my life in the hands of another." In the process of fleeing her past and fearful of an unknown future that awaited, she was oblivious to the beauty of the sunrise glistening off the waves. Instead, she thought it best to contemplate her prospects. Her impending predicament loomed large; there was no denying that. The question to answer – how was she to proceed? Lady Annabelle continued to lean against the ship's railing and allowed her mind to replay her most recent past. It pained to recall how her world had been snatched away, leaving her alone and confused; her life as a pampered debutante ending abruptly, cruelly. How could she ever have imagined that her father's continued gambling would catapult her from the pinnacle of London's elite to an object of pity and rejection? Disgraced, she hid from the world, not believing she would ever recover. But, months passed, and as one discovers, time heals most wounds. As she rose from the ruins of her former life, Annabelle realized that she was indeed fortunate to have this chance to start anew. But she also realized the huge challenges ahead; an unfamiliar country, a family she had not seen since childhood, and a fiancé duly arranged.

A fastidious, well-turned-out gentleman approached her. "There you are, my dear."

Annabelle Gainsborough groaned as once again the ingratiating voice of her father's watchdog invaded her private time and space. Would William Brumley's intrusions never end? She had no choice but to abide his company because her father, the Earl of Trent, hired him to ensure her safety on this long voyage from England. But rest assured, he would not be tolerated once she was settled with her new family.

In tandem, she and Mr. Brumley stared skyward as they were interrupted by a declaration from above. "Land ahoy! Land ahoy!" She looked up to see a young seaman pointing from his perch in the crow's nest.

Finally! She would soon make landfall in the colony of Charleston, South Carolina. She felt ready. Her first and most important life decision clear. She would allow no one to hold sway over her life. Perhaps, because her fate had been cast like a roll of the dice, she trusted no one. When he could no longer cover his losses at the gaming tables, it quickly became apparent that no amount of royal blood could erase the stain of poverty. How uncanny that her father's solution for their insolvent state was for her to be obligated to the son of his old friend, the Duke of Warrenton. She was not totally averse to this opportunity of marriage. After all, she had already turned nineteen. Jonathan Warrenton, the younger son of the Duke of Warrenton, appeared to be a complete dilemma. Annabelle would meet him halfway. She could not blame the young viscount for her recent misfortunes. But she couldn't chance being under the thumb of another man. The closer Annabelle neared Charleston; the more doubts clouded her mind. Would the Warrenton household welcome her with open arms? Did they realize the unpleasantness of her present circumstances? Being an honorable and well-connected family, Albert Warrenton would never consider reneging on a pledge such as his son's betrothal to her. Even so, his complete blessing might not be forthcoming.

Pushing these negative thoughts aside, she promised herself a retreat from any self-pity and vowed to flourish in this new land. After all, if she had survived amid the cruel snubs and distant glances from her former friends, she could handle anything life offered.

"Lady Gainsborough," William Brumley repeated with obvious impatience while dabbing beads of sweat. "We really must ready ourselves to disembark. The ship is to arrive in port within the hour. And I, for one, do not want to spend a moment longer than necessary on this 'slop chest.'"

Brought abruptly into the present, Annabelle looked up, absently nodding in agreement. "Of course, William, if you'll escort me back to my cabin, I'll prepare for our leave-taking immediately." She allowed him to enfold her arm, yet as always, holding her more closely than necessary. Annabelle quickly disengaged when they reached her door. "It shouldn't take me more than a half hour to be ready. I would appreciate it if you could return then."

Bowing, he nodded his assent and left. Annabelle eyed the half-packed trunks, knowing she would soon arrive and take her maiden step on American soil. Excitement bubbled up, as she quickly changed her ensemble. Whom and what would she encounter on this twentieth day of June 1781?

"Oh, mum, you are a sight for sore eyes, you are," said Berthe, Annabelle's cockney maid, who had volunteered to cross the Atlantic with her from England but had been stricken with 'mal de mere' the entire trip. "Blimey, but I'll be glad to be on dry land again. I surely hope we'll be likin' it here in America. It'll be a cold day in hell before I plant my arse back on a ship." Berthe stated emphatically while peeking through the porthole.

Berthe reminisced about being orphaned at a young age. Found starving in a gutter by one of the Gainsborough footmen, she became Annabelle's handmaiden. Together they grew closer, more like sisters, at the Trent country manor. Grateful, she loved Lady Annabelle dearly and was treated as one of the family.

"Well, we're ready to see our new home, Berthe. Now don't make a 'storm in a teacup.' The two of us can weather anything, so don't start your fretting. I have a feeling you're going to be right at home in our new surroundings." She wished to uplift her friend's spirits.

"Like you always say, I can be a mite prickly at times. But I'll try me best to hold me 'sauce-box'." She folded more of the gowns and smaller items in the trunks. "So, do you want me to stay 'ere with our belongings to make sure these clumsy oafs take care of 'em?"

"If you would, please. I'll catch up with you on the docks."

Mr. Brumley's knock was right on time. Annabelle stole one last glance in the mirror to be sure she appeared presentable. She had given up elaborately dressed gowns some time ago, but she was soon to meet the parents of her fiancé and felt she must look the part of privilege. She breathed in deeply and tried to ignore her uneasiness in facing a future that was uncertain. Holding her head high and shoulders rigid, she pushed aside her misgivings and opened the door to allow William Brumley into her stateroom.

If not such a practiced deceiver, her paid chaperone would have been rendered speechless. Annabelle's raven hair rested like a jewel crown atop her head, while a creamy pink satin gown accentuated her curvaceous figure. William's beady eyes remained riveted on her ample breasts, which pressed against the low-cut bodice by a stomacher. His fleshy mouth hung slightly open as he stared at the ancestral medallion that seductively dangled above her cleavage. Slowly his eyes turned downward, to her tiny, corseted waist from which flared a long train of gathered silk, fastened with braids of satin ribbon. Her discomfort with his perusal was evident by the trapped expression displayed in her dark blue eyes.

"You are the picture of perfection," spoke William as he attempted to smile warmly at the innocent face. "It's an honor to be your escort and guide. Shall we?" He extended his arm for her to grasp.

With little enthusiasm, she lightly rested her hand on the older man's thickset arm while opening her parasol to avoid the direct rays of the sun. Her escort's groveling demeanor made her uncomfortable as the two walked around the deck of the ship about to arrive at the Port of Charleston. He pressed too closely, behaving more like a man trying to court her than a companion arranged by her father.

William was mesmerized by her delicate beauty while they strolled about arm in arm. He had taken this assignment knowing he would have plenty of time to subtly influence Annabelle for his own purposes. He had not heard about her father's misfortune and still believed her to be an heiress to an immense fortune. Scheming, he meant to use their acquaintance to increase his assets both in the colonies and back in his homeland. He carefully orchestrated his manner for Annabelle's benefit. When the vessel neared the shoreline in the distance, William slyly pulled her closer as he pointed to the sandy dunes and peninsula ahead.

His inappropriate endearments did not go undetected as Annabelle abruptly slipped away from him. Trying to focus on the shore, she watched the waves lap against the high, grassy embankments, and the sea gulls dip into the breakers.

"The shoreline is beautiful; look at all the colors," Annabelle said with wonder as she viewed the tall pine trees swaying over the pink and lavender crape myrtles and oleanders in bloom. The sun glistened off the rolling waves while the vessel rounded Sullivan Island toward the harbor. Her gaze was interrupted by the shouts and orders of the crewmen behind her, as she turned to see the yards of white sails being dropped and furled. The mainmast stood naked against the lengthy hull of the four-mast vessel. Annabelle had not given much attention to the ten guns mounted on each side, until the boom of the four small cannons on the spar deck signaled their entry near the junction of the Ashley and Cooper Rivers.

"I know it seems like Charleston has more flowers and wildlife than all of England, but its outer beauty is sometimes deceiving," Brumley said in distaste. "Snakes, alligators, and other vermin lie just beneath the surface." He loathed this low country that bred infinite insects and reptiles, not to mention the suffocating humidity.

"You must admit, it is a sight to behold," she insisted, although she was beginning to feel the oppressive heat in her elaborate ensemble. William's overbearing presence wasn't helping matters.

"This time of year, the foliage is in full bloom, so I hope that you'll allow me to give you a private tour." He cupped her hands against his lips.

She abruptly pulled her hands from his grasp. "That will not be necessary. I'm afraid my time is already spoken for." She was repulsed by the feel of his wet lips on her palm. Quickly changing the subject, Annabelle turned toward the harbor and asked. "Are those church bells I hear chiming in the distance?"

"Yes, those are the bells of St. Michael's Church on the square. The ringer is signaling our arrival as well as welcoming us."

While waiting her turn to disembark, Annabelle scanned the approaching passengers on deck for a glimpse of a seafaring traveler named George Spencer, but by the time the vessel was anchored, she realized her disappointment. This mysterious passenger had piqued her interest on their many encounters on board. He captivated her with his tales of adventure and his dry sense of humor. His handsome face with the crooked smile would not be easy to forget, nor his sun-streaked hair and clear blue eyes. Although obviously not part of the peerage, she still hoped to see him again. How and where she had not a clue, but his effect on her could not be denied.

Just thinking about George brought Annabelle back to the first time they met. She still felt somewhat guilty for being so captivated by this stranger. Berthe had been desperately ill in the stateroom, which forced Annabelle above deck before she too became seasick. She looked forward to the endless blue ocean and its spraying mist. Coming toward her appeared an appealing young man with an engaging grin. Her heart pounded when he closed the gap between them. His mellow voice seemed to draw her in. Introducing himself, this unassuming young man asked her name and destination. After Annabelle revealed herself, she noticed a fleeting look of shock just before he smiled, instantly covering his awkwardness. Perhaps, humble beginnings made him uncomfortable with her title. She shrugged, giving his reaction no thought. At first, she felt self-conscious and reticent, yet at the same time very much alive. Their conversation flowed easily while they strolled the length of the ship. After that initial encounter, she made her daily walk a habit.

Annabelle would never have guessed that George Spencer had already disembarked onto a small vessel that waited for him over the side of the larger ship. His Patriot friends rowed him to a hidden inlet where he would not be seen. In truth, his name was not George; it was Viscount Jonathan Spencer Warrenton. He had many aliases and disguises which he used to secret his way from place to place in the British occupied territory of South Carolina.

What a coincidence that the lovely young lady he met from London turned out to be Annabelle Gainsborough. She had come all this way to marry him. But the truth was he had no time for thoughts of marriage – to anyone. Consumed with ridding the American shores of the British, he vowed nothing would stand in his way. However, with Annabelle, he supposed, just for a moment, what it would be like to be carefree with no obstacles nor agendas. He enjoyed their daily walks, looked forward to them even. She did not resemble the spoiled, uppity socialite that he had imagined she would be. But still, he could not trust her with his secrets. What the future held; he did not know.

William Brumley's hands around her waist balanced her when the ship rolled unexpectedly. After righting herself, Annabelle felt suddenly overcome by fatigue. Reluctantly, she allowed William to help her as they finally disembarked and approached other groups of weary travelers. She was apprehensive about meeting Albert and Amelia, the Duke and Countess of Warrenton. What would it be like living with Jonathan's parents and would they accept her?

Chapter 2

"We must hurry, Amelia; we can't allow our son's fiancée to be kept waiting."

Upon hearing the gong of church bells, Albert summoned his staff and carriage drivers for immediate departure to the harbor. His duchess, Amelia, on the other hand felt no urgency. This was, after all, a most inappropriate time for anyone to arrive on their doorstep. The British occupation of Charleston had bled them dry, and she was in no mood to entertain visitors, especially a young woman, expecting to marry her favorite son. But good manners behooved her to join her husband in one of the carriages. Wheeling over the cobblestone streets to the Battery, the Warrentons halted their caravan on a slight knoll overlooking the harbor below. From this vantage point, Albert could see many of the passengers as they gathered their belongings.

It did not take long for the duke to recognize Annabelle from the details in her father's letter. Catching sight of a dapper man escorting a young woman of Annabelle's description, Albert surmised correctly that he had found her. Signaling the driver to proceed, he and the others rode the short distance to the docks. Albert stepped out of his carriage to present himself to Annabelle. "How do you do? It is such a pleasure to meet you, my lady. I pray your journey wasn't too much of a hardship."

"Perhaps a bit, but after the first week, I really quite enjoyed it," Annabelle responded as she noticed that neither Albert nor Amelia was dressed in formal English attire. Already she felt out of place. However, by the way they carried themselves she could tell instantly that they were British nobility. Albert welcomed her warmly. Amelia showed no emotion except eyeing her keenly.

William Brumley made the formal introductions, including Berthe who was waiting by the luggage on the dock. Albert then signaled for the footmen to load one of the carriages with Annabelle's many trunks.

Unabashed, the cockney maid proceeded to give these men a proper dressing down. "Be careful with them trunks; yer not loadin' bloomin' rocks, you know!" She ordered loudly in her fishmonger's voice.

"Hush, His Grace will take care," Annabelle reprimanded, sensing Amelia's nearness. Once again, she noticed her tightened lips and narrowed eyes. The three women climbed into the first carriage while Albert boarded the other that carried their luggage. Fanning themselves in the stuffy confines, Amelia turned to look at Annabelle as she would a scullery maid who had just dropped her bucket. "I am so sorry you had to come all this way for nothing. Your father must have experienced quite a come-down if he felt the need to ship you here at such an inopportune time."

Annabelle regarded her with a look of misunderstanding. "Nothing?" Was this woman casting blame for her father's sins?

"However, Albert is adamant about his friendship with your father, so we will, of course, welcome you with open arms for the time being." Then Amelia leaned forward, and patted Annabelle's folded hands and continued in her most conciliatory voice, "If what you are presently wearing is any indication, I'm sure we can both agree that your wardrobe will need refreshing. Do not worry; I will call my seamstress immediately. I would never allow a guest of our family to become a laughingstock."

Amelia's words cut to the quick. Annabelle felt a resistance rise within, but she remembered her father's advice to be accommodating. She'd sort things out tomorrow.

Annabelle's turned face and continued silence compelled Amelia to soften. "I apologize for speaking so bluntly. I did not mean to offend. But your arrival is ill-timed." Amelia tried to make amends for her sharp tongue. "I realize that you couldn't have known, but we are an occupied city, which is a nice way of saying that we are at war. Everyone is on edge. Jonathan, our younger son, has joined the militia. He has no time for distractions."

Slowly, Annabelle raised her eyes to Amelia. "I am sorry if I have intruded; I would never want to be a burden."

"Now, now, my dear."

"If I had known…"

"Well, you're a 'fish out of water,' so let's just make the best of it, shall we? You must adjust to the circumstances in which you find yourself, even if you don't have two shillings to rub together." She raised an eyebrow while fanning herself.

Before Annabelle knew it, the abrupt halt and whinny of the horses made everyone aware that they arrived at their destination. She peered out the carriage window, not wanting to believe that they were at the Warrenton home already. It seemed like such a short ride from the harbor. She wished she could appreciate how charming the row of townhouses appeared, but all she could reflect upon was Amelia's inhospitable manner. Beautiful patios and breezeways surrounded the two-story brick homes and afforded a perfect view of the bay. The door of the carriage opened, and the coachmen aided the ladies as they stepped down.

When they were not in jeopardy of being overheard, Berthe turned to Annabelle and in a low voice she began, "'Pardon my French,' but this 'addle-pot' needs to 'eat humble pie'!"

"I agree," Annabelle said under her breath, "but..."

"Well, somebody needs to put her in her place," Berthe continued as she toted a small trunk.

"It's not going to be you. So, hush."

"Then when are you going to stand up to her?"

"Not yet, give me time to get my bearings."

Berthe continued muttering under her breath while they walked the short distance to the front door.

"Pray, do be still," Annabelle insisted.

Later that evening, after Annabelle and Berthe had settled in and shared a delicious evening meal with their new family, Albert bid everyone to join him in his small but comfortable parlor. Unaware of Amelia's thoughtless conversation with Annabelle, he thought it best to explain the unfortunate and perilous situation in Charleston. It also afforded him the opportunity to counter the glaring discourtesy of his son's absence.

"Annabelle, I realize your father felt it an absolute priority that you leave London immediately to escape the fallout of his disgrace. But I'm afraid he's landed you in an even more precarious position. You see, on May 12 of last year, Major General Benjamin Lincoln, leader of the Charleston militia, surrendered to Sir Henry Clinton, negotiator for the British." He took a deep breath before continuing. "The result for us who reside here is that the British military have not only stolen our sovereignty but have begun billeting themselves among the populace."

"Could they choose to reside here at your home?" Annabelle asked. "Or do they stay away because you are a titled Englishman?"

"For now, my title may make them pause before they bully their way in here, but it won't last. Sooner or later, the wolf will be at our door." He answered, sounding bitter and angry. "All the people of Charleston must be on guard lest they be considered traitors and executed." He insisted, "So, you must be incredibly careful. They have the right to arrest anyone, on any charge, whether you are guilty or not. You must learn to bite your tongue and be agreeable at all times."

"I had no idea," Annabelle considered. "What is their goal? I thought America was a British colony."

"The British Empire hasn't ruled the colonies since 4 July 1776, when the Declaration of Independence was signed. But the king has decided not to recognize that declaration as law. He will not give up this land without a fight."

"But Your Grace, aren't we British citizens? Shouldn't we be on the side of our king?"

"Officially, we as a family have not taken sides. At this point, I will not raise arms against England, nor will I fight here against my neighbors and friends," The duke answered with anguish. "But this will not be the case if King George stays the course. Every citizen of Charleston is fearful. The soldiers have been unnecessarily rough and harsh. Even women and children do not escape their cruelty."

"Is that why Jonathan's not here? Is he involved in this war against England?" Annabelle asked with deep concern.

"Yes, Annabelle, he is involved. But I can't discuss his whereabouts at this time. Just have faith that he sends his best regards and will welcome your acquaintance when it is safe to do so."

"So, what am I to do?" Annabelle asked.

"You live your life normally. Little by little, you will ascertain the situation here and be able to make your own decision about this blasted occupation. Whether you prefer to side with freedom or tyranny is up to you."

Annabelle rubbed her temples. "How long will this conflict continue?"

"It's been well over a year, and the demands from the king get worse by the day. There is no end in sight, Lady Annabelle, no end in sight."

Chapter 3

Tensions rose steadily in Charleston during this summer of 1781. Many of the citizens openly sided with the British, yet others secretly aligned with the Americans. The British soldiers, at first more a nuisance than a threat, became more unruly, administering harsh punishment for minor infractions and harassing the populace for their own perverse amusement. Slowly, the tides of opinion were changing with sympathy rising swiftly for the American cause.

At times, William Brumley claimed to be a Patriot; but, when necessary, he declared himself a British sympathizer. In truth, he was a crass opportunist looking out for number one. He was not part of the British military but became an asset to their cause by spying on the opposition. He helped Cornwallis's forces ferret out American sympathizers wherever he could expose them. Yet the one man who had eluded him for over six months was the renowned Jonathan Warrenton. This Patriot was known to be an active part of Francis Marion's swamp brigade. As a small colonial militia, they had surprising success routing much larger forces, such as, defeating the Tories at Blue Savannah, Black Mango, and Tear-court Swamp, South Carolina. Cornwallis was fit to be tied, while Colonel Tarleton had shown his anger by using barbaric tactics on and off the battlefield.

After completing his assignment as Annabelle's escort and depositing her with the in-laws, Brumley climbed back into his carriage and gave specific instructions to his coachman. Reclining his weary head against the leather seats, he mulled over his upcoming appointment. The subject at hand being the demise of Jonathan Warrenton. Jealousy coursed through him as this British spy considered all the wealth and privilege that the young viscount was willing to sacrifice for American freedom. No, he didn't understand him at all. For he craved money and power so intensely that he would sell his own mother to acquire what he desired. Presently, he would meet with a captain in the British Army, under the command of the infamous butcher Colonel Banastre Tarleton.

Together, they would finalize their plan to put an end to the Swamp Fox as well as Jonathan Warrenton.

After taking a slight detour around the next corner in Charleston, Brumley's driver halted the coach for him to make a surreptitious departure behind a well-known Tory pub. He wanted no one to recognize him when he went about his dirty business. Stepping onto the street, William preened his neck against the hot June sun while mopping his sweat-coated brow in disdain. He hated this humidity that clung to his skin and left him feeling damp and unkempt. He used his fastidious appearance to create an impression that he was a part of the upper echelon of English society.

Removing the gold-chained pocket watch from his vest, William viewed the dial with satisfaction. As usual, he was precisely on time as he entered the side alley leading to the back door of the Poinsettia Tavern. After one quick rap, the door opened and he was allowed entry by his associate, who led him to a secluded corner table. The adjusted change of light revealed an ideal rendezvous spot concealed by a high-backed booth and easy access to the exit. Only the barmaid had view of the twosome, but with the ales already placed on the table, her services weren't needed again. But with her keen eyes and ear to the wall, she was often able to gather a treasure trove of secrets. Only a privileged few were aware of her Patriot leanings.

William sat across from his collaborator Captain Percy. They regarded each other with some distaste. After all, one was spying on his friends and neighbors and the other an intruder within the Charleston community.

"Well, has that squirrelly bastard shown his face yet?" William demanded to know, wanting the young Viscount Jonathan Warrenton found and dispensed with as soon as possible.

"Hell no, I thought that was why you took an interest in Warrenton's fiancée – to locate his whereabouts. It's your job to find him. It's mine to dispense with him." Captain Percy flashed a cruel smirk as he handed a neatly folded document across the table.

Brumley looked it over carefully. "A warrant for his arrest?" He said in a hushed voice. "How did you get a judge to authorize this, knowing Jonathan's status as a nobleman?"

"I didn't. It's a forgery, and a bloody good one. Who's going to stop us? We're the only ones who know the truth except for Tarleton, of course."

Malevolence emanated from Percy's deep-set sinister eyes. Beneath his polished veneer masqueraded a cruel, vicious man.

"If we can get our hands on that arrogant scum, we can have him hanged before a judge has time to rule on it." William gritted out between clenched teeth and a set jaw.

"Damn right, he'll hang if I have to tie the knot myself!" Percy spoke, seething with fury and veins pulsating at his temples. Percy's anger elevated as he mentally replayed every assignment that Jonathan had thwarted. The young Patriot had not only humiliated him by stealing the stamps needed to implement the Stamp Act, which left Percy red-faced in front of his commanding officer, but had stolen a huge munitions shipment from right under his nose. His hatred consumed him.

Observing Percy's crimson face and neck, William decided he'd change the subject. "I'll maintain a close watch on his family. I've already offered to accompany Lady Annabelle on a tour around Charleston. Hopefully, our friendship will allow me access to the family's comings and goings. Surely, the duke has a way of keeping in touch with his son."

"Is Lady Annabelle the daughter of the Earl of Trent?"

"The same. Her father hired my services to be her escort to Charleston. My hope is that she will unwittingly provide us with young Warrenton's head on a platter."

"That's going to be more difficult than you might think. He's not known as the 'Ghost' for nothing." Percy sneered.

William had had enough. "Until the next time." He stated as he left inconspicuously as he had arrived.

Chapter 4

The next morning, Annabelle had awakened refreshed with more questions than answers. Looking around her surroundings, she found the colonial townhouse lovely and quite different from the ones in London. The salmon pink roof tiles added beauty to the glazed finish which glittered in the sun. She noticed the steep pitch of the roof with several dormers and chimneys at intervals. The eaves were flared out in a bell cast over the thick brick walls. The stucco was composed of burnt oyster shell lime, which contrasted with the wrought-iron balconies on the second-floor windows.

"Oh, there you are. I hope all your trunks and other baggage have been brought directly to your room." Albert's voice pulled Annabelle's gaze as he opened the iron gate to the high garden wall.

"Yes, Your Grace, everything is here and nicely situated. Thank you so much for all your kind consideration."

"My pleasure, Annabelle. Amelia will help familiarize you with the house, then, if you wish, you both can go out on the town."

"Thank you, I'd like that," Annabelle responded just before she blurted hastily, "I need to know more about Jonathan's situation. He is, after all, the reason I'm here. I'm beginning to worry that he may be in danger. I don't understand all this intrigue."

"I know, dear, and I'm sorry." The duke explained as best he could, "Soon you will understand. But for now, you must try to be patient." Albert turned quickly away, abruptly excusing himself.

Annabelle stared after him. She was not at all satisfied with Albert's answer. She needed to know more. Now. *I'll find out one way or another,* she vowed.

After covertly leaving the ship, George, aka Jonathan, found a saddled horse waiting for him. Stuffing his saddle bags with his secret missives, he headed for the Patriot camp located between the Pee Dee and Santee Rivers. Its swampy location remained hidden to outsiders. He checked his back trail often while switching occasionally off course to confuse anyone who might try to follow. As he weaved through the dense forest listening to the blended chirps and croaking frogs, his thoughts returned to Annabelle. He wanted to reconnect with her soon to explain his subterfuge on their voyage. He owed his fiancée that much. Hopefully, she would forgive his necessary act of pretense. Jonathan found her interesting, attractive, and surprisingly fun. Surely, she would give him a second chance after learning the truth. But what if Annabelle was a tool of the king? Then she would consider him a traitor to the Crown. It was possible that she was totally aligned with the Tories. Having spent so much time with William Brumley onboard ship, she could have been influenced and persuaded by his politics. If so, he'd have to find a way to convince her of his position and counter the British.

Yet for now he must stay focused on his mission and the Patriots' cause. He was bringing important news from the French Ministry to George Washington. A courier would be waiting for him as soon as he reached camp to forward his portfolio. When the British forces retook Charleston, in 1781, Francis Marion trained a new Patriot militia. With a shortage of troops to defeat the British, he used the guerilla tactics he had learned from the natives in the French and Indian Wars. The name "Swamp Fox" soon became revered for stealing supply trains and interfering with communications between the British forces.

At sundown, Jonathan rode into the camp amid welcome shouts. It felt like coming home. He reveled at the faces of the finest, bravest men he had ever known. These dedicated Patriots joined this fight from every walk of life and treated each other as equals. No titles allowed. However, Jonathan's two best friends had emerged from aristocratic lineage. Brian Burns, better known as 'Skirt' and son of a Scottish laird, was a burly fellow with red hair and a contagious smile. Patrick 'Whiskey' O'Brien migrated from Dublin. His home in Ireland had been confiscated and deeded to an English Duke by King George. This heinous act fueled a deep hatred for all things English. The lad vowed not to allow this fraud here as well. Jonathan's nickname was 'Smoke,' because of his many disguises and the ability to appear and disappear in the blink of an eye. Because of their titles and notoriety back home, their real

23

names could never be bandied about. The bounties on their heads would prove to be a tempting enticement if anyone knew the truth.

"Where's the Colonel?" Jonathan asked the group surrounding him while he dismounted.

"He's been gone for a couple days. Do you have any news from the Frenchies? Are they willing to help?" An older man inquired as he took Jonathan's horse from him.

"Well, they didn't say no, but they didn't promise anything either." Jonathan looked around. "Where are Skirt and Whiskey?"

"They're leading a raid on a supply train travelling overland to Cornwallis's camp, so hopefully we'll be having a real fine supper this evening, right, boys?"

"I sure hope so," said another. "I am truly tired of scrawny rabbits and slimy frogs."

"That's the price you pay for being a hero, Bubba," one man shouted.

Signaling in advance, a band of Patriots galloped to the center of the camp. One man dangled a small cage stuffed with chickens, while another toted a huge bag of flour. Each rider displayed the spoils of war – coffee, sugar, bacon, and beans.

Bubba smiled from ear to ear, rubbing his stomach with glee. "Looks like you gentlemen kissed the Blarney Stone!"

"We didn't have to fire a shot, to be sure," Whiskey said to the cluster of men surrounding him. "Those 'Radgers' obliged us by putting down their guns but not before 'blathering' among themselves."

"It was 'pure gravy.'" Skirt laughed. "Although a wee bit of force was needed to get them to behave."

"Aye right," added Whiskey, "but then what's a dunk in the creek between friends?"

"I'm glad to see you two haven't changed while I've been gone." Smoke laughed as he embraced his comrades in arms. "The camp looks good. It's almost liked a real town."

"Yeah, we've been building cabins and campfires. The river provides us plenty of clean water. It's starting to feel more like home," Skirt explained. "Food and blankets were all we really needed."

"Luck of the Irish today," added Whiskey as he pointed to 'a rake' of blankets dropped on the ground near the campfire.

"You two must be getting some top-secret info if you were able to find out about a supply caravan on its way to Cornwallis," Jonathan remarked to his two friends.

"I do know a young lady who is a barmaid at the Poinsettia Tavern," Whiskey explained. "There is nothing said in that Tory haven that she does not hear. She is a bonnie lass indeed, for her hatred of the British knows no bounds."

"Tell Smoke what she heard Percy and Brumley gobbing about," Skirt added.

"Oh yeah, it seems that there is a warrant out for your arrest. Not official, of course, but real enough to get you hung. So, you better not show your pretty face anywhere in Charleston. You are being hunted by Tarleton."

"I know that Tarleton is obsessed with capturing the 'Swamp Fox' and his men; that's what he calls us. He doesn't know how to stop us," Jonathan added. "But don't worry about me. I just regret that I can't go on the next raid with you."

"It's going to be a mite tricky one. Our spies multiply daily as the British continue to mistreat the decent people of Charleston," Whiskey explained. "But it's still hard to trust. Smoke, some of our moles have heard your name on Tory lips – you are a big target. Your family may be singled out as a billeting location for troops."

"I know. That's why I must find a way into Charleston. I haven't decided how yet," Smoke answered thoughtfully. "What are your plans?"

"We'll have to take as many mounted raiders as possible. It's a munitions supply train and will be heavily guarded. First, the boys will ride through the woods and swamps of the back country. Our most important weapon is surprise. We'll attack swiftly and remove the guards, then grab our prize and vanish before reinforcements can arrive," Skirt added.

"Sounds like a plan. I wish I could join you, but I've some affairs to put in order that I can procrastinate no longer," Smoke replied. "But now I'm tired and hungry. How about the old man cooking up some 'scran'?"

"Then we'll try out those new blankets. The grounds are going to feel like a feather bed tonight," Whiskey quipped as they all walked toward the campfire with hope on their faces.

Chapter 5

Warm rays through the open shutters stirred Annabelle from her night's slumber. She sat up abruptly. What time was it? Amelia had insisted she be ready at nine o'clock for a tour of Charleston with William Brumley. Overreaching, as usual, Jonathan's mother arranged this entire outing without consulting her.

Yawning and stretching catlike under the covers, Annabelle quickly rolled out of bed and yanked on the bell pull. She was annoyed. The last thing she wanted was to spend a morning with the toadyish Brumley. But what would she accomplish by refusing? Nothing but hurt feelings and animosity. It had only been a week since arriving in the New World, and still, in spite of much effort, she couldn't completely grasp the political intrigue that swirled around her daily. Annabelle found it worrisome that Jonathan still had not made himself available. Even worse, boredom was setting into her routine, and as irksome as William was, she was looking forward to a change of scenery.

"Berthe, hurry! Why on earth did you allow me to oversleep when you knew that I had an appointment with Mr. Brumley?"

"Oi was 'oping he'd get tired of waiting and skedaddle off before yer got up," Berthe stated as she poured the last of the hot water into a basin for her mistress. "He's a smarmy bugger, he is, Mum. I wouldn't turn me back on the likes 'f him. The 'pod-snapper' fair gives me the creeps."

"Everyone gives you the creepy crawlers. By the way, how are you getting along with the staff? You're not being churlish, I hope," scolded Annabelle with a twinkle in her eye. She hoped but was not at all sure that Berthe would somehow fit into the household without an undue amount of fuss.

"Not bloody likely, seein' 'ow nobody knows what the 'ell I'm saying 'alf the time. All we do is smile and play charades with one another." Berthe sashayed with a disgusted look on her face.

Brushing aside Berthe's concerns, Annabelle added, "Well, it sounds as if everyone is being very accommodating. Hurry now and get out my yellow day dress and matching parasol. I must not tarry."

By the time Annabelle was dressed and ready for the carriage ride, Albert and William were waiting in the parlor.

"Oh, there you are, my dear," Albert said warmly, rising when she entered.

"I'm so sorry that I'm late this morning. Apparently, it's taking me longer to acclimate than I anticipated," Annabelle clarified. Forcing a smile, she watched William gallantly gesture a chaste kiss on her extended hand. Inwardly, she cringed. How could she have forgotten his grating and over-solicitous manner?

William beamed with self-satisfaction, sure that he had impressed the young lady with his courtly manners. "You, Annabelle, are worth waiting for. And since I promised your father that I would make certain you are safely situated here; it is my honor to escort you around the sites of Charleston."

Beneath his polished veneer, William was more determined than ever to get his hands on both Annabelle and her sizable dowry. Plotting all the while, he also hoped to entangle her in his scheme to capture Jonathan.

When the doors to the carriage closed, Annabelle felt uneasy, even apprehensive being alone with him. But why? She did not understand the air of danger that surrounded her, since he appeared the perfect gentleman.

While the carriage moved onto the cobblestone streets, William tried his best to impress her. Yet he noticed she remained oblivious to his regard, and silently stared out her window. So, instead of describing the various landmarks they passed, he began to talk incessantly about his lineage and affluence, hoping Lady Annabelle would begin to feel they were equals within the layers of English society.

Instead, Annabelle was appalled at his gaucheness; his voice reminded her of a persistent gnat. She wanted nothing more than to scream with frustration. Blocking the drone of his voice, Annabelle's thoughts returned to her fiancé. Where was he? Was he safe? Did he look forward to meeting her? And what was the danger that plagued his every move?

After crossing Broad Street, William halted the carriage on Main Street to rest the horses under the shade of the cypress trees which lined the thoroughfare.

Stepping down for a brief respite, Annabelle opened her parasol to shield the sun and waited for her escort to return with refreshments. Enjoying her solitude, she strolled to the square, taking notice of the town's gridiron pattern of streets fronting the Cooper River. Overlooking the Battery Wall in the distance were two walled gates, fortified to protect the Colonists from attack. The daytime scenery of the inland waterway with its drawbridge and bustling trade ships was in stark contrast to the peaceful view at night, thought Annabelle. Lost in daydreams, she re-crossed the street on return to the carriage.

Earlier that morning, Jonathan had secluded himself nearby at the Harbor Pub. Its Patriotic leanings were known only to a precious few who used the location for clandestine meetings in the hidden cellar beneath the main taproom.

He needed to find out as much as he could about the warrants for his arrest. So, dressed as an aging farmer and sporting a long beard with unkempt hair, he was unrecognizable for the time being. After learning how intense the search for him appeared to be, he rapidly climbed the secret stairway that led to the owner's private door. Exiting, he looked in every direction to ascertain his best access into the crowd. Suddenly, he froze. Out of the corner of his eye he caught sight of William Brumley's carriage, passing down Main Street. Mistrust instantly pervaded him with the sight of Annabelle seated next to the Tory.

Without thought of his own safety, the young viscount pushed his way through the crowded masses of artisans, vendors, and sailors, until he finally spotted the Brumley crest parked among the other carriages. He obscured his whereabouts in a narrow alley to observe the couple's activity. He watched intently as Annabelle crossed the street alone and looked at the beautiful scenery on the Battery. Then, seemingly unaware of her surroundings, began the walk back to Brumley's carriage. Realizing that she was in no danger, Jonathan turned to leave. Just as he was about to slip away, he heard a loud whinny followed by screeching buggy wheels. Lost in her daydreams, Annabelle was unaware of the carriage careening dangerously toward her.

The driver was desperately trying to rein in the spooked horses amid the loud warning shout.

At the last moment, Annabelle turned at the alarm. Realizing she was about to be run over by a team of horses, she tried to reach safety but tripped and fell to her knees. Raw fear gripped her as she witnessed the horses' hooves rise high above her.

Anticipating the accident about to happen, Jonathan rushed to scoop her up out of harm's way. He barely made it in time.

Astonished with her timely rescue and frightened beyond her imagination, Annabelle could hardly comprehend what had just occurred. All she could remember were a horse and carriage about to descend on her. Not about to let go of her rescuer, she leaned back in his arms to thank him. At first glance, he looked like an older man, a farmer. But there was something so familiar – not the beard or the hair. It was his eyes!

"George? Is it really you?"

Jonathan was taken aback. He hadn't wanted their first encounter to be under these circumstances, and he certainly wasn't ready to reveal his real identity here and now. To explain his situation adequately, the Patriot needed to keep up pretenses for the time being. "I'm only grateful I happened by and realized the looming danger." He looked into her eyes, then kissed her lightly on her forehead. "It's a miracle you're not injured. You sure you're all right?"

"I don't think I'm hurt seriously, perhaps a few bumps and bruises. But George, where on earth did you come from? Out of nowhere, you saved me. I could have been killed."

With his arms around her, Jonathan could feel Annabelle's entire body shaking from the shock. As much as he longed to linger and comfort her, he also knew staying was a risk. So, he gently released her, leaving her by William's carriage before turning away.

Annabelle reached out. "Wait! I'm staying at the Warrenton's townhouse on Tradd Street. There's a small garden shed at the rear of the property. Meet me there tonight. Midnight."

He acknowledged her request with a slight nod, and within seconds had blended into the onlookers and away from her view.

Still trembling, Annabelle inhaled deeply. Relief flowed through her with the reality of encountering George again. Whatever could have possessed her to ask him to meet secretly? It was so very wrong. What had come over her to suggest such a thing? Of course, she mustn't meet him alone tonight. But deep down, she was certain that wild horses couldn't keep her away.

William watched the horrific scene from a safe distance. Standing with him was his old friend and sometime paramour, Miriam Worthington. Together they had caused untold damage to the Patriot cause.

"Dammit, Miriam, I told you to scare her, not murder her on the crowded streets of Charleston." He was furious. Miriam's mess could blow up all his plans.

"I'm sorry. I had no idea my coachman was so inept. But really, what difference does it make? She's just a little nobody."

Brumley gritted his teeth. "She's the daughter of the Earl of Trent and Jonathan Warrenton's fiancée."

"Bloody hell! You should have imparted that information before you asked me to scare the hell out of her." She couldn't believe he'd kept that detail from her.

"That shouldn't have been necessary." He sneered. "I wanted her to require my protection to feel safe. To want me. To need me."

"Again, you should have told me," Miriam insisted.

"Well, let's see if we can salvage anything from this fiasco."

"Lead on."

Once the horses were reined in and settled, William and Miriam rushed to her side. "Oh, my dear, what on earth happened? I should never have left your side. I am so sorry." Her escort's gushiness and false concern became more apparent with every uttered word and overture.

Annabelle shrugged him off. "I'm fine." The look she cast Brumley let him know that his help was too little, too late. She enjoyed watching him flush under her scrutiny.

"You've had quite a fright!" The auburn-haired woman accompanying him exclaimed with a haughty look and insincere tone. "I would never have forgiven myself if my carriage had injured you."

"It was your carriage that nearly ran over me?" Annabelle couldn't believe this women's audacity. "Shouldn't you be instructing your driver on how to avoid injuring more innocent pedestrians?"

Brumley grabbed both Annabelle's hands in remorse. "Forgive me for leaving you alone, even if for only minutes. From now on, I promise I won't let you out of my sight."

Annabelle wasn't buying any of their hapless apologies. Something was amiss with these two, and she wanted none of their fake platitudes. "That will not be necessary. Return me home immediately." Much to her chagrin, this woman insisted that she accompany her and William in his coach.

"Annabelle, I want you to officially meet my good friend, Mrs. Miriam Worthington, the widow of Lord Samuel Worthington. Our families were close neighbors in England. I trust you two will become fast friends."

"I hardly think that we run in the same circles." Normally, Annabelle would never lord her title over others, but her distrust for these two seemed increasingly justified.

Immediately, William tried a different tact. "Perhaps, a light lunch would be in order; just the thing to put the roses back in your cheeks."

"Thank you, no."

Miriam tried changing the subject. She desperately wanted a relationship with this young chit. Annabelle could open many doors to the Warrenton's world and her chance to seek revenge. Oh, how she loathed the duke with every part of her being. "William says you're staying with Albert and Amelia? I have been acquainted with them for quite some time. Upstanding family."

"Yes, I am living with the Duke and Duchess of Warrenton. They are soon to be my in-laws." Annabelle found Miriam's easy use of the Warrenton family's given names gauche. Not wanting to continue this conversation, she kept her answers short and clipped.

Miriam inwardly seethed. With good reason to hate the entire Warrenton family, she felt Albert had mistreated her husband and was insistent that his influence had ruined her husband; socially, politically, but most of all, financially. She would get her revenge, but for now, she would wisely bide her time and continue the charade.

"I just adore Albert and Amelia, and of course, Jonathan, their son." Miriam lied. "I quite consider him a very good friend." She allowed a sly smile to reach her lips as she glanced in Annabelle's direction.

"Somehow, I doubt that." Annabelle answered curtly, then turned to gaze out the coach's window. She remained transfixed until they arrived at her destination.

Chapter 6

Home at last, Annabelle was able to rest in the solitude of her chamber. Until this moment, she hadn't dwelled upon how truly terrified she had been. But now, she could relax and permit the warmth of the sun to quell her fear. While allowing her memories to sort the events of the day, hazy recollections eventually led her to believe there had been conspiracy behind the scenes. But why would anyone want her harmed? She needed answers.

First and foremost: How could a gentle carriage horse suddenly become frenzied when on a quiet street with little traffic? From past carriage outings in London, Annabelle knew it would have taken quite a jolt to rattle a trained team. Thinking back, she had heard no such commotion until... Secondly, how in the world did George Spencer appear out of nowhere and rescue her? It was like a fairy tale come true. He must have been following her; how else would he have exacted the place and time she needed him? And lastly, what would have happened if she was not rescued? She shivered at an image of being trampled to death. Annabelle had much to consider and clarify. But, although uncertain of the chain of events, there was one undeniable truth – she must keep a keen eye on both Brumley and Miriam Worthington. Those two most certainly contributed to today's near tragedy; yet again, why? What did they have to gain by her death?

Hours passed, but Annabelle dared not fall asleep and miss a moment of her star-crossed evening with George Spencer. Astutely aware of the recklessness in meeting him alone, she brushed aside any notion of consequence. For once in her life, she was throwing caution to the wind. The hallway clock chimed at eleven o'clock. A stillness filled the bedroom chambers down the hall. Annabelle's excitement rose with each passing moment while she watched Berthe nearby.

Berthe pampered and tucked her mistress into bed. "You had quite a scare today. The gossip downstairs thinks it was purposed. But I don't figure how that could be, Mum?"

Annabelle decided not to share her real feelings with the household. "I'm sure they're mistaken. Anyway, I'm fine, really. A good night's rest will make me right as rain." Annabelle avoided the inquisitive watch. "I won't need your services again tonight, nor do I want to be disturbed."

"Yes, of course. I'll see you first thing in the morn' then."

Annabelle remained in her chambers, until she tiptoed downstairs and crept out the back door. Under the cover of the moon, she scurried to the small garden shed discovered on her backyard walks. Tall oleander bushes concealed its entrance, so she was able to enter with no one the wiser. The full moon shone through the grimy window, creating a ghostly effect. Annabelle paced the small space with uncertainty. Had George forgotten the midnight meeting? Every sound became a disappointment, until her anticipation soon turned to annoyance. Perhaps he had no intention of coming. After almost an hour had passed, she gave up, deciding she would wait no longer. Then, the door creaked on rusty hinges and caused her to jump. Dressed in black, George slipped inside with catlike grace. He removed his cap as his blue eyes fixed on hers.

"You look lovely as usual, Lady Belle."

His appearance caught her breath – so rugged and handsome with an air of danger about him. It took a moment to regain her composure before speaking. There was a slight edge to her voice. "You're late; I was just about to leave."

"I'm sorry. It couldn't be helped. But I'm here now." His smile, so boyish and sincere, instantly convinced her to forgive his tardiness.

She smiled playfully. "I don't approve of lateness, but I am pleased to see you've shed your whiskers and dirty clothes." Even in the dim light of the little shed, she could not help but notice his impressive height as well as powerful arms and shoulders. She couldn't pull her eyes away.

George nodded agreeably as he continued to assess Annabelle. He fervently hoped he hadn't ruined their future by his deception. "Belle, I'm here tonight because I have much to explain. I want you to listen to me with your whole heart, and when I'm finished, I hope you will forgive me. I never meant to lie or deceive. I needed to protect us both." He pulled out a chair by the door and offered her a seat across from him.

"George, what have you done?" Annabelle felt alarm bells ringing in her head.

He took both her hands in his. "First things first; my name is not George."

She stepped back cautiously. "But…" She was confused. "Then who are you?"

"I'm Jonathan Warrenton, your fiancé." He watched as her mouth opened in shock, but before she could say a word, he continued, "I wanted to tell you onboard ship, but I just couldn't take the chance. I had to protect my real identity at all costs. That was why I was travelling under an assumed name. The British have spies everywhere. It would be a feather in anyone's cap to capture me. Besides, I couldn't risk you'd tip off the British."

She was in total disbelief. "I don't know whether I'm more upset about your being a wanted man, or that you thought I would turn you over to your enemies."

"We were strangers. It was possible that you were an agent of the Crown."

"But you knew I was your betrothed! You knew, and you still lied to me. I would have kept your secret."

"How could I know that? You were promenading daily around the deck with William Brumley, who's a well-known Tory."

"That's not fair." Her voice was rising. "I loathed him. I had no choice but to put up with him. My father hired him to watch over me."

"Well, that's like the fox guarding the hen house. How could I have known your father would retain such a man? No matter, I wouldn't have taken the risk anyway. If you had known who I really am, I feared that soon the whole ship would have figured it out. A secret like that is impossible to conceal."

"Maybe. But, even so, when you were safely home, you could have at least written a letter, sent a note, or somehow let me know your situation. It felt like you had abandoned me."

"I am sorry, but any letter from a Patriot could end up in the wrong hands, and then your life would be in danger as well. Besides, it was imperative that I report back immediately to my commander about my findings in France."

"I see. So, am I to take a backseat to this war?"

"Listen carefully and try to understand. The British want to hang me. Remaining a safe distance from my family protects their well-being as well as my own neck."

They both sat in silence for a while as Annabelle tried to digest all that Jonathan had shared.

Suddenly, Annabelle questioned. "But you're British. Why are you fighting against your own country?"

"That's just it, Belle. I'm not an Englishman anymore. I'm an American. I am part of a militia that is commanded by a man named Francis Marion. We live in the swamps and have been highly successful in making the Redcoats miserable."

"The Swamp Fox. I heard talk of him on our voyage. You are truly part of his gang?"

"It's not a 'gang.' It's an American militia. And, yes, I serve under his command. And I'm proud to do so. Believe me, I don't want to fight Englishmen. It's not their fault but the king's. He refuses to give up his foothold here in America." He was almost pleading for her to understand. "I will not stand idle and let the king prevail. I am fighting for my home, my family, my very life."

"Men and their wars," she said thoughtfully. "There's much I don't understand, but I promise to stand with you."

"That sounds fair…for now." Jonathan rose from his chair as if to leave. Annabelle followed suit. Tentatively, he walked over to her and wrapped his arms around her.

"Hold on." She stopped him. "I'm not through being angry at you for your deception. Embarrassed too."

"Embarrassed? What for?"

"For flirting with George. Didn't it upset you that I was willing to spend so much time with another man?"

"But it wasn't another man; it was me."

"But I didn't know that. Tell me the truth, were you pretending to enjoy my company when you were George, or were you just keeping an eye on me?"

"I treasured every moment with you. You made that miserable trip bearable. I couldn't believe my good fortune when you revealed your name. I never imagined a woman who was beautiful both on the inside and out."

"I don't believe that claptrap for a minute." She tried to conceal her smile but failed miserably.

"I meant every word." He gently tried once again to pull her into his arms. Feeling her reluctance, he cupped her chin to look into her eyes, then kissed her sweetly.

Mesmerized by the feel of his lips, Annabelle sensed a headiness. It felt so right; she rose on her tiptoes to draw him closer. She was eager for Jonathan's kisses even before he tightened his embrace. Allowing their romantic interlude to last much longer than it should, Jonathan unwillingly broke away.

"Before you go down this road, you need to be sure of your convictions."

Annabelle knew he was right. But how was she to be sure of anything when she was told only half-truths and innuendos? She had many more questions for Jonathan, but for now, she wanted to procrastinate the asking. She felt shaken by unknown feelings that she needed to explore. "Let's talk about the future."

"What do you want to know?"

"How can you just stop being an Englishman?"

"I'm only an Englishman by birth. But here in this new world, we have choices. My choice is to be a citizen of America."

"So, you've abandoned your country to fight for another?"

"I've abandoned my country to fight for my freedom!"

"You're the son of a duke. What more could anyone want?"

"I want the freedom of not being a titled gentleman, to be able to work for a living if I choose. It should be my decision, not a privilege of birth. In America, everyone has equal opportunity. We can decide our own fate."

"Will I have the same freedom as you do, to live as I choose? To marry as I choose. To work as I choose?"

"Of course."

"Have you forgotten; I'm a woman. Men tend to have privilege over a woman's life, money, and future. I can't believe that it would be much different in America."

"Ah, but it is. Here, you can marry whom you want, and own property as well as a business."

"I wish I could believe you."

"Since I haven't been able to convince you of all the great opportunities here, I'd like to ask you some questions."

"I'm ready."

He moved in front of Annabelle to watch her reaction. "What would you have done without the arrangement our fathers made? Our betrothal?"

"I imagine I would have become a governess or a companion."

"What a dally of time that would have been," Jonathan opined.

"Waste or not, my father ruled without my wishes or consideration. I never questioned his motives until I was forced to flee my homeland and sail across the sea. The hurt and humiliation were almost unbearable."

"I am sorry for all you've had to endure, but that is exactly the reason that you should take advantage of all America has to offer. You can be the master of your own fate and choose your destiny."

"Not if we marry." She pushed. "If we wed, you'll be the master of my fate and destiny."

He disagreed. "I promise never to make decisions about your future without your full accord."

She gave him a look of disbelief. "Anyway, how could you possibly think that a rag-tag colony like this can defeat the vast power of the British Empire?"

"We will win because we have right on our side." He vowed.

"Convenient words." She dismissed his certainty. "Can you tell me more about your militia?"

"Sure, as I said earlier, my militia is led by a man named Colonel Francis Marion. The British have given him the name of Swamp Fox. This small band of men camp in the woods and attack the British forces wherever and whenever they can. We hit and run. It's like poking a stick in a pit of vipers. So far, they have not been able to catch, find, or stop us." He explained.

"It sounds incredibly dangerous!"

"It can be." Jonathan wanted to downplay the daily risk he faced. "This war can't last forever."

"What if I don't want to be part of this great new America?" Annabelle's thoughts were becoming muddled.

"You'll have plenty of time to make decisions. I know this is difficult, but I have faith you will discover the truth. But for now, just wait and follow my parents' lead. Don't reveal to anyone that you have seen me. Trust no one. There are crafty wolves in sheep's clothing just waiting to entice you into giving information about me." He studied her face while his arms brought her ever closer.

"I would never willingly put you in danger." She looked up at him as she rested in the circle of his arms. "You can trust me to keep your secrets. But I'm finding it hard to give my allegiance to a country that isn't really a country."

"Understood," he answered, and then placed a sweet kiss on her cheek.

She didn't object or pull away. Nor did she encourage him to more intimacy. Smiling up at him, she put her hands on his chest. "Life was much easier when you were the unassuming George Spencer."

"Then, just for tonight, George Spencer I will be." Leaning down he pressed his lips to hers, for a chaste kiss. Then they sat at the small potting table and talked well into the night. Just before daybreak, Jonathan accompanied her back in secrecy.

Annabelle sneaked in the back door as quiet as a mouse while her senses were singing a love song. Deep in her heart, she fervently hoped that love could overcome any obstacle.

Chapter 7

Annabelle slept until almost noon the following morning, ignoring Berthe's attempts to wake her. She felt confident the family believed her exhaustion a result of yesterday's near mishap, so no explanation would be necessary. Going forward, it was going to be a challenge to keep her knowledge of Jonathan only to herself. But a promise made is a promise kept, even though their conversation raised more questions than answers. With so much to contemplate, she could feel mounting pressure to decide her loyalties, without harming these newfound relationships.

The muted sounds from the street below beckoned her to the window. Gazing out to a glorious sunshine on the glistening coastal waters, Annabelle never tired of that view. This particular morning filled her with a sense of serenity that she had not felt since her fall from grace in London. Her affection for Charleston was increasing daily: blossoming flowers, balmy weather, extraordinary architecture, and especially the clean brisk scent of the sea. Perhaps, she could find happiness here with Jonathan and his family. But until she learned more about the current situation, she would keep her own counsel.

Today would be spent preparing tonight's dinner party for Albert and Amelia's closest friends. It could be intriguing if the Colonists spoke honestly of politics and war, not just trivial banalities. How she wished Jonathan could be there, but no one expected him to risk his life. She was disappointed yet understood his circumstance completely.

Coming downstairs and not immediately finding Amelia, Annabelle crossed the hallway from the parlor and opened the closed doors to the dining room. Twelve tapestried chairs surrounded the huge glossy mahogany table, which was centered underneath a sparkling chandelier. The costly English china with the Warrenton emblem was elegantly placed with Waterford goblets and silverware. Annabelle admired the paneled walls, and the mantel carved in Chippendale with rococo. The hand-crafted furniture, made by a good friend,

Thomas Elfe, was much more refined than the heavy pieces they were accustomed to in England. She thought it showcased the oil portrait of Albert's mother.

Since the preparations looked complete, Annabelle decided to stroll down to the harbor and view the bustling trade. It seemed a pleasant way to pass the time, and perhaps, Berthe would accompany her. It would be a deserving respite for her friend.

Watching a few newly arrived ships and its passengers, Annabelle felt a sense of homecoming. Turning toward Berthe, she asked, "Are you missing London? I worry that I've brought you on a wild goose chase. Tell me the truth now. Do you want to return home and everything you hold dear?"

"And what exactly do I have in 'Jolly old England' to hold on to?" Berthe was sarcastic as usual. "The only person in this life that means anything to me, ma'am, is you. Your kindness has kept me going many a time. Besides, I must admit, I feel more comfortable here."

Annabelle smiled, amused at Berthe's point of view. "So, I guess that means life in America suits you."

"Right you are, ma'am. It's starting to grow on me, fer sure. But how about you? Do you miss life in London or perhaps your father?"

"Not a bit. My friends in the 'Ton' failed me miserably, and my father's gambling took precedent. I was only a pawn. I'm a bit surprised he didn't wager me in a poker game. Why not? He lost everything else he owned." She continued. "But I haven't made my mind up about life in America."

"By the way, where'd you slip out to last night?"

"You saw me!"

"Don't worry, the house was silent. And you know I'd never give away your secrets." Berthe assured her. "Now tell me."

"I met Jonathan at the garden shed. You remember the seafarer George onboard ship? They are one in the same."

"How cheeky! Well, I'm chuffed to bits for you."

"No more questions. I can't tell you anything else. And no one, I mean no one is to know."

"Don't worry, me trap is shut. But just know, you can trust me with anything."

"I know Berthe. Thank you." A warm embrace ensued.

"What do you think will happen at the dinner party tonight?"

"I have no idea. I just hope their conversation won't be dribble. I want to learn something about what's going on."

"Careful what you wish for." Berthe's eyes twinkled.

"I guess we'd better head back and prepare. You'll have to help me dress. I'd hate to embarrass Amelia with my 'dreary wardrobe.'" Annabelle mocked with a perfect imitation of her hostess.

Together they laughed.

"Let's go," Berthe agreed. "It sounds like I've got my work cut out for me."

Reenergized by the fresh sea breeze along the promenade, both Berthe and Annabelle strolled home to prepare for tonight's event. Passing through the entryway, they breathed in the sweet aroma of oleander and Jasmine flowers arranged beautifully in an antique vase. The color and fragrance were symbolic of the Low Country and its hospitality. Berthe proceeded ahead of her as they climbed the stairs to Annabelle's chamber.

With arms folded and toe tapping, Jonathan's mother stood ramrod. As Annabelle moved closer, Amelia showed her impatience by emitting a weary sigh. "It's about time you returned. How are we to ensure that you dress appropriately if you insist on being tardy?"

It took every bit of self-control before she was able to respond to the glaring insult. "As much as I appreciate your advice, Your Grace, I assure you I am quite capable of choosing my own wardrobe, having successfully completed my first season under the watch of the 'Ton' without your assistance." She spoke with staccato finality but could not hold back a tear.

Amelia raised her eyebrow. "Charleston is not London." She remained stoic in her criticism. "I only wanted to spare you embarrassment at being meagerly schooled. I am sorry if I offended, dear, but you need to learn the social mores of this area. No one here cares a wit about what is 'all the rage' in London."

Giving in slightly, Annabelle responded. "I understand that you only want to help, and I appreciate that. But you need to realize that I need to make my own decisions as well as my own mistakes. Snickers behind my back have no effect on me."

"I recognize when my advice and wisdom are not welcome." Amelia sniffed loudly, then lifted her head high and marched back to her own boudoir.

Annabelle waited until Amelia disappeared behind closed doors before she sank on the edge of her bed and covered her face. "Why can't I hold my tongue? I've ruined everything! Now she'll hate me forever!"

"It's time somebody put her in her place," Berthe said as she fondly embraced her. "Maybe now she'll think twice before twistin' yer knickers."

"She'll never forgive me. She thinks I'm ill-mannered and disrespectful. She'll never accept me as her future daughter-in-law."

"You'll wear the perfect dress, dazzling everyone, and behaving as if this whole ordeal never even happened."

Albert greeted Annabelle with a warm embrace just before she entered the dining room to meet the guests. "You look lovely this evening, dear."

"Thank you. I hope I don't embarrass you." Berthe had worked wonders, curling her raven hair into ringlets with strands pinned up with decorative hairpins. She was also aware that her rose colored evening attire accentuated her dark blue eyes.

"Of course not," he said, perplexed that she would ever think such a thing. "You could never do that." He continued, "These are only our closest friends, so you may hear some politics discussed. Don't be put off and keep an open mind. Sometimes, it seems like nobody knows whom to trust anymore, but tonight we can be ourselves. I think you'll enjoy it."

"I'm sure I will. The more I learn; the more assured I'll become."

Annabelle genuinely liked the guests she engaged while enjoying their meal. They seemed more informal and personable.

The conversation soon turned to politics as it often did back in London, but that was the end of the similarities. The Colonists looked at things from a different perspective than she was used to hearing.

"Does anyone here know of friends or neighbors who have British soldiers quartered at their residence?" Albert asked of his guests.

"I do," answered a baronet from Wales in a furious tone. "I have several acquaintances who were forced at gunpoint to relinquish their home to British soldiers. It's unconscionable that the owners must cook and clean for the buggers. Our colonists only have access to the servants' quarters while the troops destroy their homes."

"Why that's outrageous!" Amelia cried. "Surely, that can't be true. British troops are supposed to comport themselves with honor and dignity."

"These are the troops that serve under Colonel Tarleton. He is an abomination. He will do anything to find and kill Patriots, requiring no other authority than his own viciousness."

"I'll be damned if I'll let those leeches come in and live off my sweat and hard work!" Lord Pomeroy shouted. This was totally out of character since he was usually a soft-spoken gentleman.

"And how do you propose to stop them when they come crashing through your front door?" Albert questioned. "Do you think that if you tell them they're not welcome, they'll tuck their tails and be on their way? Not bloody likely!"

"You know," added Dave Morgan, "I had no time for this Patriot business until the Quartering Act came up. But this is the last straw. If we're to pay taxes as English citizens, then by damn we should have the rights of English citizens."

"Here, here," they replied in unison while Albert refilled their cognac glasses.

"I have heard through the grapevine that our townhouse is on the list. My son is a part of Francis Marion's militia. So, he's at the top of Tarleton's roll to be hunted down and hanged. Luckily, he has been able to stay one step ahead of him, but with all those British troops, it's only a matter of time before they catch him," Albert shared his deep worries with his friends.

"We will help you and Jonathan any way we can. We all think very highly of him," one of the wives said, trying to reassure Albert and Amelia.

Annabelle's mind soaked in the buzzing conversation while trying to incorporate it with all that Jonathan had told her. Could this Colonel Tarleton be as terrifying as Albert's guests seemed to believe? A sudden persistent pounding broke her pensive mood before she could ask for further explanation.

"Are you expecting another guest?" Amelia asked, turning to her husband.

"No. It's someone who demands entrance by the sound of it!" Albert left the sidebar and walked to the entrance.

Just as Albert opened the door, Captain Percy and his officers rudely shoved him aside and marched directly into the dining room in military fashion.

Reading from a large scroll, Captain Percy's voice boomed. "This property is being commandeered by the British government for the express purpose of quartering its commanding officers. We will take control of the property including any servants you have on the premises. The previous owners will be allowed to remain here as long as they reside in the servant quarters and stay out of our way." His pompous attitude exuded with effect, frightening everyone at the table.

"I advise your guests to leave immediately. As for the Warrentons, I suggest you begin packing your personal possessions before we confiscate them too." When one of the guests began to argue with him, Percy stomped over and backhanded the elder gentleman.

One by one, the guests stood. They raced for the door and out of sight, taking special care of the wounded man. Albert, Amelia, and Annabelle were left alone with the British Army breathing down their necks.

"You'll pay for this, you bastard. You're nothing but thieves and murderers." Albert spat out venom, then turned and marched up the stairs with his wife and Annabelle in his wake.

Chapter 8

Terrified, Annabelle could barely catch her breath as she ran up the stairs to join Albert and Amelia. Down below, she could hear the splintering of furniture with boisterous laughs, crude remarks, and much celebration as the soldiers toasted one another from Albert's spirits.

"What are they doing? They're going to ruin all your beautiful antiques and heirlooms!"

Albert circled his arm around Annabelle's shoulder. "I'm afraid we have no recourse now. But that doesn't mean we will stay here under their thumb."

"What have you planned, dear?" his wife asked, sounding confident that he had anticipated their predicament.

"Have no fear, my darling. I have been expecting Captain Percy and his troops for weeks. General Nathanael Greene has been having great success pushing the Redcoats out of South Carolina, so Cornwallis is retaliating. He attempts to put fear in the patriot's heart by flaunting his ability to billet his troops even in the houses of titled Englishmen. He wants us all cowed and subservient. But I have implemented a strategy of my own."

Albert continued to explain his plans. "No need to worry about our possessions. I've removed everything we truly value. The staff had orders to sneak out quietly, should Percy show up at our door. Their coach should already be on its way to New Hope."

"New Hope? Where's that?" Annabelle asked.

"New Hope is the name of our plantation. It lies between Goose Creek and Mount Holly on the prettiest piece of land you've ever seen. So, what do you say, ladies? Shall we carry on?"

"Come on, Berthe, hurry!"

Percy and his men continued to settle into the townhouse as the Warrentons hurriedly made their way across the sandy flatlands. Albert had calculated well.

The Warrenton property was located a half day's carriage ride from the Charleston residence. Because they had departed after dinner, darkness surrounded them. Luckily, a full moon allowed the horses to easily find their way along the well-trod road. The rocking motion of their conveyance, along with the soothing nocturnal sounds lulled Annabelle, Berthe, and Amelia into a deep sleep.

Soon the morning sun peeked through the treetops and awakened Annabelle with its warmth. Her mind was whirling with questions and fears about her future. Would she be safe? What if the British soldiers followed them? How would Jonathan know where they had gone? Facing the unknown left her queasy and uncertain. One thing she now understood; Jonathan had good reason to give his loyalty to the Patriot cause.

Deciding not to give in to her fears, Annabelle breathed in the lush scents of morning. She observed acre upon acre of violet blue flowers, blooming all along the road and into the forest. These must be the indigo plants that were in such demand in England for their dye. Passing several brooks, the carriage crossed a low bridge that spanned a marsh of some kind. These bogs seemed to be swallowed by dense foliage. Could this be one of the swamps that Jonathan had described as a hide-out?

Amelia stirred, interrupting Annabelle's musings. "This bridge is the last landmark before we turn into our drive. Don't worry, dear, you'll be very comfortable there, and it will give you time to acclimate yourself to living in the colonies. Perhaps, in time you'll lose all those London airs that can be a bit off-putting."

Before answering, Annabelle paused a moment. "I'll do my best."

Amelia patted her hand. "I'm sure you will, dear."

Annabelle pulled her hand away quickly, before preening her neck for a better view. Majestic pecan trees dotted the open landscape, and a low hanging canopy of oaks shadowed their conveyance near the entrance. The moment the carriage halted, she pushed wide the door to regard her new home. The Warrenton country home turned out to be a mansion that took her breath away. Eight grand pillars lengthened the entire wrap-around front porch.

Riveted on the stately plantation, Annabelle wasn't aware of Jonathan at the carriage door. Her heart quickened at the sight of his familiar crooked smile as he offered her his hand.

Jonathan and his band of Patriots had learned through secret missives well in advance of Percy's plan to billet his troops at the Warrenton townhouse. Realizing that his family would need to relocate to Goose Creek, he and his friends combed the woods for signs of British spies or regiments in the vicinity. A small group of Jonathan's militia remained on guard, making it possible for him to welcome his family on arrival. He knew a prolonged visit was improbable, but he could manage a few days' reunion.

When the carriage wheeled to the front entrance, Jonathan ran eagerly down the steps to greet his loved ones. He could feel the beating of his heart when he watched Annabelle about to climb down. Rushing forward, he flashed his smile. "May I be of service, milady?"

At first, surprise shown in her eyes but quickly changed to shyness. "I was beginning to think you were a figment of my imagination."

Securing her waist, he lifted her to the ground. "I'm very real, as you can see, and very pleased to make your acquaintance, Lady Annabelle." Both Annabelle and Jonathan were convincing in pretending that this was their initial meeting.

"As I am yours, Sir Jonathan," she answered, offering him both cheeks to kiss. "How did you manage to take time out from pushing those Tories into the sea?"

"When it comes to the safety of my family, nothing can keep me away. I had to be sure you escaped the wrath of Percy. He's an abomination and very, very dangerous."

"I was scared out of my wits! That monster actually struck an elderly guest at the dinner table."

"I'm not surprised. It was only a matter of time before he made his move," added Jonathan. "But strategically, he acted a bit premature. Perhaps, he's getting impatient, which marks him reckless and unpredictable." Jonathan detected a light shiver of fear on Annabelle. Instantly, he regretted his openness, so he took her arm. "You'll be safe here."

Annabelle stepped aside, as the other household members embraced him. It warmed her heart to see such genuine love. Unlike other men of his lineage, she noticed how he helped the coachmen transport the many trunks into the house.

Later that evening, the whole family gathered for dinner to discuss business and future planning. Annabelle discovered that this working plantation produced the cash crops of indigo and rice. She never dreamed that this burgeoning countryside would rival the estates in England. With overly proper manners, Amelia led the conversation in a way that included everyone. "Annabelle, the staff will show you and Berthe your accommodations. Perhaps, here at the farm, you'll finally find something useful to pursue. That would be a nice change of pace. Hmmm?"

Annabelle hesitated before answering. "A change of pace for whom?"

Amelia was obviously trying to make her feel she was becoming a burden. If Amelia wanted her to acknowledge her insults, she was going to be disappointed. Smiling to herself, Annabelle decided to lavish her with kindness…until her future mother-in-law had to eat her words.

Jonathan interrupted her reverie. "Do you ride?"

"Of course. I especially love an early outing, but as you know, English weather does not always co-operate. Here in Charleston, it'll be much more favorable. Maybe I'll experience some of that freedom I've heard everyone talking about."

Jonathan smiled. "Why don't we meet at the stables tomorrow morning and you can pick a perfect mount."

"I'll look forward to it," she responded, with one reservation. "You promise I'll be choosing my own horse."

A well-spoken butler entered the room. "Excuse me, Lord Warrenton, but you have a visitor. He states that he is a friend of the viscount. Whatever the young man is about; it does seem to be of some urgency."

"Send him back, please. We'll all hear what he has to report."

Jonathan rose to greet the scraggly, well-traveled courier. "Welcome, Tommy. You must by hungry. You'll be joining us for dinner."

Looking down at himself, he said, "I couldn't, sir."

"Nonsense. You can and you will. We're honored to have you as our guest."

With dinner complete and English trifle served, Jonathan sat back and prompted, "So, Tommy, what is so urgent that you rode all the way here at this time of night?"

"It's a shipment of English weapons – cannons, long guns, bayonets, pistols! Every firearm you can think of. Our spies have it on good authority that these armaments will arrive in New York two weeks hence. A large mule train will bring them to Charleston. Cornwallis plans a large push against

General Nathanael Greene with these added weapons. Greene is gaining on the British regulars. Cornwallis is wavering. If we could stop these munitions, we could end this bloody war."

"Then by God, that's what we must do. Stop those freight trains before they burn the Low Country to the ground!" Albert exclaimed.

"They will if they have the means. The British are determined to find and destroy Francis Marion and his men. They cannot believe that a ragtag militia that camps in the swampland and forages off the land could have such a damaging effect to their Army regulars," Jonathan explained with passion.

"I heard one General complain that the British army was being destroyed by these damned driblets. Apparently, our guerilla tactics have been very successful," Tommy added with a smile.

"But how are we going to stop this shipment? Won't they be expecting us to interfere?" Albert pondered aloud.

"What do you think, Tommy?" Jonathan wanted to hear what had been planned back at camp.

"Well, Captain, we were thinking if we could come up with a big enough diversion, we might be able to pull it off. They have no idea we are aware of the guns they're hauling down here. We have to figure how to keep the British officers occupied for an entire evening." Tommy looked directly at Amelia and Annabelle. "Do either of you have an idea?"

Amelia appeared taken aback. "I'm not sure. Albert, do you remember hearing of a large fete the Army wives put on in Belgium during Napoleon's forward march? It was quite the successful diversion. Do you think if we host a large ball here at the plantation and invite the British officers that they will participate? They certainly didn't have much respect for our position in society as they ransacked our townhouse."

Albert smiled to himself. "I remember it well, and it worked like a charm. I think it could be just the thing."

"Everybody loves a party and you'd be surprised at how powerful the preface Duke can be when associated with a large social event. Since I have never openly opined on this war, there is nothing to deter them. We'll make it the most prestigious event of the season. So much so, that a refusal will be unthinkable."

Appealing to his wife's sensibilities, he asked, "What theme do you suggest, dear?"

Pensive for a moment and considering all her options, she announced to everyone. "A masquerade party!"

"Brilliant!" Annabelle chimed. "Jonathan and his friends can hide in plain sight. The British will never recognize who is coming and going. We must insist on elaborate disguises and serve an overabundance of spirits."

"I require an exact date for this revelry," Amelia asked her son and his fellow militiaman.

"I would say a month, with Marion's approval. That should give you plenty of time to send out invitations and make preparations."

"With help, I believe so," Amelia answered assuredly. Then turning to Annabelle, she added. "You see, dear, you've not even been here a day, and already we've finally found a project for you to pass the time. Of course, I'll direct all the planning, but I'll be sure to find some small bits for you to fill in."

"Perhaps I'm better suited to work in the stables, Amelia. After all, I wouldn't want you to think I didn't know my place."

Annabelle smiled inwardly and ambled upstairs to her chamber. Boredom was the last thing on her mind. Not with the war that was boiling all around them.

Chapter 9

Heavy dew glistened like small diamonds on the grass as Annabelle peered below from her open window. Soon she would be riding across these manicured grounds with Jonathan. Excited to spend more time with her fiancé, she quickly dressed and bounded out the back door. The Warrentons privileged a very diverse stable, like the one at her father's estate in Trent. Trained as a competitive equestrian since childhood, Annabelle looked forward to riding and caring for the horses.

After passing through a copse of mimosas, Annabelle breathed in the surrounding landscape. The vista revealed several small storage barns and an impressive stable resting close to a wooded area. Gazing westward, she observed acres of blue indigo extending across the meadows in a crisscrossed pattern. She was surprised but pleased to hear swift footsteps approaching. Peering over her shoulder, she eyed Jonathan's silhouette against the sun.

"There was no need for you to get up so early." He offered, catching up handily. "It would have been fine if you wanted to sleep in; we've the whole day to ourselves. We can be as carefree as we please."

"The way trouble follows you, I think 'carefree' is stretching it. But we can surely try. Riding horseback makes me feel liberated." She twirled around with abandon but soon changed her demeanor. Teasing, she challenged in her loftiest airs, "I'm considered one of the finest woman equestrians in England. So, please don't worry, it's nothing to be ashamed of if you're not able to keep up with me."

He looked incredulous as though she was daft. "That sounds like a dare."

"Not at all, I wouldn't want to damage your ego. I know how insecure men act when they lose." She paused a moment. "But I wouldn't turn down a friendly wager."

"You led me to believe you abhorred gambling."

"Gambling is such an ugly word. Besides, it's not a risk, when it's a sure thing."

He laughed aloud. "You are your father's daughter, aren't you?" Damn, he found her appealing. Yet at the same time he still wanted to take her down a peg. Her smugness had gotten under his skin.

"The difference between me and my father is that I never lose," she said, hoping to get a rise out of him.

Instead, he flashed his memorable, crooked smile. "How about winner take all?"

She grinned back. "Fine with me. But I hate to see a grown man cry." Then she started racing to the barn. "Can't catch me."

Jonathan, bolted after her, quickly eliminating the distance. Before she could utter a word, his mouth covered hers.

Annabelle was short of breath from running, and now he had stolen what little remained. Reacting to his boldness, she laughed happily before encouraging his advances. Excitement flowed through her in response.

"Who's the winner now?" he teased. Then, sensing her willingness, Jonathan pulled her more tightly against him. While deepening their kiss, he felt desire flow through him. But that wasn't all; he also sensed some deeper emotion. Is this what it feels like to fall in love? All he knew was that he never wanted this moment to end.

Should she pull back or succumb to this headiness? The correct thing to do was to stop this embrace immediately. But instead, she urged him closer, reveling in the newness of passion.

Reality began to intrude by the sound of voices moving closer.

Jonathan also heard the voices. He hesitantly lifted his head, trying to temper his breathing. "Do you hear that?" He carefully moved her out of his arms and to his side.

"Yes. And now, I can see them. Are they familiar?"

"They're our farmhands." Jonathan motioned for them to join him and Annabelle, and the four walked together toward the barns as if nothing were amiss.

After much conversation just between the men, Jonathan saddled both their horses. He was right at home, laughing and joking as they usually did. Annabelle felt a bit awkward. He behaved as if she were only a distant family acquaintance, treating her with respectful formality.

As they traversed the property, Jonathan tried to return to a carefree state of mind. But his thoughts began drifting toward the forest, where strangers had recently been seen; men spying on his estate. "I'm sorry I ignored you at the barn, but I don't dare even trust my own workers. I don't want anyone outside the family to know of our relationship. I would hate for the British to use you as a pawn against me."

"I understand," she admitted.

Jonathan dreaded disappointing Annabelle yet again. He had noticed something skulking in the woods nearby while he was in the stable. And now, as they were riding, he noticed even more clandestine movement beyond the tree line. He chose not to alert the culprits that he was aware of their presence; that is, not until he could safely return Annabelle.

He turned in the saddle to show obvious concern. "Please understand that I don't want to cut our outing short, but we could be in danger."

She was growing weary of all his undercover activities. "There are no problems. The weather is beautiful, and we've got a lovely picnic planned. Stop worrying about the damn war. I'm sick of it!"

"So am I, believe me. But there could be enemies in these dense woods, and I would be none the wiser. Just now, I saw the shadow of a man's silhouette nearby, and that's not the first one. I must return to base camp and get instructions. I'll return soon. I must know what I'm dealing with if I'm to protect New Hope."

"I still don't understand why anyone would hide in our woods. What do they have to gain?"

"Me. I am their prime catch. If I stay, not only am I in danger but I'd be placing my whole family in jeopardy – especially if Percy and his men are searching the area. I need to let Francis Marion aware of any looming threats."

"So, you're leaving right now?" Annabelle didn't look understanding. "Really?"

When they reached the stables, he helped her dismount with a lasting embrace. "I don't want to leave you. But if I don't know what's going on, I can't protect you. Try not to worry; I'll return soon, I promise."

"I'm not going to pretend that your promises are very reassuring." She looked at him askance.

"The hands will take care of your horse. Don't ride alone, ever. Michael, my overseer, will walk you back up to the house."

"I don't need a nanny."

"Nevertheless, humor me." Allowing no time for argument, he cupped her neck and brought her lips to his. The kiss was bittersweet, sweet to the point of sadness.

Riding into Francis Marion's camp, Jonathan found it almost deserted. *Where is everybody?* He wondered. "Anybody here?" he shouted within hearing range, as he dismounted and settled in.

It wasn't long before a band of Patriots approached from the river. "Smoke is back." Bubba yelled to those behind him since he was the first to notice him.

"Whattaya doing here? I thought you'd be stayin' with your folks for a while."

"This morning, I noticed men lurking in the woods surrounding my property. I was wondering if you still had anybody watching the place?"

"Marion sends Whiskey and Skirt out there to check on things from time to time. They've seen 'em too. We're thinkin' they're Brits, but they could be local Tories. The only reason for their assignment is to either snatch your sorry ass or kidnap a member of your family."

Jonathan agreed. "So, what's the plan?"

"We're letting them be for now. Patience is the word of the day," Bubba explained. "They'll give themselves away in time."

"I agree that's the way to go," Jonathan answered. "Where's Marion?"

"Marion left last night. He's to give General Nathanael Greene a heads-up about the arms shipment. Our small militia doesn't have the manpower to carry out this mission. But Greene can handle it easily. Marion will also be briefing him about our masquerade distraction."

"What did the rest of the men think of that?"

"They laughed like hell!"

"So, you're sure our militia is not on this assignment?"

"Nope, not a one of us."

"Phew, I'm relieved. We don't want the enemy to conclude that this party was merely a diversion tactic. Tarleton and Percy could easily burn down the entire Low Country."

"There's no way the Brits can connect this heist with your family, especially when General Greene has yet to engage the British in the Charleston area."

"I agree," Jonathan said. "I'll wait here for Marion's return, then sneak back home with Whiskey and Skirt to find out firsthand what's going on."

"That'll work. We all understand your need to protect family," Bubba reassured him. "You know what? It's almost time for dinner. Why don't we raise a glass of 'who-hit-John' before we eat?"

Chapter 10

The day of the masquerade party finally arrived. Annabelle had been anticipating this for weeks, but not because of the gala that evening. Her every thought was of Jonathan. Not knowing his location or what danger he may be facing piqued a reckless speculation. It helped that her hostess kept her pre-occupied with every detail, allowing Annabelle to oblige Amelia's numerous demands of perfection.

She thought of these last two weeks as both industrious and thought provoking. Realizing her inexperience in household matters, she learned quickly from both Amelia and a dutiful staff. Annabelle spent hours polishing the Reed and Barton silverware and washing the Georgian Balustrade glassware. Then with much collaboration she enjoyed hanging the crème-colored drapes and decorations. And even though the gilded paintings of couples in Minuet were too heavy to lift, she volunteered to guide their placement. She felt a sense of accomplishment for the first time since landing in the New World.

After finalizing all their arrangements and with Amelia satisfied with the décor, Annabelle could finally relax and step outside on the wide veranda. Breathing deeply, she watched the low-setting sun beckon soon changing leaves of autumn. Summer was passing too quickly. Maybe fall and winter would bring some needed tranquility. Shaking off her daydreams, she eventually returned upstairs to prepare for the party.

Berthe was waiting in Annabelle's chamber, holding two stunning blue feathers and a beautifully beaded full-length Indian dress made from deerskin. "I found this ideal costume in a trunk brought down from the attic. It will be perfect for you. Young, modest, and lovely – just like you, m'lady."

"It's pretty, and so soft to the touch. I can't wait to try it on. But how will you style my hair? Do you know anything about Indian maidens?"

"I've only seen pictures of Indians, and they all have long braids. That should be easy enough to copy."

"Can you show me?"

"After you're bathed and dressed to perfection. We're rushed for time."

"Did you see any other costumes in that trunk?"

"Yes, there were quite a few. I believe that Amelia and Albert are going to be Antony and Cleopatra. There were also several pirate costumes and a few King and Queen ensembles. Really impressive. But none that suited you."

Annabelle trusted Berthe's instincts when it came to her wardrobe and smiled with her reflection. She looked youthful yet refined, which accentuated her natural beauty.

Soon she descended the stairs to join Amelia and Albert. Greeting the first guests, Annabelle wondered when Jonathan would arrive. He promised he would be there – dressed as a pirate with a fire-red bandana. All the Patriots agreed to wear a bandana of red, white, or blue somewhere on their garb for easy recognition.

More guests had begun to arrive with carriages lining the front entrance. Annabelle relied on English protocol while she, with Amelia and Albert, greeted each couple separately. She delighted in the oohs and aahs from their guests when they entered the nearby ballroom. She noticed that the British officers attired themselves formally with decorative medals. But their wives all attempted to overshadow one another with elaborate ensembles. Their costumes were not to be outshined by any local bumpkins.

Amelia and Albert's stately presence made a very convincing Antony and Cleopatra. Most of the British outfitted as characters from Shakespeare or Chaucer, while most of their country neighbors dressed as preachers, blacksmiths, and schoolteachers. Proud of their simple life, the attention given to their creations was impeccable. Annabelle began circling the dance floor while keeping her eyes open for any anomaly. The music had commenced, and the swirl of dancers had lined in unison. It suddenly occurred to her that this was going to be a splendid gala: a ball to rival any she had ever attended. Could the couple dressed as Queen Elizabeth and her courtier Sir Walter Raleigh be William Brumley and Miriam Worthington? Walking over, she greeted them solely out of obligation.

Both lowered their masks momentarily. Miriam wanted to show off her perfect visage. Much attention had been given to the jeweled jade gown, which accentuated her green cat-like eyes.

"Welcome to our home. I hope you've had a chance to dance. The musicians are outstanding." She reached out her hand.

"Not yet, but we are looking forward to it," Brumley answered, caressing her hand to his lips. "I hope you'll save a dance for me before the night is over. I think you look enchanting."

"I'm sure that can be arranged," Annabelle answered out of courtesy.

Turning to Miriam, the hostess forced a smile. "So glad you could make it. Your costumes are impressive indeed."

Miriam preened under her flattery, but deep down she seethed with jealousy toward Annabelle. "It was my idea to dress as Sir Walter Raleigh and Queen Elizabeth. It suits our social backgrounds, don't you think?"

With an uncomfortable pause, Annabelle answered. "I haven't any knowledge of your place in society. Besides, I thought Americans scoffed at such snobbery."

Incensed with Annabelle's rationale, she perused the Indian outfit with a sour look. "Simplicity suits you; I suppose. I can see that you've taken a liking to all things American. Is Jonathan expected this evening? Or is he still in hiding?"

"I don't believe that Jonathan will be here this evening. But you never know, now do you? He is an enigma and always seems to do the unexpected." Annabelle's smile was starting to slip.

Seeing that William had turned to another couple, Miriam leaned in. "Well, he promised me that he would be here tonight. Alone. You need to understand what good friends Jonathan and I had become. I had come to depend on him," Miriam hissed, hoping Annabelle would infer that she and Jonathan were paramours.

"It looks to me as if you've found a new friend to rely on," Annabelle answered as she tilted her head to indicate William Brumley. "I think he's a more appropriate companion for a woman of your maturity." Before Miriam could respond, Annabelle turned her back to converse with another couple.

Miriam stewed like a boiling cauldron. To be truthful, she didn't care a whit about Annabelle's fiancé, *How dare she, that little tart. First, she claims Jonathan, and now she has William drooling all over her.* Since her husband's death, she had relied solely on William's wisdom. Recently, she realized that she had developed deeper feelings for the man. Romantic feelings. She just wasn't ready to express them yet.

William, on the other hand, could not rivet his eyes from Annabelle. She consumed his delusional thoughts night and day. At first, it was only her money that enticed him, but his infatuation grew the more he remained in her company.

Unaware of Miriam and William's speculation, Annabelle mingled among the guests while searching for Patriots. Still, she could not spot any pirates with red, white, or blue sashes. Tired of dancing, she headed to the kitchen to peruse more trays of food. Music and laughter filled the hallways. No talk of war. No talk of politics, and no talk of Jonathan. In the kitchen scurrying among the caterers, Annabelle finally spied several pirates – dressed identically with red bandanas. Her heart skipped with joy. One of these had to be Jonathan. She teased each man while peeking behind every mask. Finally, she found her prize. Squealing, she threw herself into his arms.

"You're here; I can't believe you actually came." Without guile, she planted a kiss on his unsuspecting lips. Stepping back, she watched Jonathan's cohorts cheer for their friend's good luck.

"Let's get our plan in play, shall we?" Whiskey rubbed his hands together, anxious to begin the ruse. "Smoke, you and Annabelle need to twirl out on that ballroom floor. Let everyone see two people in love. We want them all to recognize it's your fiancée in your arms."

Soon, Jonathan and Annabelle glided in unison with the other couples. Their bodies entwined with love and happiness, as more and more of the Tory guests noticed their identities. When they were sure they had been seen by everyone, they passed through the paneled hallway doors, where Jonathan discreetly whispered good-bye and changed places with one of his friends waiting in the wings.

In the wink of an eye, Whiskey swirled Annabelle in a Minuet, pleased with his charade. "Someone is going to come and try to arrest me, thinking I am Smoke. That's when the jest begins."

The Irishman's assessment was correct. Several British soldiers parted the dancing couples to confront her partner. Fear rushed in, as she watched them advance. What was she supposed to say? How was she to act?

Two overbearing soldiers abruptly addressed the pirate. "Viscount Warrenton, you are under arrest. Release the lady and come with us."

"How dare you interrupt our dance?" Whiskey accused while removing his mask, in a posh, high ton accent. "What is the meaning of this?"

Both military men stood down and begged his pardon. "We were assured that you were the young Viscount Jonathan Warrenton. We have a warrant for his arrest."

"That may well be, but you can be assured that I am not he."

"Please accept our apologies, sir. And ma'am."

The dashing couple glided from the dance floor and returned to their co-conspirators in the kitchen. As the night progressed, Annabelle took turns dancing with each pirate, confounding the British officers who watched them. Strangely enough, euphoria replaced her fear despite Jonathan's absence. Annabelle prayed that her fiancé remained safe and out of harm's way. She wondered what it was like to be on the run, to have an enemy searching for you night and day? And where could her fiancé have vanished? His ability to disappear like smoke was not only a mystery but an enigma that continued to save his life.

Chapter 11

After inconspicuously leaving the ballroom, Jonathan climbed the attic stairs to his favorite look-out spot. As an imaginative lad he had spent hours spying on make-believe pirates from this vantage point. Presently, he was watching for any suspicious activity outside. So far, nothing appeared amiss, until a lone carriage wheeled down the drive and delivered its passengers.

The late arrivals were none other than Captain Percy and his First Lieutenant! Jonathan eyed the arrogant twosome barge past the butlers with boisterous degrades.

Wanting to scrutinize the two troublemakers, he hurried to the kitchen and quickly changed into a server's uniform. After grabbing a plain black mask, he hoped no one would question his appearance among the guests.

Exiting the scullery, he sneaked to the wrap-around front porch, where he spied on Captain Percy and his friend. He watched them meander on the grounds until they took seats in the rocking chairs on the porch. Their raucous laughter and crude remarks penetrated the night, making the surrounding couples hasten past them in displeasure.

Damn, thought Jonathan, *were those 'bollocks' drunk already? They hadn't even entered the ballroom for refreshments.*

Stumbling down the steps, Captain Percy pointed toward a new direction and his officer followed.

Where could they be going? Jonathan followed them as they weaved down a darkened path and away from the manor. Careful to remain undiscovered, he lingered behind some well-placed trees. He did not worry that he would lose them; their obscene jokes followed them to the fieldworkers' cabins. What could they possibly be looking for? Those buggers were up to no good. Of this he had no doubt.

Abruptly, the lieutenant was ordered to stay put while Percy continued further ahead. This hindered Jonathan's forward movement, but he inched ahead as quickly as possible without being seen. He stopped when the inebriated man staggered while relieving himself against a tree. In disbelief, he eyed the officer withdraw a pistol and bellow a British tune. Before the underling could fire his pistol, Jonathan acted.

Realizing a discharged gun would attract the guests and interfere with his surveillance, Jonathan crept around the thicket of bushes and struck a swift blow. He then dragged the Tory into the underbrush and out of sight, swiftly scurrying after Percy.

Loud sobs and moans filled the air as Jonathan drew closer to the slave cabins. Now, realizing exactly what Percy had in mind, he ran to the last secluded cabin. A small family lived in that cabin, but the parents were at the manor helping with the ball. He had to reach their children before that filthy bastard hurt them.

"Leave me alone!" the voice of a teenage girl cried out. "Mister Michael, our boss man, don't let nobody mess with us. He'll hurt you."

"I don't see him anywhere around, do you? Now stop your caterwauling and get out of that dress before I tear it off."

"No! No! I won't. I won't. Leave me be!" The helpless girl struggled against cloying hands.

Just when Jonathan neared the open door, he heard sinister chuckles.

The captain snickered as he backhanded his hostage, watching her stagger backward and hit her head. "Don't cross me, girl. I'll have you one way or another." Percy's vicious threats created louder sobs from the shielded face.

Unbuttoning his breeches, Percy moved into position against her. "Pull up that dress further, before I rip it right off!" Unaware of anyone observing, he roughly fondled her.

Jonathan stood ramrod behind the culprit and poked his saber at Percy's bare buttocks. "Looks like I caught you with your pants down," Jonathan said evenly but with resolve. "Your ass is a convenient target, and this tip is exceedingly sharp. I'd stand real still if I were you."

"It's you, isn't it? Damn you, Warrenton! You can't tell me what to do," he hissed. "I have rank in the British Army. You'd better leave while you're able. My men have orders to shoot you on sight. Lieutenant! Lieutenant!" Percy cried out to the silent darkness.

"He won't be answering your call; he's indisposed at the moment."

"What have you done with him? I'll make you pay!" Percy teetered with expletives.

"I don't think you're in any position to threaten me; do you, Captain?" Jonathan asked the girl in a placid voice, "Hand me some rope. You're about to witness a lynching."

Percy grasped in horror when the rope dangled in view under the lantern's light.

Jonathan grabbed the cord and tied Percy's hands behind his back, while Alma covered herself. "Now apologize to this young lady, you swill-belly!"

"I will not! She has no right to say no to me...to me!" Percy spat.

"As long as she lives and breathes, she has every right. If you want to live to see tomorrow, I suggest you do as I ask."

"I apologize," Percy mumbled.

"So, she can hear it!"

"I said, I'm sorry, very, very sorry."

"That's more like it. Now, shall we rejoin the party, Captain?" the Patriot prodded him forward with jabs of his saber, drawing blood with each thrust.

"You can't leave me like this. I'll be a laughingstock!" Percy begged, horrified at the realization of how he would appear before all the guests.

"Watch me."

"I won't rest until you're caught and hanged!" Percy promised.

"Looks like you'll be losing some sleep then," Jonathan retorted while holding his saber in place.

Before entering the party, Jonathan re-donned a black mask to match his clothing. He forced Percy to waddle back to the mansion with breeches around his knees and hands tied behind his back. With the gagged captain in tow, the Patriot entered the ballroom.

A hush enveloped the crowd, as the entire gathering gawked at the scandalous sight. Jonathan handed him off to a higher ranked British officer, just when the snickers began. He watched as Percy cowered by turning away.

As expediently as possible, Jonathan informed the major exactly what crimes Percy had committed and demanded that he be punished accordingly. Then he bowed and retreated before someone recognized him.

Aghast, the major marched Percy out of the limelight before berating him for his behavior unbecoming to an officer. They departed the grounds immediately, not wanting a British soldier to be seen in such poor light.

Chapter 12

During the week leading up to the masquerade party, most of Marion's militia remained in the Charleston area. Their continued presence had reassured General Charles Cornwallis that Marion's band of brothers knew nothing about the British cache of armaments arriving off the coast of Virginia. What a colossal mistake. This was to be their Army's last stand against Washington, and these weapons were imperative for victory.

While his men were otherwise occupied, a determined Francis Marion trekked northward to personally hand over to General Nathanael Greene the geographical information the colonial forces needed to appropriate these weapons. He understood that the outcome of the war could depend on his ability to reach Williamsburg in a timely manner.

The Swamp Fox forged through dense forests and rolling hills with little sleep or sustenance. Cold, tired, and miserable, he persevered with only one goal in mind; to reach his destination. After a week of relentless inclement weather, the Patriot finally arrived at the general's encampment. Pleasantly surprised by the warm welcome, he was willing to answer a multitude of questions about his notorious exploits.

Hoping to return home immediately, Marion swiftly completed his mission with the commander. He had planned to remain only long enough to ensure that the troops were given orders to either retrieve or destroy the arriving armaments. But when it was revealed that George Washington was residing at a base camp nearby, he quickly decided to follow General Greene to Yorktown and meet this legend.

They arrived there amid the numerous tents and soldiers. Soon, an envoy appeared with an invitation to dine that evening with General Washington in his personal pavilion. That night, the camp's headquarters filled with colonial officers as well as several well-known French generals.

Marion took a backseat rather than join the loud conversations or interrupt to ask questions. He just listened in awe to the greatest military minds of his time.

When strategies concluded, Marion felt an ease about the outcome of the country's independence. But he also felt that God had bestowed a great personal burden. Was he the right man to determine the fate of the South Carolina residents? He prayed fervently that he would persevere through his doubts.

The following morning, the Swamp Fox departed under cloudy, uncertain skies. Fatigue of both body and mind slowed his travel time. But it afforded him time to reflect on what was decided in Yorktown. He had been assured that under no circumstances would those armaments be allowed to reach Charleston. Greene was to confiscate the weapons and deliver them to Washington well before they began their trek south. Then the Continental Army planned to use the lot against Cornwallis at Yorktown. It appeared the Warrentons' masquerade would be successful and remain blameless for their participation.

At last, a beleaguered Marion arrived back at his swamp camp. It felt good to be home with his compatriots again. He was immediately hailed with questions.

"It's been almost a month! We were beginning to think you'd been caught and hanged by those Tory sods!" Everyone was talking at once.

"Attention!" Marion ordered. A hush encircled the campfire. "Let me clean up and eat. Then we'll sit around the fire and I'll tell you my tale."

"Yes, sir," his men replied in unison, as they gathered around the pit.

After freshening up, their leader returned. "It was a hard slog up through North Carolina and Virginia, but finally, I found the camp of General Greene."

"Were they successful in appropriating the weapons?" someone asked.

"I have no idea," he answered. "I accomplished my mission. I expect they will do their part too; we should hear soon." Marion stood and stretched. "Instead of returning immediately, I was given an opportunity to meet, face-to-face, General George Washington. After introductions, we had a small repast, and then all in attendance discussed strategy. Apparently, Yorktown is where they expect to make their last stand. Believe me, they are ready."

"They allowed you to be privy to their war plans?" Bubba added.

"I admit to being shocked when the Brass invited me to the meetings. I listened well. If I had ventured an opinion, I would have been tongue-tied for sure." Marion laughed at his remembered discomfort.

"That's a first!" Smoke joked while the others nodded in jovial agreement. "Exactly who was at this meeting?"

"Well, let me get this straight. There was George Washington, of course, also Alexander Hamilton. But what I found extremely interesting were the French officers present; Admiral De Grasse, General Rochambeau, and even Le Marquis de Lafayette."

"Lafayette agreed to join the fight?" asked Jonathan. "Why? What do the French have to gain by helping us?"

"Everybody knows that the French love to take a jab at the English every chance they get."

"But is that a reason to trust them? There's been no love lost between our countries."

"Washington seems to think he's to be our savior."

All the men turned quiet, deep in thought.

"I guess there's nothing to do but wait and see," Jonathan opined.

"As usual, we'll probably be the last to find out," Marion affirmed. "All I know is if we go down, be assured we'll have fought to the last man."

Chapter 13

Daylight was dwindling rapidly on this early autumn evening. As the streetlamps were lit one by one, they cast an eerie glow to the darkened door of Miriam Worthington's townhouse. The widow was just about to light the sconces near her front door when she spied two men moving cautiously between her home and the neighbors. Before she could retreat into her foyer, the gentlemen had reached her doorway and pushed their way inside.

"Miriam, don't be alarmed. It's William. And this is Captain Percy, a close associate," Brumley spoke quickly to ease Miriam's mind. "I apologize for our lack of manners, but we are here on urgent and secretive business."

Gradually, Miriam's racing heart slowed. "Really William, you gave me a fright. Next time, I'd appreciate a small message of warning before you barge in uninvited."

The sight of Percy's uniform stopped her from continuing a tirade. Her first thought was that the British Army had come to billet her home. But with the sound of William's pressing plea, she began to feel more relaxed. Yet, she wondered, what could they want with her? Turning to her intrusive guests, she warned, "William, you know I will assist you if I am able; you've been so kind to me since Samuel died. But I will not openly take sides in this war."

With comfortable ease, William removed his hat. "We are hoping to change your mind. You are a necessary part of our plan, and I can assure that you will willingly help us when you learn the name of our target."

"I'm ready to listen, but I make no promises. Although, I admit, you've made it sound intriguing." She didn't want to disappoint her friend. "Why don't I have Maggie put the kettle on, then we can relax in the parlor while we discuss exactly why you two gentlemen are here."

"Be sure to put some brandy in my cup," Percy ordered in his usual brash manner. He scanned the lush furnishings around him and surmised that Miriam could indeed be a valuable contributor.

"Might as well put some in mine, too," Brumley agreed.

"Why don't I just bring a flask of brandy out with two glasses? I assume that's your preference?" she asked with a raised eyebrow.

"Indeed," they answered in unison.

As she walked back to the kitchen to relay the visiting gentlemen's wishes, she remembered how she and her late husband, Samuel, had enjoyed entertaining. Now she was alone – so alone. She had loved him so much; together they made the perfect couple. But then life had thrown her a fateful blow. Cringing inwardly, she knew that the death of her husband had turned her into a woman consumed with hate and a desire for revenge. Her husband's downfall had been in trusting the wrong person – a man who claimed to be his friend and then betrayed him. That man was Albert Warrenton! He had convinced Samuel to invest in the trade ships sailing to the Caribbean.

"Easy money." She recounted hearing. "You invest a little and receive a handsome return." But in the end, her husband had lost. Watching the love of her life die, clutching his chest and falling face down on their parlor floor was etched in her mind.

She recalled William's solicitousness in her time of grief; how he had arranged the funeral and taken care of all the paperwork. Shocked when he told her of Warrenton's betrayal, Miriam would never have imagined that Albert could have done such a thing! But her confidante had assured her it was true. Now, she owed all she had to Brumley. After all, he had been a savior in her time of need.

Returning with the brandy, Miriam noticed that William acted as if he was a practiced guest, immediately stoking the fire and adding more logs to the roaring flames. She could get used to the sight of him relaxing in her parlor.

He had also seen that the drapes were drawn across the front window and no lamps aglow on the tables. When the parlor met his satisfaction, he turned back to Miriam and Captain Percy. "Let's get started, shall we?"

Before their concourse began, however, Percy spoke, "So, just how close is your friendship?" He perused her up and down in a provocative manner; his eyes resting on her ample breasts.

Miriam's gaze moved to William Brumley, expecting him to set Percy straight, but he appeared deep in thought and never even turned toward her. Not wanting to encourage the despicable man, she answered stiffly. "I'm not quite sure what you're implying, but William and I have been friends since my late husband's demise. I don't know what I would have done without him."

"I was hoping that maybe you and I could be good friends too. Perhaps, more." Percy's unctuous inference was made crystal clear.

With a look of disgust, Miriam motioned for both men to sit closer to the fire in the surrounding chairs. "Shall we, gentlemen?"

After pouring himself and Percy another drink, William leaned back on the Victorian and stated, "I want to apologize again for the subterfuge, but we could not take the chance of being seen. Normally, we use couriers between us. It has been our most reliable and secretive way of communicating. However, we needed to speak with you in person, this once. The fewer times we meet face-to-face, the better."

"We must not be discovered by those swamp rats! Not again!" Percy explained to Miriam, with rising fury in his voice. "That bastard, Jonathan Warrenton, has more spies and friends in Charleston than there are mosquitos in the swamp. He always seems to know what we're planning. This time, it's going to be different! We will catch him, and we will hang him!"

"When are you going to explain this caper to me? I need to know what it is you expect me to do," Miriam asked, tired of Percy's tirade.

"The point of this assignment is for you to write a missive to that titled traitor about an upcoming payroll shipment. You make him believe that you overheard this information by chance. You give him the time and the place of its arrival. All the while you will assure your loyalty to the colonists. When he appears to steal the shipment at a time and place of our choosing, we'll grab him. He'll never know that it was you who betrayed him."

"Why Jonathan? Why not his father? He's the one I want punished."

"Don't tell me you have a soft spot for the cub?" Percy sneered.

"I don't have anything against him, except that he's a Warrenton."

"Isn't that enough?" William chimed in. "Hurting the son will hurt the father more deeply than anything you could do to ruin him."

"I want to see that sack of dung hang from the highest tree in Charleston!" Percy declared unequivocally.

"Do you really think that I can convince him I'm a Patriot?"

"Of course, no one knows your true leanings. We need you to lure Jonathan out in the open so we can trap him," William insisted. "This is a perfect way to seek revenge and get your money back from the Duke of Warrenton."

"Is that possible?" Miriam leaned forward with rising interest.

"You'll see." Percy exhaled a disgusting belch. "You get back your husband's money, William gets his lovely Annabelle, and I get promoted to major."

Miriam cringed with the thought that William still wanted Annabelle. But now she assessed what the men had told her and exactly what part she was to play. Would all three of them come out winners in the end? She never doubted her own capabilities, but her loyalty to Percy was nil. He acted so uncouth and unlike other British officers. She wanted nothing to do with him.

Looking at William, she concluded, "Yes, I'm in. Where do you want me to send the missive?" How she wished William would turn to her and forget that little witch. Hopefully in obliging him she would gain his favor.

William removed a blank note from his vest pocket and handed her the quill from the scrolled desk. Miriam proceeded to write a missive to Jonathan about the upcoming payroll shipment, for the approval of both men.

Soon she would attempt to lure the young viscount to her townhouse with the promise of further information and to convince him of her loyalty to the colonists. Capt. Percy assured her that he and his men would capture Jonathan at the Paymaster's office. No one would suspect either her or Brumley's involvement in this sinister plot since they would be conveniently elsewhere. William would be the eyes and ears at the local pub. He would maintain a low profile and unsuspecting – only passing information to Percy when Jonathan took the bait.

The thought of scheming with a man of Percy's character made Miriam a bit squeamish. Both men seemed so consumed with hatred; it scared her. But was she any different or innocent with her own desire for revenge? Probably not.

The front door closed on the backs of these collaborators. Would their treacherous plot expand her opportunities to move forward in her life or trap her more deeply into the darkness she wished to escape?

Chapter 14

The sunshine danced off the bathroom's crystal candle holder, illuminating the walls with a spectrum of iridescent colors. Watching its play of light renewed Annabelle's feeling of well-being, as she waited patiently for Berthe to ready her bath.

"Here we go, ma'am," Berthe said while pouring the last pitcher of warm water into the claw-footed tub. "I've put some rose water in yer bath so just plunk yer bum down in there and you'll smell pretty as a flower."

"Thanks," Annabelle replied, smiling at her handmaiden's choice of words. Sponging with a loofah, she continued. "Have you any plans today?"

"Daisy's goin' to be teachin' me all about herbs and medicine. Later, it'll be back to the kitchen. It appears I can't cook to save me life. But I ain't given up. I'll learn to chop vegetables if it kills me."

"I'm glad that you've found such a good friend in Daisy. And I'm so proud of how you've accepted all the strange and wonderful ways of our new home." Pausing as she reflected on Berthe's smiling face, she asked, "Are you as content as you seem?"

"I'm chuffed to bits, I am." Berthe's face lit up as her thoughts turned to her friend Patrick, causing her to blurt out, "Patrick O'Hearn, the delivery boy from the Mercantile, wants to court me." Realizing she had spoken those words aloud, she turned away in embarrassment. "Can you believe such rubbish? A nobody like me with a beau?"

"Why, I think your beau must be absolutely smashing to have picked such a fine Irish girl as yourself." Annabelle enthused before a worrisome thought crossed her mind. "But be careful; are you sure he's a Patriot?"

"He and his family emigrated a few years back from Dublin," Berthe explained. "They own the Mercantile Store near Goose Creek. He comes here a couple days a week and always asks for me."

"Does he talk politics or ask questions about Jonathan?"

"No, mum, he's a hard worker, just like me. We take walks and talk about our life back home and how fortunate we are to be living in America." Shaking her head, she continued, "His older brothers are all in the colonial militia. He's no Tory, that's a fact."

"I trust your judgment, but you must never lose sight that we are in a war, and you must keep your guard up at all times."

"Yes, mum, of course." Berthe draped a towel over the tub and busied herself with laying out a riding outfit on the bed. "I'm guessing you're taking your morning ride with Lady as usual?"

"You're exactly right; my only obstacle is that annoying William Brumley. I've made it quite clear that I am not interested in him, but he won't take no for an answer. His visits have increased with frequency, while I'm trying to escape his prying eyes and questions. He acts as if he's courting me, despite my engagement to Jonathan."

"He's a sneaky worm who's used to getting what he wants. I've seen his shifty eyes move over you. There is no doubt he wants you. Patrick and I have spotted Brumley and his nasty companion Percy hanging around in our woods several times during our walks. What are they doing here, anyway?"

"I'm not sure if it's me he's watching or Jonathan, but he's up to no good, that's certain."

"I'll keep me eyes peeled, don't ye worry none about that."

After Berthe had cleaned the upstairs living quarters, she left to unearth herbs in the forest with Daisy.

Annabelle remained looking out her window while pondering her new life. Each new day at the Warrenton's country home became an adventure. Annabelle had much to learn about the business from cash crops to the raising of animals for profit. She attained this information by watching and listening to anyone who would allow her incessant questions. Without Jonathan and alone most nights, she availed herself to the extensive Warrenton library. But, by far her favorite pastime was working in the impressive barn and outbuildings which sheltered superb horseflesh, along with many family pets. Jonathan had gifted her with a beautiful well-mannered mare named Lady, and she quickly became Annabelle's constant companion. Hardly a morning went by that she didn't dash to the barn at first light, reveling in the freedom of racing across the meadows as the sun slowly rose in the morning sky.

This fall day was no different when she approached the horse barn shortly after breakfast. Knowing she would arrive at the barn before Michael, the overseer, Annabelle took her time, stopping at the root cellar to pick up some raw carrots and apples to treat the horses and goats. Both horse and rider looked forward to their grooming sessions.

Before entering Lady's stall, Annabelle stopped at the tack room to collect a bridle along with the curry comb and brush. But before she exited the storage room, she heard two unusual men's voices. Their words grew more distinct as they ambled in her direction. Annabelle quickly hid behind the door when she recognized one of those voices; William Brumley's. Why was he sneaking around the Warrentons' barn? Up to no good, that was for sure, she surmised. Needing to remain hidden, she slipped behind several large bins of grain while leaving the door slightly ajar. The men must have stopped a short distance away; their voices came through clear as a bell.

"What the hell are we doing here anyway?" Brumley asked. "We're not going to catch that traitor hiding here. He's much too smart for that."

"One of my spies claims that black stallion of his has been in the side corral for days. I've never known him to go anywhere without that beast. Since nobody else can ride the fiend, why is he here? So, it's safe to reason that the cub is somewhere near." Captain Percy's tone imparted impatience.

"Even if he is here, we'll never find him. He knows these grounds well enough to stay hidden until hell freezes over. I've done my best to become better acquainted with the Warrentons by calling on Annabelle as often as is seemly."

"Doesn't matter. We'll have him dead to rights soon enough. With Miriam's help, we'll flush him out and have a noose around his neck before anyone's the wiser," Percy insisted.

"Has she sent her missive yet? Are you sure she understands how to find the messenger? We don't have much time."

"Stop worrying. We have plenty of time. Let's just hope that he takes the bait we've set for him. Then we'll all get what we want. Maybe, when your lovely lady hears of her young viscount's death, she'll fall into your open arms."

"That's the plan," Brumley said in a thoughtful tone. "But what if she doesn't? I'm determined to have her at any cost."

"So, I don't see the problem. Nobody cares how you convince her. I'm sure you'll find a solution if she doesn't co-operate. Just do what you need to do. However, she is the daughter of an Earl. You'd better move quickly."

"If we're already married there won't be anything anyone can do. She'll be mine. Mine!"

"If you say so," Percy sounded bored. "All I care about is my promotion in the ranks. I damn well deserve it. Besides, it's a waste of time to pine for any female. Women can be had anytime, anywhere."

"Are we through here? We've found no guns or stolen property to give us cause to arrest the viscount. Of course, we could plant evidence and then arrest him." He knew Percy would be agreeable to anything underhanded no matter how heinous.

"Don't worry; we'll get rid of the whole family when the time comes." Percy reassured him. "I always have several men watching this place. The truth is we can occupy this property for whatever reason we please." A gruff laugh echoed in the confines.

Percy's pompous words made Annabelle's skin crawl as she stifled a gasp. She needed these collaborators to leave so she could act. Somehow, she had to find Jonathan's hideout in the swamp before her fiancé received that missive from Miriam. But how was she to convince him that Miriam was the enemy? Would he believe her? Minutes ticked by in solitude until finally, she rose and peeked out the door. No voices. No footsteps. She crept to the outer barn door, only to see the two villains galloping away. Annabelle immediately turned toward the stalls and ran with tack in hand to saddle Lady. She dared not tell anyone that she was headed deep into the swamps. This was the only way. The time it would take to convince anyone to help her could mean disaster to Jonathan. She quickly grabbed a blanket and riding vest. It was crucial that none of Percy's men who might be lurking about would question her daily routine of rides consistent with previous mornings. No one followed while she skirted the forest and quickly disappeared within. Soon she was zigzagging through a maze of thick trees and camouflaged paths. Her mind raced with the reality of being lost. How would she find her way with her only lodestone the sun? Decision made, she headed southeast through the dense woods, remembering Jonathan's description and directions.

Annabelle rode steadily for hours until late afternoon crept upon her. It was troubling that she didn't feel any closer to her destination. Creepy shadows began to appear at regular intervals. How could she find her way with only the light of a full moon? She started to second guess herself when the sudden flight of some seafaring birds from a nearby marsh sent a chill right through her. Taking deep breaths to calm herself, she soon realized that seeing these gulls meant that she was closer to her journey's end. Before she guided Lady back in the correct direction, she was suddenly surrounded by an unkempt group of men with stern faces and pointed rifles.

"What's a lady doing riding in our swamp? Give us your name and state your business." The apparent leader exchanged glances with the others.

Concluding instantly that these ruffians were part of the militia, Annabelle reasoned it would be best to just tell them the truth since there was no time to lose.

Words came tumbling out of her. "I am Lady Annabelle Gainsborough, and I have news of the utmost importance. This morning, I overheard Captain Percy and William Brumley plotting in my barn. I must inform Jonathan straightaway. They're setting a trap for him. Believe me, I would never have ventured into these woods alone if there were any other choice."

For a moment nobody spoke. Then, the leader of the group said, "Well then, Lady Annabelle, if what you say is true, we'd better get a move on." They slung their rifles over their shoulders.

A surly, distrustful man demanded, "Blindfold her, until we know she's who she says she is."

Breathing a sigh of relief, Annabelle smiled widely to all the men. "Oh, thank you. Let's hurry, shall we?"

The spokesman rode his horse next to Annabelle, and removed his dirty neckerchief, and then he tied it tightly to cover her eyes. "Hold on to your horse's neck and hand me the reins. I'll be your guide." Her trek began again in unknown territory. Soon she could smell the damp ground and fetid bogs nearby. Without her sight, the sounds of all the nocturnal insects and squawking seagulls were amplified. Her stomach reeled. How could anyone live in this foul, noisy habitat?

"We're almost at the camp, my lady." He sidled up next to her and removed her blindfold. Suddenly, Annabelle was surrounded by tall trees laced with hanging moss. She gasped aloud, surprised by the serene setting of lush ferns and flowering bushes. The smells and sounds seemed to retreat when encircled by such rustic majesty. "I had no idea…"

"I understand, my lady, I, too, was amazed by this ever-changing swampland. It's a perfect balance between beauty, danger, and heat."

She smiled. "I'm awe-struck."

He returned a smile and short nod of approval, before joining the others.

They soon rounded a corner and rode through a canopy of trees that led them directly into the center of the camp.

Chapter 15

A smoldering fire's embers rose in contrast to the full moon high above the treetops. Annabelle could feel the camaraderie among Francis Marion's militia, as she watched them huddled around with food and drink. Advancing her horse slowly, she perused the entire area looking for Jonathan. Finally, she turned toward the young recruit who escorted her. "Don't you realize how critical my information is? I need to find Jonathan, immediately."

The Patriot raised his hand to calm her. "He was here when we went out this morning. He's probably in his cabin."

"Well, then, take me there." She timbered her voice to such degree that the whole group turned to see who was causing the commotion.

"Who is this lass, brazen enough to invade our camp, and start giving orders?" one of the older men questioned heatedly while he rose to confront.

"She's Smoke's lady friend," the young recruit answered. "She's uncovered a plot against us, and she's anxious to share it."

"It really is a matter of life and death," she chimed in. "Won't somebody please help me find Jonathan?"

"And why should we believe anything you have to say?" a loud voice sounded.

"Stand down, Karl!" a voice rang out from the darkened area near the camp's edge.

Annabelle's eyes riveted on the easily recognizable man approaching from the shadows. He moved like a soldier, tall, straight and in complete control. Why had she never noticed his look of competence and strength? She watched him steadily close the distance between them. Her eyes never left his as he made his way to where she was waiting and gently took her in his arms and kissed her lightly. The moment she relaxed and felt the safety of his embrace, she broke down, losing control as tears began streaming down her face.

"Whoa." He lifted his head to study her face. "You're safe now. You made it." He knew enough to let her cry it out. He could feel all the fear and dread she had suppressed for hours evaporate. Inch by inch, she returned to normalcy. He slowly released her and stepped away. "I am furious with you. How could you plunge headfirst into the Low Country? You had no idea where this camp was, never mind all the alligators and quicksand out here. Your recklessness could have turned out much differently, you know."

"I didn't think about anything but arriving here on time to warn you. Brumley and Percy want you dead. They'll do anything to catch you," Annabelle warned emphatically.

Smoke took a deep breath. "You're safe now, Belle. That's all that matters. Promise me you'll never do anything so foolhardy again! I realize that everything worked out this time, but it could have had a disastrous ending. Come, it's time to sit by the fire so you can warm yourself and have some food."

Jonathan's reassuring voice and touch seemed to calm her. Soon, she was settled comfortably before the fire with the others.

When she had relaxed and eaten, she began to tell her story to the cluster of men. Showing interest and respect, they were unusually quiet. Annabelle explained from the beginning why she was in the stables that morning when Captain Percy and William Brumley sneaked in.

Jonathan broke in. "I can't believe those bastards were sniffing 'round my barn."

Ignoring his outburst, she continued, "Fine. Now, back to my story. When I heard their voices, I hid in the tack room; they never knew I was there. They have no idea that I overheard their nefarious plans."

"That's why you were so determined to warn us. Correct?" Francis Marion poured himself another cup of coffee. He too, was very interested in what Annabelle had to say.

"Exactly." She smiled at the notorious legend. He didn't frighten her, but she was a bit in awe.

Annabelle recapped her story by telling everyone how Miriam Worthington was in cahoots with Brumley and that horrible Capt. Percy. How they had hatched a plan that included Miriam sending Jonathan a missive to meet her. And when he agreed, she would set him up. They didn't go into detail about exactly what the plan entailed, but they seemed dead certain that it would work. A quick and unlawful hanging was to follow. The hatred and jealousy these two villains felt toward Jonathan will not be assuaged until his death.

When she was through, there was complete silence while all the men digested what she had relayed to them. War tactics were one thing, but the actions of these two unstable men were beyond the pale.

"Well," exclaimed Marion. "Has anyone here seen such a missive?"

"Somethin' came in the other day. I found it in the cedar tree where we exchange information with the Patriots in town," said Bubba. "I put it on the colonel's desk as usual."

"One of you privates hotfoot it over there and retrieve it! NOW!" Marion bellowed. "Those fools must have forgotten who they're dealing with. We'll teach those bastards not to underestimate us!" His presence commanded respect and obedience.

The young militiaman returned out of breath with the missive in his shaky hands. He immediately handed it over to Colonel Marion. Ripping it open with little fanfare, he read it aloud. "Dearest Jonathan, please meet me at my townhouse a week from today. I have some information that will be of great interest to you. I have found a way to get back at the British for quartering its filthy soldiers in your home and spying on us. This will benefit both of us. I will expect you on Wednesday, the ninth. Loving regards, Miriam."

"Now the planning must begin. Whiskey. Skirt. You both come with me. We will plan as we go since we are still in the dark about their actual plans. More information is the key. You boys get into Charleston. See who comes and goes. Watch and listen."

"Smoke, you will take your lady home first thing in the morning. Then hightail it into Charleston and find out what the hell is going on. And damn it! Stay out of sight."

When the evening ebbed, Jonathan reached for Annabelle's hand to lead her back to his cabin. Both could hear the night song of the swamp, as they slowly weaved their way through the woods. "Every man here was impressed by your bravery, Belle. What you've accomplished this day will save many lives."

Embarrassed by the praise, Annabelle tentatively crossed the threshold. Was she expected to stay overnight with him? Although, she was aware that would be immensely inappropriate, Annabelle was so exhausted; she would be willing to rest her head on a bale of hay.

"Come," Jonathan said gently. "I'll try to make you as comfortable as possible in this rustic pile of sticks I claim as my cabin. The bed lies in the far corner – and is comfortable – of course, not up to your standards, but…"

"Hush." She stopped his rambling. "At this moment, I have no standards, only a longing for a soft spot to lay my head." She smiled up at him weakly.

"Belle," he said, shaking his head. "You amaze me. Not only are you beautiful, but you are unbelievably courageous. I never imagined that a woman would care enough for me to risk her life. And as thankful as I am, I can't help but shudder to think what would have happened if the British had found you first."

"I'm sorry, but my only thoughts were of saving you from those monsters," she answered softly. "And I'd do it again. I didn't realize how much you meant to me until I heard those horrid men planning your demise."

"I feel the same about you," he spoke from his heart.

Slowly, he turned Annabelle to face him and lifted her chin to gaze into her eyes. After a moment's pause, he touched her lips with his. Lifting his head, he tried to clarify his thoughts. "I find myself thinking about you when my concentration should be elsewhere. You haunt me in my sleep. There seems no cure for how deeply you've touched me. How will I ever recover?"

"You've only to marry me. Isn't that the plan?" Her heart was soaring with happiness. Could he really be falling in love with her?

"Nothing would make me happier. However, this is America. You are free, with the whole world at your fingertips. You have no obligation to me. You may marry whomever you choose."

"Well, I choose you. I fell under your spell the first time you smiled at me on the deck of that smelly old ship." She slipped into his arms and lifted her head to meet his kiss again.

Without faltering, he deepened the embrace while tightening his arms around her. This time, he led his fiancée to the bed and laid her down with obvious desire. Her eyes welcomed him, and her smile enticed. Removing his coat, he moved to join her as he sat down to take off his boots. As he reached for the unwanted footwear, a sharp knock sounded against the door.

"Hurry up, lad!" Whiskey shouted. "We've got plans to make to save your ornery hide. The Colonel's waiting."

Chapter 16

Annabelle was awakened the next morning by a persistent knocking. Looking through the open window, she could see that the sky was still dark. "Who on earth?" she murmured to herself as she slowly moved to open the door.

Whiskey stood in her doorway with a morning greeting. "Time to get up, buttercup. Jonathan's getting the horses ready. You two need to be on your way before the sun rises. The earlier you depart, the easier to dodge the British. You only made it here yesterday because some of our boys led the Redcoats on a goose chase. Believe me, those bastards were too close for comfort."

"Fine." She sent him a sour look. Why was he here instead of Jonathan? With no fresh water, and little time, she readied herself for the long trek home.

Her stomach rumbled as she inhaled the yummy aromas coming from the campfire and realized that Jonathan had breakfast waiting for her. Annabelle had nothing to pack, so was surprised to see a bedroll and other necessities already behind her saddle. She realized in a moment of clarity that Jonathan did indeed take her needs seriously. It would have been a perfect time for them to linger over their coffee, but before the sun fully poked through the darkness, Jonathan insisted they retreat from camp.

Annabelle followed Jonathan's lead and rode in silence, until he turned in his saddle to check on her progress. "This doesn't look like the same path I took," she remarked as they crossed a rickety bridge.

"It may not be the exact route, but terrain looks completely different when you're coming back home from a destination. That's why it's always a good idea to look back at intervals when you're traveling."

"Are you accompanying me all the way?"

"No, it wouldn't be safe. I'm going to leave you with the Campbells. It'll be an easy ride from there to the manor. I doubt the Redcoats will bother you."

"I can do that. I hope Colonel Marion has come up with a plan to keep you from hanging?" Annabelle asked in a lighthearted manner. "I'd quite miss you, if you were to be so unfortunate."

"Would you now," he answered with a smile. "I believe it's best if I take responsibility for my own neck; Marion has enough to attend to. The boys will be very thorough with their detective work, have no fear. We've been taught to take one step at a time. And we've not been caught yet." Looking over at Annabelle, he rather abruptly changed the subject. "It's still hard for me to believe that Miriam could be involved with those two cretins."

"Believe it," she insisted. "I knew she was a nasty piece of work the first time I encountered the floozy."

"Floozy, is it?" Jonathan almost started to laugh.

"She tried to make me believe that you and she were lovers. If that's not being a floozy, then what is?"

"Whoa! I never once considered her anything but a family friend. My apologies if she attempted to convince you otherwise; you are absolutely correct." He was still grinning. "Except that she's a bit long in the tooth for my taste. So, you can see how I find the whole idea of Miriam as a femme fatale a little over the top."

"Don't sell her short. She's smart and she's mean. Don't oblige her, whatever you do. From the little I heard in the barn, I trust she has a deep-seeded hatred for your family, especially your father."

"I can't even begin to understand why she might hold grudges against the family, but don't worry; I'll not turn my back on her or allow myself to believe a word she says."

"That makes me feel a wee bit better, but you still need to take her seriously. She's dangerous! Berthe and I will go on an extended shopping trip to Charleston so we will be handy if you need us."

"I don't think that's wise."

"Of course, you don't. You probably want me to stay at home and sit by the fire. Well, I'm not going to do it," Annabelle fired back.

"Well, I'll leave that up to your better judgment, but beware; don't get in the middle of this mess. You've already done your part."

Annabelle swayed in the saddle as a sudden wave of fatigue overcame her. "Can we stop for a few minutes?" She didn't want him to think her weak, but even less did she want to fall from her horse. "All of a sudden, I find myself starving. Do you think we could take our tea a bit early?"

"Of course. We can sup here. But then, no more stops. It is too dangerous for us to be lurking in these forests," he said as he lifted her down from her perch. Once again, he found her in his arms. He held her close. Before letting her go, he leaned down to kiss her softly, thinking she would surely push back from his clumsy embrace, but no, she melted into him. They fit so perfectly together. Moments passed before either one pulled away. They both knew this was neither the time nor place, for the hell of it was, they were in a swamp surrounded by English soldiers.

Annabelle held on to him for a few more moments before stepping back. It felt like her heart was breaking, but she stoically kept her thoughts to herself as she helped make a comfortable camp for lunch. After eating mostly in silence, they mounted for an uneventful ride to the Campbells' place. After reaching their destination, they separated, as usual travelling in opposite directions.

Not long after Jonathan was taking leave of his betrothed, his two best friends, Skirt and Whiskey were crouched down in the shadows behind Miriam Worthington's townhouse. Their mission was to discover exactly what the British had in mind, which included where, when, and how Capt. Percy planned to execute his devious plan.

They slipped into Charleston a few hours earlier, dressed as local farmers, easily mingling among the populace and the crowded city streets. They located Percy exactly where their compatriots had indicated – the Poinsettia Tavern. Sitting in the shadows observing, the Patriots overheard a frosty exchange between the British officer and William Brumley.

"I thought I had made myself clear that you were not to acknowledge me in public. Yet here you are sitting across from me in this bloody booth," Brumley snarled at the Redcoated Percy.

"Stop your whining. There's no turning back. You're up to your eyeballs in this double-cross. You've passed the point of trying to convince anyone that you're neutral," Percy shot back.

"I will not be espied around Charleston with the likes of you. Not now, not ever. Again, it's up to you and Miriam to finalize this escapade. I've played my part. Now I'm out."

"You're out when I say you're out." Percy sneered. "Until then, you'll do as you're told as long as I need you." Percy patted his sword so that Brumley would know that he meant business.

The two men continued their conversation in muted tones, but both were scowling and appeared uncompromising. Abruptly, Percy rose and left the tavern.

Whiskey and Skirt decided their best bet was to follow Percy. They soon realized he was leading them to Miriam's townhouse.

"Can you believe the bloke led us straight to the horse's mouth?" Whiskey asked. "The luck of the Irish, eh?"

"I believe it's more the wisdom of the Scots." Skirt elbowed his friend. "But either way, we still don't know their plans. It's a pleasant fall evening; surely a window or two must be open to let in a breeze."

"Stay close to the townhouse. There's plenty of cover with all these bushes and trees. I'll walk east. You walk west. We'll meet when we locate them."

The two men rendezvoused at the front of the townhouse under an open hurricane shutter above some oleanders. Apparently, this room was the parlor, where Miriam received guests. The windows allowed the voices of a man and a woman to be clearly heard. Crouching down low, they were glad not to be seen from the street or any other residence. Grinning with satisfaction, they settled in to listen. The stillness of the night helped the clarity of voices within.

"Have you heard back from the golden boy?" Percy spoke with a voice of authority.

"As a matter of fact, I received a reply this morning. Jonathan is very interested in hearing more. He should arrive here sometime tomorrow evening."

"So, he's just going to walk right in, not knowing who or what he has waiting for him? I would assume he'd be more careful. He's still a wanted man."

"He trusts me. Besides, I'm sure he'll have his scouts making sure all is well," Miriam responded. "But since you know where he'll be tomorrow night, why don't you just grab him here? It should be easy with enough men."

"I want to catch him in a treasonous act. I want to hang him with no trial. Visiting his mistress is hardly an act of war." Percy dismissed her premise.

"I am nobody's mistress. The sole reason for this plan is for me to get my revenge on his father," she responded angrily.

"If you ever thought to convince me that you are lily white, I'm here to tell you that ship has sailed. You've been servicing Brumley for months. I've had a hundred women like you." Percy gave her a knowing smile.

"That's a lie! How dare you! Get out!" The two Patriots heard a chair suddenly scrape on the wooden flooring.

"Don't pretend to be outraged," he scoffed. "You should be flattered I'm willing to take Brumley's leftovers. He's obviously tired of you. Why else would he refuse to come here with me? You're nothing to him."

"I don't believe you. William's my friend and confidante. He's always taken care of me," she responded desperately.

"I guess we'll see about that, won't we?" he retorted with a nasty smirk. "But for now, sit down and let's get our facts straight. Do you remember what to tell Jonathan tomorrow night?"

"I'm to tell him the payroll is rolling into the purser's office on Friday. But in reality, it will already be safely locked up. So, by the time he rounds up his friends, all he'll get for his trouble is a bogus wagon full of rocks."

"And a hangman's noose. They'll be twenty soldiers following that wagon, and more sentries waiting at Post Headquarters. When they reach the purser's office, there will be twenty more soldiers ready to arrest Jonathan and his men," Percy reminded her. "They'll be surrounded with no escape."

"How many guards will you have on Thursday night when the payroll actually arrives? Surely you have some protection for the safe?"

"I'm not an idiot. I'll have two guards posted on the outside door and another two in the hallway. Few will know about the arrival of the payroll. If we put too many soldiers on patrol at the purser's office, someone might become suspicious. So, we'll keep it normal with four guards. Two inside and two out. It's up to you, Miriam, to make sure Jonathan's at the right place and time we want him. You must entice him to take the bait we are dangling right beneath his nose."

"I'll do my best," Miriam answered, growing weary of this whole ordeal.

"You better be ready to do what's necessary to ensnare this man. And he best not suspect a thing." He flashed a look of pure lechery. "I have faith in your powers of persuasion."

"I said I'll do my part." She felt sick to her stomach. "After this caper, I want nothing to do with you Tories."

"I don't know about Brumley, but you and I have some unfinished business. And I never leave a friendship such as ours…incomplete. Besides, soon I'll be a rich man. Colonel Tarleton has given me permission for one more raid. The Warrenton estate and all that they own is about to fall under my command."

Miriam trembled with fear as she closed the door firmly behind the revolting man. What had she gotten herself into? Was revenge going to be worth the cost?

Chapter 17

The multi-colored leaves had fallen at the Warrentons' plantation. An early October crispness filled the air. All the crops were harvested and there was a feeling of celebration with town festivals and pumpkin carvings. But what had begun as a day of promise had quickly turned to one of fear and dread. The servants and farm workers were hastily sorting through the valuables, packing up anything they could find of worth. The entire household scurried about, trying to decide what to keep and what to leave.

Only hours earlier, the family had received a missive from Jonathan to prepare for departure. His spies had heard that British soldiers were converging to raid their home. Preparation for another coming invasion must begin immediately. His letter gave explicit instructions to evacuate the premises and retreat to the swamp where Marion's men would lead them to safety.

Annabelle, Berthe, Amelia and Albert were directed to the Mercantile Store, owned by the O'Hearn family. Patrick O'Hearn remained Berthe's beau and had been a great asset to the Patriot's cause. His family had willingly offered their storage facilities behind the store to house the family during this time of crisis.

"NO! I don't want to leave my home again! They have no right to do this." Amelia sounded as if she could burst into tears at any moment. "We're not even a part of this war. Why can't they leave us alone?"

Albert was just as furious as his wife. Incapable of sugarcoating their situation, he put his explanation into plain words for her. "It's that bastard Percy. He will stop at nothing to capture our son. He's even resorted to putting a bounty on his head. Jonathan didn't make it clear in his missive how he discovered the enemy's plan, but, for now, let's just be grateful he found out in time to save Marion's militia as well as our family."

Annabelle and Berthe were working diligently beside the older couple. Annabelle wasn't sure how to tell the family of her involvement. She cleared her throat to get everyone's attention. "I overheard Brumley and Percy planning a trap for Jonathan."

They gasped.

"What do you mean you overheard Brumley and Percy?" Amelia asked in disbelief. "Where were you?"

"They were trespassing in our barn while I was working in the tack room. When I heard their voices, I hid, and I listened. When they finally left and rode away, Lady and I rushed to find Jonathan."

"Why on earth didn't you come to us first? We would never have allowed you anywhere near those wetlands. They're very dangerous." Albert couldn't believe what he was hearing.

"That's exactly why I didn't tell you! I was desperate to warn him at any cost. Of course, I got lost, but his friends found me and brought me to his camp. When I told Colonel Marion what I had heard, he immediately gave orders and made plans. What those orders were, I do not know, but when the Swamp Fox gets through with the British, they'll be on the warpath, and Jonathan's afraid they'll come here and destroy everything."

"How could we not know you were missing for a night?" Amelia asked in amazement. She still didn't comprehend how Annabelle could have made such a foolhardy decision.

"Berthe covered for me. Remember, she told you I felt a little under the weather that night," Annabelle explained. "We didn't want to worry anyone."

Amelia nodded in understanding.

"Thank you, Annabelle, for your remarkable bravery," Albert commented. "However, as much as I admire your courage, I beseech you never again act so foolhardy."

"I promise, I won't leave again without telling you."

"All right then," Albert said. "I guess we better get back to work."

The day passed quickly as everyone packed, buried, moved, or hid anything of value; then they collected what they needed for their journey. As nightfall crept upon them, they gathered to share one last meal together. Excitement and sadness filled the air. The entire staff realized how fortunate they were that their safety had been insured by Albert, who was not only a dependable man with his peers but a kind and caring overseer to them.

A loud rap at the door froze everyone. Could the British have started their rampage early?

"It's just another missive from Jonathan." Albert read it to his family. One could feel the relief in the air. "He's in Charleston with his men. He says they're ready for action but not to worry. However, he sent a special request to you, Berthe."

Berthe puffed with pride at the thought of the militia needing her assistance. "I'd be proud to help the cause in any way that I can. You can be sure of that."

Albert continued, "He needs Berthe to gather the herb valerian from our garden and take it to Charleston."

Then he turned to the others. "We better all get some sleep. Tomorrow's going to be a long day. Let's just think of what's to come as a great adventure. An experience we'll be able to tell our grandchildren." He hoped he was able to cover his misgivings.

Berthe tampered the candles and allowed the darkness to prevail.

That same night Jonathan's family was turning out their lights for the evening, he unobtrusively entered a dockside pub, called the Harbor. Waiting for him in the basement of this American watering hole were his best friends, Whiskey and Skirt. In hushed voices, Jonathan's two compatriots in disguise hashed out the situation before them. The flickering hue from one lone candle cast a somber glow to their serious faces.

"It sounds like Miriam's in over her head," Jonathan remarked thoughtfully. "This will not end well for her."

"I agree," Whiskey answered. "But she's only herself to blame. How on earth could your father have wronged her so deeply that she would want to harm you?"

"We can't concern ourselves with her viciousness now. After listening to what she and Percy have planned for my family, I'm going to need enormous self-control to hold my tongue while I try to convince Miriam I believe every lying word she utters. It's a bit ironic that after I've persuaded her of my complete faith and trust in her words, we will soon be thieving the real payroll that will arrive early tomorrow morning."

"We mustn't gloat too soon," Skirt warned. "As soon as you finish with Miriam, you hightail it back to the Harbor Pub. We'll be waiting – ready to go. I shouldn't have to remind you how important it is that you are not followed or recognized. There must be no proof of our presence in Charleston during this heist. None. After we've loaded the payroll onto our horses behind the pub, we'll take the road east of the city into the swamp." Whiskey was adamant about the importance of their deniability.

"Where are you two going now?" Jonathan asked.

"We're to wait here for Patrick O'Hearn to bring us the valerian the girls brought from the manor. Then, we're going to pay a little visit to Maggie and Kate, the prettiest Irish lassies west of County Cork," he said with a wink. "The payroll should arrive with no fanfare or acknowledgement. Our barmaids will deliver evening meals to the soldiers on duty at the Purser's headquarters. If all goes well, the guards will be taking a nap shortly after they eat, and we will be in and out in less than ten minutes," Whiskey quickly explained.

"If all goes well," Skirt said skeptically. "Since when does anything we do turn out to be that easy?"

"Since tonight," Whiskey answered smiling. "We've got the luck of the Irish sittin' on our shoulders."

The broad daylight with many passersby made it easier to blend in with the busy thoroughfare. Jonathan made sure nothing seemed amiss as he approached Miriam's front door. Not even a token soldier was watching her townhouse, near or far. Percy's obvious set-up almost made him laugh. Almost. This was still a dangerous business he was about.

Miriam answered the door at his first knock. "Welcome. It's been such a long time since I've seen you." She offered both her cheeks for him to kiss. "I'm so glad that you agreed to come hear me out. I think you'll find what I have to say very interesting and perhaps beneficial to your cause." She escorted him on one arm into the parlor and offered him a seat.

The wide smile she flashed at him made him feel like she was the spider and he the fly. An involuntary shiver coursed through him, but he maintained his cool demeanor. "To be honest, I really don't understand how you could be in possession of any information that could aid my cause. You are well known to keep company with William Brumley. And although he pretends to align himself with Patriots, it is obvious to anyone with eyes that he has sold himself to the British."

For a moment, Miriam looked nonplussed, but she readily regained her poise. "My association with Mr. Brumley ended shortly after my husband's estate was finalized. I have no knowledge or interest in where his loyalties lie."

With raised eyebrows, Jonathan continued, "At one time my father considered your husband one of his dearest friends. But since Samuel's death, you have not darkened our door. So, why should I believe anything that you tell me? It appears to me that you have spurned every overture that my father has made."

For a moment, Miriam looked like she had swallowed her tongue. Shaking off her inner fury at Jonathan's words, she recovered quickly. "Believe me when I say that I desire to assist you because of our family's long friendship as well as my fatigue of the British occupation of Charleston. Perhaps, you're correct about William's allegiances. I recently discovered that he is tightly aligned with the British soldier named Percy. Percy is an unscrupulous blackguard. I'll not be content until both men have paid for their sins." Her face showed real disdain for the two villains.

As Jonathan observed her performance, it reminded him of a skilled actress. If he did not know better, he would probably believe every dirty lie pouring from her mouth. "Well, then, let's hear what you've got to offer."

She began to explain to Jonathan how the payroll was due to arrive at the purser's headquarters two nights hence. She revealed the time and place the payroll shipment would begin, before ensuring him that a minimum of troops would be guarding the caravan.

"Where do you suggest we attack this caravan?" Jonathan asked, curious as to her suggestions.

"I believe anywhere along the way would work, but you might wait until they're almost to headquarters. Their guard will be down even more the closer they come to their destination."

"I will have to think about all you've told me and discuss these matters with my men. I agree there's a lot of money to be had. Money that we sorely need. But perhaps, the risk is too great." He tried to sound a bit disinterested.

"So, you aren't even going to try?" Miriam's voice cracked with worry.

"I didn't say that," he answered. "I said I would have to weigh my options. 'Tis not my decision alone."

Miriam stood and pierced his eyes. "Well, I hope you realize just what an opportunity this is for your militia. This money could keep your men in food supplies and ammunition for quite a while." Her pleading seemed unjustified. He was beginning to understand just how much she needed him to take her bait. What would Percy do to her when this whole caper was over? The captain was not a forgiving man. However, Jonathan was not about to feel sorry for this woman, who without a backward glance was ready and eager to throw him to the wolves. Not when she was planning his demise.

"You'll know soon enough, Miriam. I thank you for your information. I'll try to use it wisely."

Miriam's hands balled at her sides. "I want you to get revenge for us both!" she insisted. Walking up to him and placing her hands on his chest, she looked up into his eyes with an almost maniacal stare. "I need you to carry this through. Do you hear me? I need this!"

He gently removed her hands. "I'll try my best. That's all I can promise."

Stepping back, he recovered his hat and stepped out the front door without even a backward glance. Jonathan sucked in the fresh air. He felt like running yet too much was at stake and duty called. He made his way to the Harbor Pub as covertly as possible.

Chapter 18

Jonathan's mind filled with confusion as he made his way through the back alleys of Charleston. His encounter with Miriam left him spoiling for a fight. He had no misgivings about the assignment that lay ahead. Reaching his destination, the Harbor Pub, he waited impatiently for the owner to show him the stairs leading to a secret room where Whiskey and Skirt waited. He joined his friends as they lit an additional candle on the table, centered in the room. No windows were visible to any prying eyes from the street above. A lone lantern hung from a wall beam and cast enough light to finish their business.

"I'm glad to see you've made it back to us in one piece. We were worried that the she-wolf might have had special plans of her own leading to your demise," Whiskey remarked with real concern in his voice.

"To tell you the truth, the woman terrified me," Jonathan answered only half joking. "I couldn't get out of there fast enough."

"Did she spell out the plan?" Skirt demanded anxiously.

"Miriam laid it out exactly as she was told. She proved herself to be nothing more than a lying conniver. Although she denied it, it's obvious that she, Brumley, and Percy are in cahoots. She used all her wiles to convince me her motives were genuine and her disgust for the Tories ran deep. But the more questions I asked, the more frantic she became that I co-operate. If I hadn't been wise to the truth, I might have bought into her lies. She was that good an actress."

"You've got to admit it was an ingenious trap," Whiskey said, shaking his head. "It's only by divine providence that we found out the truth."

"Nothing divine about it," Jonathan contradicted. "It was Annabelle. Her courageous actions saved our hides."

"Hear, hear to Annabelle," they recited together, clinking their glasses in salute to her unabashed bravery.

The upstairs door creaked open, and Patrick O'Hearn joined the other men already seated. He noticed a crude design of a building mapped out in front of them.

Jonathan was the first to rise and offer his hand to their newfound friend. "I'm Jonathan Warrenton, thanks for meeting us. I see you've already met Whiskey and Skirt."

After bringing Patrick up to date on Jonathan's meeting with Miriam, they laid out their plans for the night to come.

"First things first," Skirt began. "Did Berthe remember to give you the valerian? It's the key piece to this puzzle. If administered properly, it will allow us to enter the headquarters, do our business, and slip away without any bloodshed."

"She sure did, more than enough," Patrick said as he removed a pouch from his vest and emptied its contents on a handkerchief. The dried herb valerian appeared crumbly to the touch. "It's a powerful sedative. Use too little and you get a sleepy effect; use too much, you can put someone to sleep forever. I'll be showing the two barmaids the exact amount to mix into the sentries' food. It should knock them out for at least a couple hours."

Jonathan felt it between his fingers. It didn't feel or smell lethal, but now he realized this night's confrontation depended on its exact implementation, not just good luck. Although, he had to admit it was fortunate that these two loyal American lassies delivered meals routinely to the soldiers, so no one should be the wiser.

"We've been told only four sentries will be guarding the Post Headquarters."

"Good. I'll divide the exact amount of valerian into each portion for four meals," Patrick assured them.

Whiskey and Skirt assured Jonathan that the barmaids were adept at flirting and would stick around until the meals were completely consumed. "They plan to mix the herb into the apple cobbler to disguise any aftertaste." Everyone agreed that anything resembling apple pie never goes uneaten.

"Everything seems to be in place. The lassies will deliver the meals at the usual time – seven o'clock."

Jonathan asked, "Patrick, how long before the valerian takes effect?"

"Within the hour. You can make your move safely at around eight o'clock." Patrick rose and gathered the four portions to take with him. Before leaving the clandestine room, he turned to Jonathan. "Your family is well, but worried about your safety, of course. And all send their love. I believe your father plans to return to the manor soon."

"Patrick, you need to let him know what's going on. Try to make him understand the danger he'll face if he returns home. He needs to remain with the rest of the family."

After he left for the Mercantile, the three compatriots went over every detail of their plan one last time. Then, at exactly six thirty, Jonathan, Whiskey, and Skirt joined in a short prayer before departing to set their plan into action. The darkened alley made a perfect hiding place for them to position themselves behind a few empty whiskey barrels. Fortunately, no one else appeared on the street in this secluded section of Charleston. From this vantage point, they could watch the Harbor Pub barmaids deliver the meals at the scheduled time. One friendly lassie handed the food to the two sentries on the outside door. The other entered the hallway to the Purser's office. After an interlude of chatter and laughter, the women left and signaled that the meals were all eaten.

A sense of relief flowed over the men as they realized the satisfactory conclusion to the first step of their task. It amazed them that no additional soldiers or sentries were on guard when a payroll of this magnitude was locked inside their headquarters. Still, the Patriots remained diligent. The stillness of the night lent itself to covert movements with no conversation between them. Jonathan snuffed out the lighted sconce on the street when it appeared safe to approach the building.

Creeping stealthily toward the offices, they spied the British soldiers slumped against the walls of the Post Headquarters. The empty plates of food laden with valerian proved to be effective. Dragging the two bodies inside the front door, the three men nodded in agreement before they entered the hallway and quickly eased down the corridor. A wharf rat scurried out of their way and hid behind the next corner. The Patriots were glad to hear deep snoring emanating from the two sentries posted outside the Purser's office. Jonathan's plan was to slip into the office and open the safe while his friends stayed outside keeping watch.

Jonathan removed a pouch that held his safe-cracking tools and easily unlocked the hallway door and slipped inside. He could feel his heart beating faster and faster. The new moon revealed a big desk centered in the office and a floor safe positioned behind it. How fortunate that he had room to maneuver around the desk without scraping the legs on the wooden flooring.

Carefully, he knelt and used the first of his lock picks on the safe. Nothing! What the hell! He tried another to little avail. Sweat beaded on his brow, as his breathing quickened. Everything depended on him; he couldn't allow his ineptness to ruin this job. Taking a deep breath, he tried again with the last tool. Success! The safe door swung open. He felt enormous relief as he stuffed a burlap sack with the British currency. Sitting back, Jonathan swiped his forehead before quietly closing the empty chamber, careful not to leave any evidence that an unauthorized person had entered the office. Hastily, he rose and rounded the desk. As he left the premises, he signaled his two friends that all was well; it was time to bolt.

A sudden murmur and a re-positioning of a soldier stopped them in their tracks. They watched in dismay when one sentry opened his eyes and tried to stand in a stupor. Without a second thought, Whiskey knocked the man out with a swift butt of his gun. The soldier slumped down into a sitting position again.

Realizing their need for haste, the disguised Patriots picked up the pace as they raced toward the Harbor Pub where the owner had their horses waiting. Wasting no time, they were on their way back to the swamp. Riding into the night, all three men were dreadfully aware of the backlash that would follow, but they could never have imagined the terror that was to come.

Jonathan and his two best friends galloped on their hidden paths without a backward glance. With blood pumping and hearts racing, the three didn't slow down until they came to a clear pond on the edge of the woods. Relieved that no one pursued them out of Charleston, they dismounted to give their horses a brief respite.

"Hot damn!" Whiskey exclaimed.

They slapped each other on the back in celebration of their success.

"What an outlandish operation!" Jonathan agreed with excitement. "Can you believe we really pulled it off? We've just bested the high and mighty British again."

"Aye, and you can bet your ass there'll be hell to pay. So, let's not get ahead of ourselves," warned Skirt. "I, too, feel elated, don't get me wrong, but I've a rare bad premonition about what's to come. Besides, our job is not finished until we're back in camp, money in hand."

"I agree wholeheartedly," Jonathan anguished. "There will be no end to what we started this time. The real task at hand is how we face the backlash. We are of the same mind when it comes to Percy and Brumley. They will never let this theft stand. The fact that we outfoxed them will drive them mad."

Rubbing his chin with concern, Whiskey asked, "So, how do we stay one step ahead? Their revenge will be unrelenting. And they have the force of the British Army at their disposal. We can take care of ourselves, but they could inflict unforgiveable retribution on our friends and families. The question is, how do we protect them?"

Whiskey's words had shifted the mood to somberness. They remounted their horses and rode with a foreshadowing of doom hovering overhead.

In the wee hours of the morning, the Patriots reached the camp of the Swamp Fox militia. They were surprised to find that few were sleeping; most were gathered around the roaring fire pit and discussing relevant events. A welcome shout brought the remaining few out of their cabins to hear the outcome of such a high-risk mission. Volunteering to steal a British payroll right under the noses of their sworn enemy was daring indeed. The recruits admired these three Patriots not only for their audacity and wit but because their courage never faltered. Francis Marion had made certain that their willingness to volunteer for the most perilous assignments did not go unnoticed.

The morning sun peeped above the horizon while they all ate and embraced the embellished exploits. But at the end of their dramatic telling, the audience was left with the same foreboding as Jonathan, Whiskey, and Skirt. What next? Before a discussion could ensue about British retaliation, two riders galloped into the camp, as a courier dismounted from the camp of George Washington himself. With a sense of urgency, a militiaman awakened Francis Marion and asked him to join the group and read the missive from Washington. It was addressed 'For Colonel Francis Marion's Eyes Only.'

A short interval passed before Colonel Marion arrived at the fire pit. The courier handed him the document with a brief explanation. "Colonel Marion, this comes from the office of George Washington, but was written by one of his aides who wished to be remembered to you. His name is Lt. Robert Burke. Apparently, he holds a certain fondness for you and has written an addendum to Washington's announcement, to clarify the future of Charleston. He believed it would be of interest to you."

"Thank you very much, sir." He efficiently opened the missive, and then settled his glasses at the end of his nose. "Gather around, men. I want all of us to hear the news from General Washington."

To my fellow Patriot,

I hope that this document finds your militiamen and yourself in good health. I am aware of all that you and your special militia have contributed to the war effort. First and foremost, I wanted to thank you for all the success you have had in thwarting our enemy. I am sorry to announce that your work is not completed. You must stay the course for the time being. Soon this war will be over in South Carolina. But not yet; you must persevere and fight the good fight until the end.

As to the business at hand, I am pleased to report that on October 17, 1781, British General Lord Charles Cornwallis surrendered to me in the field at Yorktown, effectively ending the War for Independence.

We did not accomplish this feat alone. First and foremost, I want to credit your men. The armaments that we confiscated because of your good work in Charleston aided us greatly. I also had help from The French Navy commanded by Francois, Count de Grasse, and the French Army led by the Marquis de Lafayette. By September twenty-eight, our forces had succeeded in encircling the British Army in Yorktown with the combined American and French forces. After three weeks of continued bombardment, Cornwallis finally surrendered.

Best Regards,
George Washington/ Commander in Chief of the Continental Army of the United States of America.

Addendum by Robert Burke
My dearest friend, Colonel Marion.

The War of Independence is indeed over, but there are some codicils that you should be made aware of; the first being that Charleston is still at risk. It has been made apparent that the war will persist on the high seas and in certain other territories. The upper northern territories, southern territories, such as South Carolina, Georgia, Northern Florida, as well as certain western lands have a heavy British occupation. Because of their presence in these areas, they believe they can negotiate for these land areas at the Treaty of Paris. This treaty will include French, Spanish, British, and American delegates. Decisions will be made there that cannot be undone. General Washington's advice to Charleston is to gradually push the British out – into the sea. We will be sending more troops when possible, but you must make local plans for this resistance to be successful.

We will stay in communication. Godspeed.

Lt. Robert Burke

Chapter 19

Captain Percy climbed the stairs to Post Headquarters with renewed confidence. After reading Miriam's missive describing her assignation with Jonathan, he had good reason to believe that his newest schemes to entrap the intolerable Patriot would soon bear fruit. Today was the day he would bloody well capture the bastard. With William Brumley waiting in the wings and holding a perfectly forged document, it allowed him the authority to hang Jonathan without a trial. Percy's eagerness could not be contained.

The four sentries who had posted guard the night before stood at attention as Percy brushed by them with barely a nod. They exchanged glances of uneasiness after their commanding officer closed the door. A pact had been forged between these fearful British soldiers. They avowed the previous evening would never be spoken of, not to friend nor foe. Almost immediately, it had become clear that none could remember what had truly transpired. But each recalled enough to grasp the unchangeable fact that they had fallen asleep on the job – a humiliating court martial awaited if discovered.

Percy entered his office and emitted a contented sigh. Crossing to his desk, he settled in his chair, and propped his boots on it. Leaning his head back, he pictured his exalted stature among fellow officers when they discovered he had accomplished the impossible – the capture of 'Smoke' Warrenton. He and he alone would be the man who bested the notorious Francis Marion at his own game. The captain painfully recalled the blatant giggles and whispers after Jonathan had humiliated him at the recent masquerade party. Never again! Now he would become a legend! He would be recognized as the man who had instigated the downfall of the Swamp Fox! Percy could hardly wait to be congratulated by the other officers, especially those who had openly mocked.

He felt totally secure that the payroll shipment lay safely in the locked compartment in the Purser's office. His moment of triumph would come when he captured Jonathan and his co-conspirators as they prepared to steal the fake shipment arriving tonight. And what a feat it would be – a hanging that would be a warning to all who crossed him.

Then and only then would he pay one last visit to Miriam. He fantasized about how she would bow to his power. Her reluctance to bed him would evaporate, as she melted into his coaxing arms. But if she still dared to prove difficult, it would not hinder him. A vile smile spread across his face. A woman's unwillingness had never stopped him before. A knock on his office door broke his concentration.

"Come in," Percy ordered, standing to address the group of soldiers who entered in an orderly fashion, and stood at attention before him.

Percy barked his orders without delay. "I am counting on you men to keep this caravan punctual, and that you appear to be protecting it at every vantage point. Only four of you are to remain with the wagons. The other twenty are to follow at a safe distance, but off the main road. You must stay close enough to keep track of the payroll wagon the entire trip. I'll have another twenty waiting at the end point. Under no circumstances are any attackers to escape. I want them caught and I want them alive. DO YOU HEAR ME?"

"Yes, sir," the erect soldiers answered en masse.

"Do you have any idea how many militiamen will show up to attack the shipment?" an officer asked.

"No, I do not. It's your job to figure that out. Post some outlying sentries if you have need."

Another officer suggested. "If they attack before crossing the river into Charleston, we'll have our lookouts along the Cooper River. We'll ambush them before they know what happened."

"A sound idea. But you never know, they could attack anywhere or anytime. You must be vigilant." Percy smiled for the first time. "And all they'll get for their efforts is a payload full of rocks!"

Assessing the quick reaction of his underlings gave him a sense of supremacy. He reveled in that feeling. "Report back to me as soon as you connect with these vipers. I'll join you and take control over our prisoners. Killing is too easy for them. We're going to have a party. A hanging party."

As the sun moved across the October sky, Percy returned to his office to relax. He was optimistic that at long last he would get his revenge. It loomed so near; he could almost taste it. Early that evening he dined alone, waiting for impending news of his enemy's capture. But as the sun lowered in the sky and darkness approached, his impatience increased. Soon it would be past the time for his soldiers to have alerted him of their success. A sensation of dread crept over him. The exploit must have gone terribly wrong; he could sense it deep within. By now, Jonathan and his men should have been apprehended. He should be in the position of proclaiming them all guilty of treason. Percy continued his incessant pacing until he heard wagons rolling down the street. He rushed to the outside door while praying for deliverance. At first sight, hope arose as he spied the caravan – twenty soldiers in front and twenty soldiers as the rear guard, riding in perfect formation. But where were the prisoners? The troops and wagons looked precisely the same at the start of their journey.

"Where are the Americans?" Percy shouted almost incoherently. "I gave direct orders to capture and hold those prisoners. Did you have to kill them all?" He raced to the covered wagons to assess the situation for himself. "Hell, it doesn't look like you fired a shot!"

"No one attacked the wagons, sir. We drove all the way here with no problem."

"No attack, you say. That's not possible! Their leader was told about the payroll. He believed it was on this freight wagon. Nothing could have stopped him and his men from attacking us. Nothing! This was a foolproof plan, by damn!" As Percy's voice raised in timber, his face turned crimson, almost matching the color of the setting sky. His mind raced. What could have stopped Francis Marion's men from attempting to steal all that money? Taking a few moments to absorb the total failure of his plan to ensnare Jonathan, Percy became uncontrollably enraged. "That filthy, slippery, tosspot must have discovered our scheme," he said aloud. *But how? Could there be a traitor in our midst? Only he, Miriam, and Brumley knew the details. It couldn't be…or could it?*

His body seemed to spasm. *It's just not possible; we all had so much to gain.* His awareness seemed to be spinning in circles. Shaking his head to clear his mind, he returned to the problem at hand.

Confronting the men on horseback, Percy issued further orders. "Get those wagons off the street. You're all dismissed, for now. But I will grill each of you in the morning. There's no doubt in my mind that a traitor is in our midst. And when I find out whom, he'll wish he had never been born."

Reentering headquarters, Percy began to plot his way out of this fiasco. It shouldn't be too difficult, he supposed. He had become a master at shifting blame away from himself. When his fury subsided, and he thought through his predicament, a horrifying awareness encompassed him. What if the true payroll was stolen? What if Jonathan not only refused the bait but had found a way to steal the genuine payload? "No. No. No!" He exploded with fear and anger. A sickening sensation overtook all his emotions.

The two regular guards near him stood at attention, not daring to look him in the eye.

"Open the safe!" Percy screamed at the guards. "Now!"

The captain trembled, hardly able to move or speak as he peered into the empty safe. He couldn't believe it; no, he wouldn't believe it. He pounded the desk in front of him while cursing Jonathan Warrenton and his militiamen. He felt the color drain from his face with the realization that he had been bested again. Sinking down in the chair, he held his head between shaking hands. He didn't notice that the guards had scurried away like rats on a sinking ship. He was all alone – outplayed and defeated! What treachery could have turned his strategy on its head? There was no passing the buck now. His head would indeed be on a platter, answering to none other than his superior Colonel Tarleton.

Percy's first thought was still to shift the fault to someone else to save his hide. His sinister eyes could have bored a hole through his saber while his rage mounted to a fever pitch. Gradually, he calmed and checked his emotions before focusing on who could be responsible for this betrayal. Only one name came to mind. Miriam.

Catching Jonathan would have to take a backseat for now. But in the end, he would destroy not only Jonathan but he would erase the entire Warrenton name from history.

Chapter 20

Still riding high after learning of Cornwallis's surrender at Yorktown, Jonathan prepared to leave the swamp and give some much-needed attention to his family. But it was hard to feel celebratory when South Carolina was still wallowing in the mud and surrounded by British soldiers. He could not understand what the English King hoped to accomplish by remaining in Charleston. Did His Majesty really think Britain could continue to subjugate the southern states and Florida? Only time would tell. But for the moment, he was still 'Smoke,' and all was quiet in the city. *Not for long,* he thought; all hell was about to break loose because of the stolen payroll.

Early the next morning, Jonathan departed for Goose Creek. Frost blanketed the ground if for only a trice before it disappeared under the morning sun. He had always loved the sights and sounds of the bog on a clear, autumn day. Galloping through the forest, the Patriot was cautious that the enemy would not detect his presence. As usual, he disguised himself as a local farmer. The closer he came to his destination; the more impatient Jonathan grew as he remembered his last reunion with Annabelle. He would never forget the kindness of the O'Leary's. Not many would have had the audacity to allow his notorious family to take refuge in their home.

Jonathan approached the streets of the town with the sun sitting high in the sky. Cautiously, he circled the vicinity to make certain no Redcoats were patrolling the area. Then, discreetly, he rode to the back door of the store after the Mercantile had closed for lunch.

Patrick O'Leary welcomed him with warm surprise. "You canna know how glad I am to see you, lad. We've been sitting on pins and needles, awaiting word of your success."

"And glad I am to be here," he answered with a grin; then followed Patrick into an adjacent room to reunite with his family.

Jonathan's eyes lit up as he gazed on his loved ones, cozily gathered around the long, oak table, deep in conversation and enjoying the warmth of a roaring fire. The aroma of stewed beef permeated the air, causing his mouth to water. His favorite, a stack of corn pones, was centered in the middle waiting to be passed, along with plates of homemade bread and butter. Steaming mugs of coffee accompanied every plate.

"Is there room for one more?" Jonathan asked in a quiet timber.

Each family member turned as one, instantly recognizing his voice.

"Jonathan!!!" Albert was the first to rise and share a bear hug with his son. "If you're not a sight for sore eyes! We have surely missed you, my boy." He stepped aside quickly to allow everyone to greet him separately.

Annabelle had just entered the room with a black kettle, and almost dropped it when she met Jonathan's eyes. Placing it on the table, she ran with abandon and embraced herself in his welcoming arms. While gazing into his eyes, she felt such relief. "You're actually here! And in one piece." She couldn't seem to stop rattling on. "Have a seat, I'll fix you a plate. You must be famished. I know you have so much to tell us."

"As long as you're sitting next to me." He flashed his cheeky, crooked smile.

"I think I can manage that," she tried to sound a bit reluctant so she could get a grip on her fluttery heart.

Hanging up his coat and floppy hat, Jonathan took his seat beside Annabelle. "To be sure, I've been sick with worry that something I've been involved in would end badly for my family. That, I could not endure. So, I returned as quickly as possible. Luckily, I ran into no interference."

Albert interjected. "Is there still an arrest warrant out for you?" He sipped his coffee mug while his eyes riveted on his son.

"I won't go into details, as I wouldn't want any of you to be accessories after the fact, but I will say that our entire escapade was successful. It was carried out without a hitch. However, I have no doubt there will be hell to pay. Even without a shred of evidence, I can assure you that Captain Percy and his unit know we confiscated it. Poof, it just disappeared – like smoke. And that will make them crazy. They'll feel the need for payback. How they will do it is anyone's guess."

Annabelle took Jonathan's hand in hers. "I believe that someday, in generations to come, the Swamp Fox and his militia will be remembered with pride."

"I'd like to think that's true, but sometimes I feel like all I'm doing is dodging cannon shot. No matter how many times we claim victory, there's always another battle around the corner. It never ends."

"You're making a difference, son. You must realize that. More and more soldiers appear to be vacating the city," Albert reasoned. "Have you heard anything from the frontlines?"

"I have great news. While at camp, Marion received a missive directly from the general himself."

Everyone drew in a breath spontaneously. "You mean from George Washington?"

"Who else? Washington proclaimed General Cornwallis's surrender to him at Yorktown on October 17th."

"Oh my, do you mean the war is over?" Amelia asked hopefully.

"Not so fast, Mother. Although much of the war is over, most of South Carolina will still be occupied. Washington seems to think that they will not leave this place until we drive them into the sea. So that's exactly what we intend to do."

"Hear, hear." They raised a glass in solidarity.

While the men were being cavalier and toasting Jonathan's news about the British withdrawal from America, a feeling of dread spread over Annabelle. Dropping her shoulders in despair, she quietly interrupted everyone's jovial mood.

"Well, I for one am greatly disappointed by this news. Why should we have to keep fighting? Why doesn't the main army come down here and move those Redcoats out? Surrender or not, we are no better off. We are stuck, bogged down in this miserable conflict with no end in sight. There's nothing to celebrate."

"The lass is spot-on," Patrick chimed in. "I'd also be liking to know exactly what we, the people of Charleston, have gained from Cornwallis's surrender?"

"Don't worry, we'll be free of those bastards. It won't be long now," Jonathan tried to reassure his family.

After a moment, Jonathan glanced fleetingly at Annabelle, giving her a knowing smile. She, too, returned the gesture. It never failed; whenever she showed him the slightest interest, he wanted her. Ready for conversation to be over, he needed only to reconnect with his Belle. Alone. But he had one more piece of business to conduct before he could devote his evening solely to her.

Jonathan then stood and asked if he could speak to his father in private. He wanted answers. Walking outside together, Jonathan turned toward Albert.

"Tell me about the feud between you and Miriam Worthington. It's her hatred toward you that allowed her betrayal to our Patriotic cause and an alliance with Tories. Evidently, she's been consorting with Captain Percy and William Brumley to aid them in ridding the world of the Warrenton name."

"I don't believe that! Her husband was one of my dearest and closest friends. His death pains me still."

"Well, she believes that you betrayed him in a deep and personal way."

"That's absurd."

"I assure you; it is not."

"Then, I'll just have to hear it from the horse's mouth. What you've told me makes no sense, and I won't rest until I find the truth. Assuredly, I'll be paying Mrs. Worthington a visit." With head down, Albert retreated like fog rolling in off the coast.

Jonathan felt mucky even mentioning Miriam and her unsettling plans to his father – a man of untarnished reputation. So, after dropping that bombshell on his father, he wasted no time clearing his mind of that whole sordid tale. Turning back toward the Mercantile, he noticed Annabelle at the backdoor, watching him. Unexpectedly, he felt his heart skip a beat. She was beginning to affect him in ways he had not experienced before. Most of his adult life had been spent as a soldier, so he knew little about romance. No longer content with just being friends with Belle, he was ready to move forward with their future. With his crooked smile and an inviting nod, he motioned for her to join him.

Annabelle couldn't seem to take her eyes off him. Shivering from the nippy October breeze, she adjusted the woolen wrap around her shoulders. Then slowly, enticingly, she sauntered toward him. Moments passed, as they gazed deeply into each other's eyes, until Jonathan leaned in for a kiss. As always, Jonathan's kisses were gentle and sweet. But this time, she felt more. When he deepened the embrace, she experienced a slow burn within, tempting her to move closer still. Perhaps, this would be the night she would find out what it meant to make love to a man. Fate had a different idea.

Out of nowhere, a group of townspeople with empty baskets in hand happened to move among the row of fruit trees. Some of the children ran past them as they gleaned the fallen apples. Even one stranger commented how the O'Leary family believed in sharing good fortune with the neighbors. Reluctantly moving apart, they began to chuckle. Within seconds, they were laughing aloud. Privacy was never to be theirs. Jonathan grabbed her hand and urged her to run with him deeper into the orchard. Finally, they stopped and dropped at the base of a huge pecan tree.

"Alone, at last," Jonathan declared with a look of mischief. "How long do you think it will last this time?"

The sun's rays cast a softened glow to Annabelle's face, yet he thought she appeared unsettled. Apparently, something was on her mind. He was correct.

During her short stay at the Mercantile, Annabelle had been able to reassess her situation. She now lived in America. There was no aristocracy recognized here – and no talk of arranged marriages. She was a nobody. Jonathan and his family owed her nothing as Amelia had made clear from the beginning. She did not want to be accused of forcing Jonathan into a marriage in which he or his family had doubts.

"What's bothering you? Suddenly, you're a million miles away."

"I've been thinking about our situation and learning more about America every day. Arranged marriages are not recognized. Would you like to be released from your obligation to marry me?"

"What the hell are you talking about? Marrying you was never an obligation. Believe me, I would never have considered a lifetime with anyone I did not have feelings for."

"I wish I could believe you. Sometimes, I feel like I've been foisted upon you without your knowledge or approval."

"How can you say that? You must know that George Spencer was half in love with you during our time onboard that wretched ship. Who could have put such notions into your head?"

"I can feel that you want me – I want you, too. But do you really think you could fall in love with me? After all, we're talking about the rest of our lives."

He leaned in closer and cupped her face with tenderness. "How could you not know how much I care for you?"

"Jonathan, I know that you are the love of my life. But I want to be the love of your life, too. And as much as you care for me, I must be sure that your love is real."

"And how do I go about proving that?" He was becoming exasperated with her.

"I'm giving you time," she insisted, "to think about the future and what you really want."

"You're joking, right? I don't even have the time to court you properly. Never mind planning a future."

Tears began to roll silently down Annabelle's face. "Your mother has made it crystal clear that I am not worthy of the Warrenton name. I can't blame her. My lack of funds as well as my tainted background are a blight. I wouldn't want you to bear my shame."

A sound started to bubble up from Jonathan's chest. At first, she thought he was going to cry, but then she realized he was laughing. A big, belly laugh.

"My mother? You listened to my mother's prattle? Everyone knows she thinks too much of herself and well above the rest of society. Believe me when I say that nobody would be good enough for her son. I love her dearly, but she has some decided character flaws. I am so sorry that I didn't warn you. From now on, just nod your head and pretend to agree with her. And remember, don't necessarily believe every word she says."

Annabelle was speechless. How could he talk about his mother in that manner? "She didn't say anything that wasn't true."

"I don't care what anybody thinks about the woman I wish to marry. I am a man with a mind of my own. I care nothing for what others flap their gums about. The only opinion that matters to me is yours. Do you love me? Do you want to marry me?"

"You know that I do. But I want time for us to discover more about each other. We've just met a few months ago. We're at war and we have a new country to consider. A world we've never dreamed of is opening before us. Don't you think we should both take our time before plunging ahead with marriage on our minds?"

Jonathan's face turned stony as he pondered all she had said. After showing his displeasure, his voice sounded hard. "So, what is it that you want me to do? Do you want me to court you? Sorry, I'm still fighting a war. If I step back the way you suggest, we won't be moving ahead with anything, especially marriage."

It took only a moment to realize that Jonathan did not understand what she meant. "You're not listening to me." Annabelle stepped into his embrace as she put her arms around his neck.

"I'm listening all right. I just don't like what I am hearing." He released her hands.

Annabelle would not relent. And once again reached up to kiss him. At first, he avoided her lips until finally, sighing, he gave in to her overture. He felt her body tremble slightly when he embraced her and deepened the kiss. They remained in their timeless space, sharing passion, neither wanting to end the connection.

Annabelle felt like she was falling; her love for Jonathan growing. But in an instant, she felt her love betrayed. Jonathan laid her down while his hands wandered to places that only a doxy would allow.

"Stop. What are you doing?" She grabbed his wayward hands, thrusting them away.

"Sorry," his voice reflected no remorse at all. "Isn't that what you wanted? You've made it clear you have no interest in marriage anytime soon, yet you throw yourself in my arms. What did you expect? I can only presume that a sexual liaison is what you have in mind."

"Sexual liaison? Are you serious? Is it so wrong to want to learn the world around me? To understand myself. You should realize that doesn't change how I feel about you."

Her cracked voice and speech did not sway him a bit. She had hurt him deeply, and all he wanted to do was lash out. "The only thing you've made me aware of is that you want to meet other men to make sure I'm your best choice. You want to weigh your options. Well, good luck with that. You can be sure William Brumley is still interested. Let me know when you're ready to settle down, and maybe, just maybe, I'll listen." He walked back into the Mercantile leaving her sobbing and alone.

Chapter 21

Percy's fury was out of control. He couldn't bear the thought that his flawless plan had failed so completely. Somehow, those miserable lowlifes had found out about when the payroll was expected. But that was impossible. He had told no one. In his mind, he had pictured himself receiving accolades for saving the payroll as well as catching the elusive Jonathan Warrenton and doing away with him for good. Instead, he was being held responsible for the loss. The British investigators could find no proof as to how the payroll had been stolen. Not a single clue was found that pointed to a culprit other than himself. The money appeared to magically disappear. But, by damn, he, Percy, knew better, and he didn't need any confounded evidence. It was those no-good thieving scoundrels – Jonathan Warrenton and the Swamp Fox; and if it took his last breath, he would make them suffer.

How did they pull it off? He vowed to turn over every stone needed to reveal the evidence that would clear his name. The sentries he posted swore under oath they never abandoned their stations. That left the only three people who had possession of the facts to his ruse – William Brumley, Miriam Worthington, and himself.

And to top off this calamitous fiasco, he had just been informed that Cornwallis had surrendered to George Washington at Yorktown. It should have been a devastating blow to all the British soldiers, but the truth was that they were also sick of the war, and many were eager to return home and leave this inhospitable swampland. However, they were quickly subjected to orders from Central British Command. Their entire battalion was to remain in Charleston and continue their occupation until otherwise notified. A sea presence would be forthcoming to ensure their safety.

Confined to this insect and snake-infested hellhole increased Percy's need for revenge. He would find a way to make the Warrentons pay for his failure. Nobody made a fool of him and lived to tell about it.

After ruminating over the facts, as he knew them, Percy settled his ire on Miriam. Who else could it be? Who else had connections to the Warrentons? He could only assume that she was pretending a seething hatred toward that haughty family. Determined to find the truth, he would make her talk no matter what it took. A fierce storm pelted the windows of Post Headquarters, but Percy refused to be deterred from confronting Miriam. To witness her fear, when she realized that he discovered her treachery, aroused him. He looked forward to punishing her in ways she had never dreamed possible. Grabbing his slicker, he stormed outside to meet his femme fatale.

By the time he had reached her home, his anger had once again reached a fever-pitch. He banged at her door with a vengeance. "Open this damn door before I break it down!"

Miriam leisurely placed a napkin in her lap and sipped the expensive wine. She and Mary, her lady in service, were about to enjoy dinner together in the cozy kitchen when the banging began. Who could be calling on her at this hour? She was not expecting anyone.

"Just a moment, I'm coming," she called out hastily.

Just as Miriam unlocked and opened the door, it was pushed roughly against her.

"Get out of my way, woman," Percy shoved past her into the foyer. "Is anyone else in the house?"

"Yes, of course, I have live-in help. We were just sitting down to eat." She was not only repelled by his manner but his alcohol-reeked breath as well.

"Get her out of here!" Percy bellowed.

"I can't do that. This is her home." Miriam slowly stepped away from him. She was becoming frightened. Why was he acting like such a brute?

"Now!" he roared.

Listening to their distant exchange, Mary inched forward, scared as a mouse before running out the front door.

"At least she knows her place," the officer remarked with a smirk as he slammed and locked the door behind her.

Miriam was truly frightened now. Gathering her courage, she lifted her head and attempted to act as proprietress of the manor. "You have no right to charge in here pushing and ordering us around. We are not your soldiers. I'm sorry but I must ask you to leave." With shaking hands at her side, she faced him head-on. "Your boorishness does not belong in a lady's home."

Before she could utter another word, he backhanded her face. "Lady? I don't see any lady. All I see is a treacherous, lying wench who deceived me."

"I never—"

Suddenly, he grabbed her roughly, pushing her against the wall. Screaming in pain, Marianne tried to scramble away from him.

But he reached for her again, ready to strike.

"Stop! What are you doing?"

"You thought you could get away with your disloyalty? To me? Did you really think I wouldn't find out that it was you who divulged the real plan to young Warrenton?"

"No! No! I told Jonathan nothing. Nothing. He took the bait. I'm sure of it. He believed every word I said. If something went wrong, it was not on my behalf," Miriam appealed desperately to make him believe her.

"Save your breath."

"It wasn't me; I tell you."

"Prove it." His demeanor seemed to soften for a moment as he looked at her with a sickening longing. "What are you willing to do to convince me that you're innocent? How much does my friendship and trust mean to you?" His face looked like a mask of insanity.

"What…What do you mean?" Miriam could not breathe. Panic was coursing through her. She knew exactly what the blackguard wanted; she would die before giving in to that monster. Before she could begin to defend herself, his arm moved like a snake as it lashed out to grab her.

He jerked her toward him, knocking her off her feet. "Get up!" he barked. Roughly, he pulled her up against his chest. "Now we're going to have some fun. You owe me that."

"I don't owe you anything." Her hands flayed wildly, but he was just too strong. Miriam watched in horror while her blouse was ripped in two.

"You're starting to look better already." With malice, he laughed without humor at his own remarks. Miriam's struggles made him so angry he clouted her across the face before forcing her down on the sofa. Hearing her whimper made him more lustful before he was interrupted. A loud knock stopped Percy in his tracks. Miriam didn't dare say a word. A louder knock followed.

"Miriam, I know you're in there. Open the door. It's Albert Warrenton. I need to speak with you. It's rather urgent."

"Looks like I was right about you, you bitch." Percy rose in a fury, buttoning his trousers.

Gathering her wits, Miriam yelled. "Help! Help! Albert, I'm being attacked. Hurry!"

Albert started to beat against the door when he heard Miriam's plea. He slammed himself against the wood, until the door splintered after the third time. Frantically, he ran into the townhouse. Looking from side to side, he searched for the assailant. He realized the intruder must have run out the back as soon as he heard the knock on the door. He was nowhere to be found.

Miriam was discovered slumped in a pile on the floor, trembling uncontrollably. She was covered with bruises and welts.

"Thank goodness, you're here," she whispered while resting in soothing arms. Slowly, she spoke, "He broke in. I never saw him before. He was so filthy and cruel." Miriam sobbed as she spoke. "He smelled like he was drenched in ale. As soon as he heard you, he rushed out the back door." She looked up at Albert with thankfulness. "You saved my life!" She managed between hiccups.

When her weeping subsided, Albert gently lifted her onto the sofa. They sat quietly while her grandfather clock ticked away the minutes. Finally, Albert broke the silence.

"Do you want to tell me what happened? It is rare that a ruffian would venture into this neighborhood, and unthinkable for one to actually cross your threshold." He pondered a moment. "Do you honestly believe that the man who attacked you was a stranger? Was there nothing recognizable about him?"

"No," she insisted. "He was bearded with a slouchy hat and rough clothing. I never really got a good look at his face, but his voice was not familiar. Lower class." She shivered at the thought of him. "He must have followed me home from my walk. He seemed to slip in the door right behind me. I never had a chance to lock it."

"Sounds to me he was waiting for you. He must have been a brute by the looks of your face and arms. Do your bruises need looking after? I can have my doctor here on a moment's notice."

"No. No need. I just want to take a hot bath and go to bed. Mary should be back directly and do whatever is necessary."

"You should report this incident to the magistrate, before he attacks someone else in the same brutal manner."

"Do you really think the British care what happens to me? I would never put my trust in their hands. Never!"

"I understand your lack of faith, believe me. I lost all belief in the British system some time ago."

She smiled weakly. "Who would have thought that an English Duke and Baroness would turn their backs on their king?"

"We are not the only ones. I can assure you of that. Our government has crossed the line in their cruelty, and I for one want no part in it."

"I agree." She nodded her head before continuing, "What is the reason for your visit? I can't imagine that you would be stopping by on a whim."

"No, I am not. I heard some disturbing news from my son Jonathan. He explained that you had bitter feelings toward me; that you believed that I played a part in ruining your husband and aiding in the financial demise that led to his death."

"That's the truth." She looked at him with despair in her eyes. "I learned from an exceptionally reliable source that his investments in certain shipping lines were incurred because of your insistent advice. And that you profited greatly from his losses." Her face hardened as she let her seething rage rise to the surface.

"That's impossible." He was completely taken aback while he wondered who her reliable source could be? "I do not make deals with or invest in cargo-carrying ships. I have always found them unreliable at best. Too many of my friends have lost their fortune placing their money in a ship, hoping for that pot of gold at the end of its journey. Am I to believe that was exactly what your husband hoped to achieve? Easy money?"

"You're making him sound greedy and dimwitted. Besides, it had to be you. Whom else would he have trusted in manners of finance?"

"Since I am certain that I had no part in what is starting to sound like a set-up by some very unscrupulous men, you might start with that person who pointed you in my direction." Albert shot her a profoundly serious look. He wanted information, and he would not leave without it.

"I'm afraid that's privileged information," she stubbornly replied, refusing to cooperate.

"Instead of protecting the men who are truly responsible for your loss, you might find it beneficial to work together to find these swindlers. It might even be possible for me to aid you in recouping some of your losses."

Suddenly, she felt a dread. What had she done? Could she really have been so misguided? Could William Brumley have not only lied to her but taken advantage of her naivete in the most egregious fashion?

"You would help me? Even after my malicious accusations?"

"If you let me," he assured her. "First, you must give me a name."

"How well do you know William Brumley?"

"I hear he regularly plays both sides of this war. He is an outsider, but watches, rather than participating, until he's got a sure winner. Then he picks his side."

Miriam began to share her story. "After my husband's death, Brumley approached me with sincere condolences. Then he proceeded to tell me how you had swindled my husband out of his fortune, and that he would help to retain as much of my inheritance as possible before others came to claim the losses. I was so overcome by grief that I immediately believed him. He was so helpful with the funeral as well as all the paperwork related to the estate. He made me believe that I was left with extraordinarily little."

"That charlatan! What kind of man preys on a grieving widow? No decent one, that's for sure." Albert was furious at the blackguard's sins.

"But we have no proof. I don't think he'll just hand over any money he's stolen. Apparently, his concerned demeanor is only a façade."

"He's no gentleman, that's for certain. Do not confront him. I want to have him investigated without his knowledge. There may be a way for you to reclaim some of your inheritance."

"I can't believe you'd really help me. Not after everything I did. Did you know I even tried to entrap Jonathan? He could have been killed."

"Yes, I'm aware of your connection to the British. Since Jonathan made a clean getaway, and I can only assume that you're back on our side, I would be happy to give assistance."

She smiled with sincerity, then hugged Albert for his kindness and generosity of spirit. It had been a long time since she felt a sense of friendship, but this gentleman had given back her faith in people.

Albert stood. "Pack up, you're coming with me. You dare not remain here any longer. Something's afoot and I don't want you caught in the middle. You can stay with my family in the country. Nobody will find you there."

Miriam felt a catch in her breathing. Crying with sheer happiness, she was no longer alone, nor having only herself to depend on. Did she dare discard her troubles and unease? At least for a little while.

Chapter 22

To say the least, Annabelle and Amelia were taken aback when Albert entered the parlor with Miriam Worthington in tow. At first, neither spoke a word but looked stone-faced at the unwelcome intrusion.

"Why is that despicable woman in my home?" Fuming, Amelia stood with hands on hips in defiance.

But before his wife could spew any more venom, Albert insisted in no uncertain terms that Miriam was to be their houseguest and to deal with her accordingly.

Completely gob-smacked, Amelia made an abrupt about-face and stormed out.

With a look of repugnance, Annabelle followed in her wake, leaving her opinions to the proprietress.

"Don't worry, dear," Albert soothed Miriam, as he patted her hand. "They'll come around eventually. For now, just settle in. Remember, no one can be apprised of your whereabouts, so for now, stay hidden from visitors and passersby." He rang for the butler, who escorted her upstairs with a few trunks.

After settling into the guest quarters, Miriam sat in retrospect before her mirror. She'd been such a fool, she thought. Although she no longer trembled from paralyzing fear brought on by Percy's attack, she was left with a feeling of utter despair. Deep down, she speculated that William Brumley wasn't the man he pretended, but she had been so alone and vulnerable. He had been so convincing as her only love interest, and that made him even more enticing.

And now she must be holden to yet another – Albert Warrenton, of all people. What kind of man could so swiftly forgive the pain she had caused him and his family while offering her sanctuary as well? It seemed he was every bit the dear friend her husband had believed. Her biggest fear was that she would never be accepted by Amelia and Annabelle. Both women had good reason not to trust her goodwill. Lacking a good rapport with other women, Miriam had no idea where to start.

Amelia and Annabelle were sipping an aperitif, as they waited to be called into dinner. Both had the same problem on their mind.

"Can you believe my husband brought that malicious trollop into our home?" Amelia gasped.

"Surely, he has sound reason. But what could she possibly have done to negate the fact that she assisted in a trap that would end in Jonathan's death!"

"Not a bloody thing, as far as I'm concerned. I can't imagine how I'll be able to keep a civil tongue in my head around that woman."

"Did you realize it was her carriage that almost ran over me that day on the Battery?"

"If that's true, then she's willing to get down and dirty with her tricks. She's more callous than I imagined."

"But Albert insists that we treat her like any other guest?"

"Not on my watch." Amelia snorted.

"I'm not ashamed to admit that I'm a bit afraid of her. Not only has she insulted me at every turn, but she also tried to kill me and then laughed it off as if it were inconsequential."

"Last I heard, she detested Albert." Amelia was so confused. "What on earth is going on?"

The door to the parlor flew open. Apparently, Albert had been eavesdropping on their conversation. "I'll be glad to tell you exactly what occurred. I daresay, you both should have more faith in my judgment."

"Well, get on with it then," both women spoke in unison.

"When I arrived at her townhouse, she was being attacked by an intruder. He was viciously beating her with rape on his mind."

"And you saved her?"

"Something like that. Miriam had been grossly misinformed about my business dealings with her husband by none other than Annabelle's escort, William Brumley."

"He's a slippery bugger, that one. We need to tread lightly lest we raise his ire." Amelia was no stranger when it came to dealing with scoundrels.

"Agreed. Brumley fits in to this mess somewhere, but I'm not sure exactly where yet."

"You really feel we should give Miriam a chance to prove herself trustworthy?" Annabelle asked hesitantly.

"I'd appreciate that. I'm sure you are both up to the task."

"Humph," was Amelia's answer.

"We'll try our best. For your sake, Albert."

While the others were dining downstairs as usual, Miriam secluded herself for the time being. She needed to rest and perhaps do a little soul-searching. She had been lying to herself about William. Somewhere along the line, she had fallen in love with that reprobate. Surely, that blackguard had bilked her inheritance. Where was he now? What were his plans for her? When would he make his next move in the abhorrent game he seemed to be playing? She knew he wanted Annabelle. But to what lengths would he go to acquire the young lady? And how exactly was she going to stop him?

While Miriam was acclimating to her new accommodations, Annabelle strolled from room to room inside the manor. She loved living in the country. Never again would she take for granted the coziness and beauty of her surroundings. Truly she had been blessed in the peace and serenity it offered. But what if she had foolishly thrown it all away with her rush to judgment? Jonathan was furious with her. Of course, he misconstrued everything said to him. While she believed that she was pouring out her heart and love to him, he adamantly heard something entirely different. How could Jonathan think for even a moment she wanted another man? She understood that prolonging their engagement was the only prudent thing to do; yet he insisted she was using it as an excuse to look at other prospects. Men were idiots!

Annabelle's contemplation was interrupted by a knock on the front door and whinny of horses. She moved aside the drapes in the parlor and peeked outside to see the Brumley crest on the carriage door. *Not that addle-pot,* she groaned. Taking her time to reach the foyer, she remembered that Albert had warned not to reveal their knowledge about Brumley's criminal behavior until proven.

At the butler's invitation, the Englishman stepped inside the entrance, spying her immediately. Without pause, he embraced her warmly. "I'm chuffed to bits to see you again. Where have you all been hiding? I was about to abandon hope of ever seeing you again."

Annabelle backed away abruptly. She never could abide the man, but now that she had learned that he was a lying scoundrel as well, her fear and wariness was threefold. He was a dangerous man. She attempted to discourage him. "What can I do for you, Mr. Brumley? I can't imagine that you could have any business with me."

"Business? Heavens no. My visits with you, my dear, are sheer pleasure. And, as always, you are a sight to behold."

Mulligrub! Annabelle thought to herself. *He's speaking as if he's courting me. What game is he playing? He knows that I am engaged to another.*

Brumley continued. "I am especially fortunate that you have returned today. You see, I find myself in need of refreshment – a bit peckish. It's almost teatime. Do you think you could set another place at your afternoon repast?"

Annabelle couldn't believe what she was hearing! That shifty bugger was inviting himself to tea. "I'm not sure we're having an afternoon repast today, sir. We have just returned from a week's long visit with friends." That should deter him, she hoped.

But Amelia, having heard the distant discourse, decided to play devil's advocate. She remembered the adage, 'keep your friends close and your enemies closer.' "Why Mister Brumley, what a nice surprise. Let me take your top hat and justico; then I'll ring for some refreshments. We can visit in the parlor."

"Such a lovely hostess you are, my grace. Thank you so much for your hospitality." Brumley exuded graciousness.

Amelia led William into the parlor and directed him to the sofa while she and Annabelle took the wingback chairs facing him. An oak coffee table separated them with the tea tray.

Annabelle discreetly conveyed to the older woman not to leave her alone with their guest.

"Well, ladies, where have you been this last month? I haven't seen the usual farmhands during your departure." Brumley eased into a conversation.

"We've been vising friends. And there is no need to work the fields. Harvest is over," Amelia answered, not giving him any real information.

"Indeed, as we all know, these are troubled times. I just wanted to insure myself that all is well here. I wouldn't want anything to happen to your lovely family. The British can be ruthless, you understand."

"That is very kind of you, sir. We appreciate your concern, but we have no need of your protection," Annabelle answered in no uncertain terms.

"Still, these are trying times. The duke or his son could easily succumb to the casualties of war," he continued with a touch of hopelessness in his voice.

Annabelle gasped. His tone sounded almost threatening. She decided to return the favor.

"I can assure you that my fiancé can take care of himself, as well as guarantee he would not appreciate your unsolicited visits. He might find your interest in my wellbeing quite offensive."

Ignoring her remarks, William continued to act like a coveted guest. "Where is Albert, by the way? I haven't seen him in quite a while."

"Both his farming and business interests keep him occupied. He has no time to gallivant around the countryside, visiting neighbors unannounced." Annabelle fidgeted even more with Brumley's mere presence.

"My, look at the time," William said while pulling his watch chain out of his breast pocket. "I see that I must return to my own business affairs." He bowed. "Ladies, I believe I will take my leave." Looking straight at Annabelle, he continued, "But rest assured, I will be back to make sure all is well with the Warrenton women."

Amelia rose and returned with his outerwear.

Then, wasting no time, he tipped his hat to the ladies and gave them an unreadable smile before sauntering out the door to his carriage.

About the same time William Brumley returned home, Percy was basking in his promotion to Major. He was now the highest-ranking officer stationed in Charleston. Most of the senior commanders were aboard ship or on their way home to England. He reveled in the power he could now wield. He could finish Jonathan Warrenton, for good. He stared at the warrant for the arrest of Albert Warrenton, claiming he was guilty of sedition against the Crown. It was a false accusation, of course, but he had falsified enough documents to trick the courts. Death by hanging exacted the inevitable conclusion. He smiled because he knew that this was one scenario that the young viscount would not be able to ignore. A satisfied smirk crossed his face as he thought of what lay ahead. It was true, he didn't really want the old man. Albert was only the bait.

With Percy's preparations in order, his troops waited in the courtyard for his command. He had but one more assignment to complete before their

122

departure. Leaving his office, he assuredly readied to the Poinsettia Tavern. He had curried a missive last evening, informing William Brumley to meet him at this exact time. He loathed doing business with the double-dealing turncoat but needed him for one last task. As usual, being the first to arrive, Percy sat alone in their regular shadows at the back of the pub.

"I told you not to contact me again. I want nothing to do with your miserable schemes," Brumley hissed as he slid in the booth across from Percy.

"Too bad. I don't much care to deal with a liar and a thief, but I'm stuck with you."

"What is it you need from me? I have nothing you want."

"Ah, but you're such an accomplished spy. My moles tell me you spend almost everyday sniffing around the Warrentons' estate."

"That's none of your business," William spit out in his face before rising to leave.

"Sit down and shut up. I don't give a rat's ass why you slink around out there. So, while you continue your misguided assumption that Annabelle Gainsborough will ever be interested in an inconsequential cod like you, you can inform me of any sightings of Jonathan and his mates."

"Why do you care? The war's all but over." William still wanted no part of Percy's scheme.

"Not here, it's not. The British are still in charge, and I mean to make that clear to all of Charleston," Percy snarled.

"I see." William chuckled. "Your plan to catch Warrenton didn't pan out."

"I thought I told you to stifle it. Keep your eyes open and your mouth closed."

Realizing he had no choice, William acquiesced. "I suppose it won't be much of a hardship to give you the lay of the land. Especially, since I want Annabelle's fiancé out of the picture as much as you do."

"Right. But I expect frequent reports. And I'll want to know immediately if you spot the duke."

"He's there now, as far as I know. Don't ever ask me to meet with you again! I'm through!" Brumley's voice turned hard.

"Shut your trap before I throw you in the brig. I'll do anything I damn well please, and you'll do as I tell you, when I tell you. Now get the hell out of here."

Returning to base, Percy realized that the time had finally come. With everything aligned, he was ready to proceed. He looked over his redcoat regiment with pride.

"Prepare the troops to ride," Percy ordered his sergeant. "We have a dangerous fugitive to bring in, and I don't want any mistakes." He cringed inwardly as he remembered all the times that young viscount had bested him. He would stand for it no longer. This time there would be no escaping his wrath.

In full dress uniform, Percy mounted his horse, taking the troops' lead position. An impressive column of soldiers paraded through the streets of Charleston that afternoon. Nobody watching the spectacle realized the calamity about to take place on the South Carolina countryside.

The late fall day found the Warrenton family gathered comfortably in the rocking chairs that lined the front porch of the manor. A cool breeze stirred around them while they watched the last of the migrating geese.

"I never get tired of watching the sun descend slowly behind those tall cypresses on the far side of the meadow." Amelia sighed.

"It is a sight to behold." Albert reached over to take Amelia's hand. "I can't remember when I've felt so content."

"If only Jonathan were here; I'd be the happiest mother alive." Amelia found her son's deep involvement in the war difficult to bear. How much longer would she have to endure?

"He's exactly where he needs to be," Albert remarked. "Washington made clear that the British aren't through with South Carolina. They've dug in their claws, and they're not about to give up without a fight."

"But if the general has claimed victory over the British, and Cornwallis surrendered, why is their army still here?" Annabelle questioned.

"The actual terms of surrender have yet to be determined. A peace treaty must be agreed to by all parties. Until then, the British believe that they are still in charge. It is up to us to disavow them of those beliefs – with force, if necessary," Albert explained.

"So, what you're saying is that we in South Carolina have gained nothing. We must continue to fight," Annabelle acclaimed.

"It appears so. However, I can assure you that we will prevail." Albert patted her hand in encouragement.

Annabelle smiled in return, not wanting to bring up more uncomfortable questions.

As darkness began to descend, the three eased into silence, enjoying the tranquility of the evening. Soon, the dinner bell rang. But before they could return inside, the sound of loud pounding hooves filled the air. They turned in dread to witness an entire regiment of redcoat soldiers racing up to their entrance.

Chapter 23

Annabelle woke with a jolt. Had morning finally arrived? The dream of a looming calamity had robbed her of sleep. She couldn't forget last night's fear at the sight of a complete regiment of Redcoats arriving at their manor. Neither could she fail to recall the sight of Percy swaggering up the front stairs to forcibly arrest Albert. Then, to be sure that the family realized the severity of the moment, that vicious man conducted a mock trial on their veranda. In short order, with no jury of his peers, the duke was convicted of treason! Treason! What poppycock. His sentence? A public hanging. Then the scene unfolded. Amelia fainted. Berthe was first to procure the needed smelling salts, reviving her. After the soldiers left in a cloud of dust, the women shared the dire situation and their need to lean on one another. But reassurance was slow in coming. They could not erase the indignity of Albert being carted away, trussed up like a turkey. By the time their tears were spent, each struggled to hope for a better tomorrow.

Miriam had watched in horror the whole event from her upstairs window. A hopelessness washed over her the entire time. Cringing at the sight of Percy, she had hidden behind a drape. Luckily, none of the Redcoats noticed her nor anyone else in the household. It was like her hands were tied behind her back. She needed to keep her whereabouts a secret for now, especially from the British.

The following morning found Annabelle, Amelia, Miriam, and Berthe gathered 'round the small kitchen table.

"So, where do we begin?" Annabelle asked recalling minute details out loud.

"I haven't a clue. We have no one to stand with us. I've never felt so alone." Amelia had not been without Albert to lean on for over thirty years. "Such rubbish!" she voiced in tears. "That horrid man wants me to trade my son for my husband. I simply cannot make such an impossible choice."

"And you won't have to," declared Miriam. "I've been alone for some time now. It hasn't been easy, but I've learned that you can undertake anything you set a mind to."

"This endless agonizing over Albert's arrest is obviously pointless; we must go forward," Annabelle insisted. "Any ideas?"

"We can get off our backsides and get moving," suggested Berthe. "I'll be taking me buggy down to the Mercantile and asking Patrick to watch the prison and learn Albert's whereabouts. Maybe he can find a way in or make Albert more comfortable under the circumstances."

"Thank you, Berthe; that's a wonderful idea." Annabelle smiled, proud of her friend. "Amelia, perhaps, you and Miriam can get word to all our neighbors and friends. You can retell last night's incident that Percy has Albert and is holding him unlawfully. Hopefully, someone might know where to find an honest magistrate."

Miriam stood. "I will do everything I can to help Albert. I feel so ashamed for placing the blame onto him for my husband's ruin. Now I know otherwise. Believe me, I want nothing more than to make amends; that is, if you all will let me."

Amelia reached over for her hand. "I understand the pain you felt at Samuel's passing. He was so young, and I also understand how you could put your trust in the wrong man. It's a story as old as time."

Annabelle was not yet ready to exonerate Miriam for her past deeds. "Amelia, you know you are not alone. If we all work together, we can not only free Albert but damnify Percy in the process."

"And what exactly are you going to do, milady?" Berthe asked Annabelle. "Or do I really need to ask?"

"I imagine you've already guessed my destination. I'll be on my way to Jonathan as soon as I pack a few things. And I don't want to hear any arguments. I'm going and that's that."

"We wouldn't dream of trying to change your mind, dear," the matriarch remarked. She wiped her last tear and gathered her faculties. Amelia was now ready to fight, along with her co-conspirators. "I am so thankful for each one of you. With your help, I'm ready to go to battle for my husband and son."

"Let's rally the troops and get started," Annabelle affirmed.

Within the hour, she was on her way into the swamps. The bright sun and crisp air invigorated her. She rode non-stop through the woods until almost noon, when she came upon a familiar rock, where she and Jonathan had stopped on their last adventure. Dismounting, a lump in her throat formed as she compared their idyllic repast in this lovely spot to their last regrettable encounter. Jonathan had shown such anger. Would he ever forgive her? Surely, he would not remain distant and aloof forever? She'd find out soon.

While enjoying a light meal, Annabelle heard horses in the distance. Quickly, she gathered her things and led Lady into the deeper woods, where they could remain unseen. Whether the riders were friend or foe, she had yet to determine. Patiently, she waited behind the thick brush, as she muzzled Lady.

Less than five minutes later, she witnessed the bright red coats of the British cantering adjacent to her hiding place. Fortunately, they looked neither left nor right but rode on past without a glance. *Percy must have sent his troops this way for a reason,* she thought. He reasoned correctly that she would immediately race into the swamps to warn Jonathan. She should have known! That demon planned to ensnare her before reaching camp. But now that she witnessed his men roaming the swamps; she could take extreme precautions. Jonathan had shown her a shortcut; and with a little luck, she'd not miss the turnoff that would take her through a deeper, murkier area of swampland. It was dangerous to be sure, but Annabelle wasn't worried because Jonathan had imparted in her the markers along that path. At least the snakes, insects, and even the alligators were either hibernating or had migrated further south. Yet still, she didn't want to ride after dark. She could only pray that someone from the camp would spot her before that was necessary.

Before Annabelle could mount, another contingency of riders raced by her position – Redcoated as well. She pulled back just in time. After they passed, Annabelle decided to change her tactics. She led her horse as quietly as possible, deeper into the forest. Confident she was alone; she climbed atop Lady and began searching the area for remembered landmarks. Finally, she recognized the turnoff. Ahead, two shallow rivers joined to form a larger one. A short ride eastward took her to the sandbar that connected one bank with the other. Jonathan had shown her how to carefully cross the expanse and the difference between shifting sands and deadly quicksand. Remembering his words, she maneuvered her horse to the other side.

Beginning to feel safe, Annabelle found a well-concealed resting place. She leaned her head against the trunk of a cypress tree, while Lady drank near the riverbank. Before she knew it, she slept.

Subconsciously, she soon awakened in a panic. Frantically studying her surroundings, she noticed Lady's ears perk at the sound of pounding hooves coming toward them. Bracing herself under the moss-covered tree, she peeked through the branches to see who was pursuing. She prayed silently, *Please don't let it be the British, not this close to my destination!* She pulled back even more, hiding as best she could until a familiar voice brought a sense of relief.

"We found your horse, Annabelle; we know you're in there. Come on out and we'll take you to camp. This is no place for you to spend the night," Whiskey's Irish voice floated to her ears.

"Is that you, Whiskey?" she called.

"It sure is. Mount up. British soldiers are crawling around here like fire ants."

"I know, it's me they're looking for." Running to him, she hugged his neck, then quickly scrambled. Tired but relieved, Annabelle followed the men back to camp.

Percy stopped pacing, finally taking a seat behind his impressive oak desk. He basked in his own importance as he beheld his new domain. He marveled at how his preparations were progressing. The nobleman had been arrested with no pushback whatsoever. For now, Albert was being kept in the stockade with twelve guards surrounding the area, and his entire regiment standing in reserve. There was no way Jonathan Warrenton or Marion's militia could break him out forthwith. If they tried, he'd hang them both, side by side, with all of Charleston watching.

"Courier just arrived from headquarters," a young corporal announced. "It's marked urgent."

"Thank you," Percy replied as he reached to accept the missive from his superiors. Anxious to read it, he unsealed it immediately.

The plans for the British evacuation from Charleston were spelled out in detail. With many of the British soldiers stationed inland, Percy must use his troops to assure they reach the sea with a minimum of bloodshed. The strategy included ships waiting for these soldiers along the inlet waters surrounding Charleston. But obstacles were aplenty.

General Henry Clinton, the commander of the British Army in the Southern colonies, was ill and confined to bed. His only wish was to deter the massive desertions within the rank and remove his troops from the colonies before winter set in. The worst of his setbacks emerged from the Swamp Fox and his men.

The commander hoped to avoid this problem by sending a contingent of troops to James Island to begin preparing for evacuation. This nearby island would allow the troops to reach the ships waiting for them in Charleston Harbor. Percy was heretofore ordered to back up the small provisional militia of arriving troops with his standing regiment. This operation was to take place two days hence.

"Bollocks!" Percy raged. With a complete evacuation looming, he had little time to carry out his plans for the duke. He'd need to speed up Albert's court date and flush out Jonathan. But how could he guarantee Albert's imprisonment when he and his troops were on James Island? Of course, he thought with evil intent, he'd hide the old man where no one would ever find him.

The sound of the Patriot camp buzzed with activity when Annabelle and Whiskey rode in. She had never seen so many men milling around the area. What was going on? Had Jonathan found out about Albert's situation from someone else? Then she realized that she did not recognize many of the men in her midst.

"We'll find Jonathan and take care of your mare. You need to sit by the fire and warm up for a bit," Whiskey said while helping her dismount. After handing her the bedroll and sack hanging from her saddle, he walked the horses down to the stables.

"Thank you," Annabelle called after him. "It seems like you're always rescuing me."

"I can't think of anyone more worthy of saving." He waved with a smile.

Annabelle tentatively approached the firepit. Wrapping her arms in warmth despite the gripping cold, she found a comfortable place to sit. Observing her surroundings, she spied Jonathan trudging up the hill toward her. He wasn't smiling, nor did he seem pleased to find her in his domain again.

He looked down at her and asked with no emotion in his voice. "Why are you here?"

Annabelle felt the same sinking sensation she had in London when her friends and acquaintances had first turned their backs on her – an outcast. How long was he going to punish her for speaking the truth?

"Don't worry, this isn't a social call. I came to make you aware that your father was arrested last night by that despicable Percy. He means to hang him in three days unless you turn yourself in to take his place." She looked up at him, waiting for him to respond. When he did not, she burst. "Doesn't the fact that Percy has your father locked up in his filthy jail warrant enough urgency for me to invade your world unwelcome?"

Ignoring her heated words, he thought aloud. "That's impossible, my father hasn't committed a crime."

"Since when does Percy require permission to carry out his malicious schemes?"

"He wants me that badly, does he?"

"He wants you more, and he wants you dead. Nothing less will satisfy his insane rage."

"Well then, perhaps I should give him what he wants. Maybe then he'll leave my family alone." He shrugged his shoulders.

"You will not!" she stated firmly as she stood. "I don't care how weary you are. Your mother is frantic, your father is in jail, so you are going to fix this. Now! We have no time to waste!"

Her urgency finally grabbed his attention. Jonathan turned to look at her, really look at her. She was dead tired, her hair a raggedy mess, and her face and clothes all covered in dirt. And she had never appeared more beautiful. As their eyes touched, he felt a tightening in his groin. Damn her. He felt ashamed of his reaction to her as well as his hesitation to take her words seriously. The pain from her rejection had clouded his judgment. "So why are you the courier? How do you fit into this mess?"

Annabelle's anger was rising. How dare he question her devotion to his loved ones. "You know how much I love Albert and Amelia. I consider them my family now. I would do anything to save your father!"

"I'm surprised you haven't moved on to greener pastures by now."

"Just because I asked for a little time before we made any long-term decisions doesn't mean I don't love you. You must know that I do."

"Actually, I don't know anything of the sort. But now is not the time to hash out all our differences. So, I'm taking you down to my cabin; later we'll talk to the others."

"You need to begin planning now. We have limited time. Your father's guarded around the clock. And remember, there is no remorse in Percy. He will gladly execute an innocent man without a second thought."

"Don't worry, we'll stop that immoral bastard. While I gather Skirt and Whiskey and let them know what's up, you stay in the cabin and rest. There's a big meeting shortly after supper tonight. You can join us to discuss our plans at its conclusion." He hesitated before he took her hand and continued walking down the hill. He gazed at her one last time. "I'll be back with some food." Jonathan barged ahead to locate his friends with no sign of affection.

Annabelle could sense his frustration and determination to keep his distance. How on earth was she going to convince him that he had misunderstood her? She had to make him listen. As tired as she was, Annabelle was too restless to sleep, so she spent her time refreshing and changing into clean clothes. She was about to go stir crazy with nothing else to do but wait for Jonathan to return.

By the time he came back to retrieve her, Annabelle noticed newcomers dressed in colonial uniforms milling around and waiting for the dinner bell. They circled among the new arrivals until dinner was over, and a meeting called to order by Captain William Wilmot. They watched the officer address the camp along with his contingency of seventy soldiers.

"My fellow Patriots, I've come to ask your assistance in a minor engagement that will be taking place on James Island. We have it on good authority that most of the British troops are on the move. They are trying to position themselves to easily evacuate the Americas. We want to encourage them to leave, of course, but we have found that in their leaving, they are marching through small towns and villages, causing a great deal of harm, by stealing livestock and destroying property. We need to prevent this conduct.

"Two days hence, we are going to ambush the British soldiers on James Island. Our orders are to help them on their way before they commence to pillage the citizenry who make their home there. We need the assistance of Francis Marion and his militia. The Swamp Fox patrol is more familiar with this area, increasing our chance of success." Wilmot nodded to the crowd and stepped aside amid the buzz of conversation.

Francis Marion replaced Wilmot, raised his hand, and quieted the crowd. "I'm sure I speak for my men when I say it would be an honor to assist you in this endeavor. If we could speak in a more private setting, we can finalize our strategy. Jonathan, Whiskey, Skirt, and Bubba, join me please. We'll gather in my tent in fifteen minutes."

Jonathan decided to arrive at Marion's tent ahead of time, so he could talk to his leader in privacy. The chain of command needed to grant permission for him to leave his post, so it was imperative that Marion understood the peril of his father's arrest. Maps of the inlet waterways and Charleston Harbor covered the table. Pinpointing the strategic areas, Marion did not appear surprised to see Jonathan arrive early. The commander had observed Annabelle's presence and knew something must be amiss with the Warrenton family.

Hastily, Jonathan explained his father's ordeal.

The Swamp Fox listened intently to the account of Albert's predicament. Then, after a few moments of mulling over a viable solution, Marion offered, "I believe our excursion to James Island could be the perfect diversion for your rescue mission. Percy's troops will surely be required to assist the evacuees as they prepare to cross the island. That should leave him short on guards in his barracks. So, while we're busy trying to stop the British soldiers from stealing livestock and pillaging homes, you should have time to slip into Charleston and find your father."

"I'll need to take Skirt and Whiskey."

"Of course," he smiled. "I think we can do without you three this time."

"We'll return as soon as possible. With my father in tow, hopefully."

"Godspeed."

After thanking Francis Marion and exiting, Jonathan watched Captain Wilmot and three of his officers walk by. He saluted the notorious officer before spying his friends approach Marion's tent. A quick interlude followed.

"I guess we're on our way to Charleston." Both nodded in agreement. "How in the hell are we going to break your father out of the stockade?"

"We'll figure that out when we get there." He laughed. "Same as always. Let's gear up and meet at the stables in ten minutes."

"Another impossible task!" Whiskey joked. "Out of the frying pan and into the fire."

"We Scots like a good hot fire," Skirt replied good naturedly.

"We Irish only like it in our whiskey!"

"Don't worry, we'll have plenty to drink after we've beaten that lowlife scum Percy one last time!"

Jonathan returned to his cabin, ready to pack and explain his scheme to Annabelle. "I'm on my way to Charleston tonight."

"To rescue your father. You can't go charging in; it's way too dangerous. They'll be waiting for you."

"Don't worry so much. You know Whiskey, Skirt, and I will come up with something. We always do."

"How cavalier you sound. You're not as invincible as you think. And what about me? Am I to return with you?" Annabelle felt so weary; she didn't think she could stay on a horse long enough to reach the city.

"No, of course not. You need to rest after the ordeal you've been through. It's no picnic riding through the swamps, especially with the British Army stalking you. You'll wait here until I return…and I will return with my father. Both the cook and the stablemaster will be staying here at camp, so you and Lady will get plenty to eat." He looked up from his packing to impart an uneasy option. "Maybe you'll find the time to think through what it is you really want."

She was startled by his bluntness. "I already know what I want. I want you."

"I don't think you're as sure as you sound."

"You just choose not to believe me. It's easier for you to doubt me."

"No, you just talk in circles. On one hand you assume we both need time to discover our 'real feelings,' then, you continue to profess your love to me. My head is spinning with your contradictions. So, until you are sure of where you stand, just keep your feelings to yourself. You must realize how beautiful you are. Your choices are limitless."

"Is that supposed to be a compliment?"

"No. It means, without our marital agreement, you have no reason to choose me."

"But I do choose you. Only you."

He smiled sadly. "I will always want you, Annabelle; I can't seem to help myself. But until I'm sure of your state of mind, we can't be together."

She stepped close to him and reached up to touched his face. "Kiss me before you go. Please."

"I don't think that's such a good idea." He shook his head.

"Are you afraid?"

"Terrified."

"I would never hurt you." She rose onto her tiptoes and gave him the sweetest, softest kiss.

Jonathan couldn't resist kissing her firmly in return. The attraction between them was undeniable. He pulled her close enough that she melted into him. He sensed her willingness, so he deepened the kiss and lay her down wantonly on his bed. Before he could join her, the increasing volume of voices jolted him back to reality. What was he thinking reopening his heart to this woman? Not with his head, that's for sure. More confused than ever, he pulled away and grabbed his gear. "It's best I leave. I'll be back to take you home."

And just like that he was gone. Gone. Annabelle was left alone still wanting him while she worried continuously for his safety and Albert's release. She hoped against hope that her prayers would be answered.

Chapter 24

Jonathan and his friends set out immediately for Charleston, taking no time to explain their coming absence from the conflict on James Island. Each was focused, intent on freeing Albert from Percy's clutches. The full moon might make their journey less perilous, but with the British regulars posted throughout the swamp, extra vigilance was in order.

Dawn broke through just as they stopped at a hidden alcove to rest the horses and consider the task at hand.

"What's our first move?" Skirt asked as he led his horse to the bubbling stream nearby.

Jonathan followed. "Annabelle mentioned that Patrick was keeping watch on the situation. He's attempting to scout out as much information as he possibly can. I imagine he can lead us in the right direction before we make our final plans."

"If Percy left with his company for James Island, our mission shouldn't be too complicated," Skirt shared his optimism.

"It'll depend on how many guards he left posted, or if he's moved him out of our reach," Whiskey added.

After emptying their knapsacks of food, they checked their gun chambers one last time.

"Can you believe that this interminable war is really over?" asked Jonathan.

"I still don't trust the bastards," answered Skirt. "If the war is over, how does Percy have the authority to hang Albert for treason? Doesn't make sense."

"Arresting my father has nothing to do with treason or the war. It's about Percy's vendetta against me. He wants me to pay for thwarting him time and time again."

"Well, I'm still hopeful," insisted Whiskey. "I've heard the British are evacuating like roaches in the sunlight. Of course, we might have to oblige them along a bit, but it's a certainty they're well on their way."

"Too bad Percy couldn't just leave quietly," said Jonathan. "This is not the time to be taking care of personal grudges."

"It couldn't be helped, man. Marion knows that," Skirt explained. "We've all done our part in this war. Many times, more than asked of us." They all nodded in agreement.

While his friends perused various maps, Jonathan's mind wandered to the days ahead. He had so much to live for; the birth of a new nation that he helped to build, the land he had inherited and wanted to flourish. And, of course, Annabelle. He had made a true hash of that.

The horses' ears pricked as if they heard someone approaching. Rushing to muzzle their horses, they silently receded into dense foliage, camouflaged yet continuing to watch the main road.

In the distance, pounding hooves sounded an alarm – first, came horses with a platoon of at least fifty mounted soldiers; scores of infantry followed. These warriors were riding to the coast. It was a safe bet that they were part of Percy's company on their way to James Island.

"Wow," remarked Skirt. "They look ready for action."

"Looks like it's going to be a long slog on James Island." Whiskey shook his head.

"Well, at least we know they won't be causing us any trouble." Jonathan smiled. "Did either of you notice Percy?"

"A captain maybe, but not Percy."

"Let's get moving. We've got a job to do."

As the Patriots approached the business section of Charleston, they were relieved to see the shops opening. Jonathan, Whiskey, and Skirt blended in well with the merchants, shoppers, and farmers bustling along the road. The trio soon arrived in the back alley of the Harbor Pub. No one seemed to notice anything out of the ordinary as they congregated near some empty whisky barrels.

Patrick O'Leary stepped out of the pub and walked around the corner at the pre-arranged meeting time. "Right on time, boys." Patrick welcomed them as he led their horses around the back of the business. "I've just returned from the Watch House, and the only thing I know for sure is that only a few guards are on duty. At first, I thought it might be a trap, but then I watched as most of Percy's soldiers left this morning. I have no idea of their destination."

"They're on their way to James Island to help a company of infantrymen evacuate to a ship waiting in the harbor. It'll be a boon if they have cause to stay on the island all day. So, we really have no time to waste in breaking Albert out of that hell-hole," Jonathan explained.

"There was something very strange going on at the prison last evening. I feel confident that it's connected to Albert. Wagons coming and going, carrying guards and officers alike. Arms and equipment were being loaded on freight carriers." Patrick pondered. "It just didn't make sense, especially since only four guards appear to be stationed in the guard house."

"Maybe the soldiers are hiding inside, just waiting for us to make a move," Whiskey suggested.

"Perhaps," he answered doubtfully. "Do you remember the barmaid, Caroline from the Poinsettia Tavern? She's the one who delivered the doctored meals to the guards. The meals that knocked them out."

"I remember the bonnie lass." Skirt smiled. "And a good job she did."

"Well, I couldn't shake this feeling that something odd was transpiring last evening at the prison. Although the guards know me well from my daily supply deliveries, last night they insisted I leave immediately. They were even ready to use force if necessary. So, after leaving quietly, I stopped by the tavern and pleaded with Caroline to be my eyes and ears outside the Watch House. The courageous lass was more than eager to oblige. I still haven't heard from her, but let's hope she found out something that will help us find Albert."

"Good job, mate." Jonathan patted Patrick on the back. "Now we need to become invisible. Are you prepared to turn us into farm workers? Maybe some broad brimmed hats to go along."

"No problem, I've got everything you need ready and waiting."

"Well then, let's get started." Jonathan adjusted his gun belt under his jacket.

Near the wharf, the mammoth gray structure that held Jonathan's father stood easily visible. Discreetly, the four men sauntered up Main Street and reached the turn-off to the Watch House. Nonchalantly, splitting off in different directions, they encircled the building.

Whiskey served as lookout, after finding a vantage point that allowed a clear view of the surrounding wharf and any possible movement of soldiers.

The thick, humid air carried the voices of the two outside sentries, who were positioned at opposite ends of the Watch House. His eyes followed as Jonathan, Patrick, and Skirt easily rendered the guards unconscious, tied them up and dragged them between a stack of wooden crates. He then saw his friends advance to the back door of the prison. Patrick masterfully unbolted the locked door and slipped inside. Jonathan and Skirt followed his lead. A stillness filled the air, and darkness enveloped them. The storekeeper moved through the familiar layout of the corridor.

Jonathan hung back a few paces, while Skirt remained inside the back door armed and ready to silence any unsuspected guards.

Looking back to ensure Jonathan was following, Patrick led him by candlelight through the dark prison maze. Although he felt confident with the information given, Patrick could only approximate Albert's location. So, even though it was time-consuming, they both thought it prudent to check every passing cell. The further they crept into the abyss, the stronger the stench. Patrick and Jonathan looked at each other, silently agreeing that this dungeon was an abomination. While Jonathan and Patrick were searching for any sign of Albert, Skirt had disabled two more soldiers. He had hidden in an alcove and as each passed by, knocked them unconscious, trussed them up and stashed them out of sight. Skirt knew Jonathan and Patrick still had to find the ungainly keeper of the keys. But for now, he would keep his post at the front door.

Most of the dungeon was empty. Even so, Jonathan called loudly to any who could hear. "Albert Warrenton, I'm looking for Albert Warrenton!" All he heard were the echoed groans of pain and anguish.

Turning down the next corridor, they noticed a lone lantern hanging from the wall in contrast. They had almost reached the last cell block when a giant of a man lumbered forward with a pitchfork pointed directly at their midsection. His straggly, greasy hair, flat face and lifeless eyes were frightening enough, but when he lifted his head, growling and moving his head back and forth like a charging bull, both became terrified. But before the man could prod them, Jonathan crouched low and launched himself at the ogre's feet, knocking him off balance. With a loud thud, the giant sprawled on his back.

The floor shook, as the giant let out an unearthly bellow. When he attempted to rise, Patrick swung straight at his huge head with a heavy slop bucket. The ogre's eyes rolled back in his head – lights out.

Staggering to catch their breath, Patrick and Jonathan looked at each other in disbelief. "That was a close one. He's a beast!"

"That's a hell of an understatement! Still, did you have to use a full bucket? I'll never get this stench off me."

"It suits you," Patrick replied, trying not to laugh. "Friends and foes alike will be able to smell you coming. Why don't you detach those keys from the giant's key chain? I'll just go on ahead."

"Wait just a doggone minute. How about you remove the keys, and I'll go on ahead?"

"So, you admit you're chicken?"

"Hell yea, I'm scared to death. Together we'll tie him, the tighter the better. When he wakes up, he's going to be crazy mad," Jonathan proclaimed unnecessarily.

"There's plenty of loose chain in here; let's get started. I don't want to have to deal with his wrath a second time." With keys in hand, they searched more cells.

A weakened prisoner answered their calls. "Yes, Albert Warrenton was here, but they removed him last evening. They probably hanged the poor man. I'll surely be next." He began weeping quietly before shuffling away from the bars. Still, Jonathan and Patrick finished their search, leaving no stone unturned. They found nothing. Both were deeply discouraged, not knowing what to do or where to go next.

"NOT HERE!" Jonathan shouted in desperation at the top of his voice. "We've got to find him. Time is running out! Where do we look? How do we find him? He could be anywhere! Anywhere at all."

"I told you I thought something was afoot. We've got to find Caroline and find out what she knows. We will find Albert, I promise." Patrick felt responsible. He knew that Caroline would have the answer, but would they reach him in time?

Exiting into the sunlight, they could hear shots fired from across the peninsula on St. James Island. Their only hope was that the skirmishes would continue throughout the day. They hurried to meet Whiskey and Skirt to tell them of a missing Albert.

"The luck of the Irish! Look who's coming! Caroline's our best bet." Patrick was excited. "She'll know where Albert's being kept. Mark my words."

"I'm so glad I found you. I checked at the pub, but no one knew your whereabouts. I do know where Lord Warrenton is being held." Trying to catch her breath from the long climb, she began her story. "I watched for hours. Nothing happened. I thought that was the end of it. But then I spied two guards drag a man out the back door with a sack over his head. Staying out of sight, I followed the buggers. Those pod-snappers thought they were alone and threw him in the back of a hay wagon. So sure of themselves, neither noticed when I slipped in the back and hid under the hay. Soon they were too busy tipping ale to worry about keeping their traps shut. They referred to their prisoner by name, repeatedly."

"Where did they take him?" Jonathan pleaded.

"I'm getting to that. It was a jumble-gut ride, all the way to Morris Island. They stopped at the point. I kept hidden while they removed him to the lighthouse."

"You mean to say, he's locked up somewhere in that lighthouse?"

"Absolutely, I saw it with my own eyes."

Jonathan grabbed the barmaid, spinning her around, and placing kisses on both her cheeks. "How can I ever thank you? You risked your life to aid my father."

"It was an honor. I'd walk barefoot over hot coals to cause pain for that bastard Percy. What a tortuous man – a beast who forces himself on any woman who catches his fancy. Many of my friends still carry his scars. He needs to be stopped."

"We have no time to lose," Whiskey announced.

They retrieved the horses and headed for Morris Island. As the hard-packed road softened into a marshy ground, they slowed, carefully making their way over the sandy wetlands that led to their destination. Blasts of explosives and gunfire could be heard from across the water with acrid smells of sulfur following. While they pushed onward, a dense fog rose out of the mist encircling them. Even so, the lighthouse seemed to rise into view like a beacon showing the way. With unwavering conviction, Jonathan led the group. The octagonal brick structure towered one hundred feet over them, with a base for the keeper's quarters.

"I pray my father's in there; it's our last hope," Jonathan said as they dismounted in the dense foliage. "Does anyone notice any guards?"

With guns drawn, Whiskey checked the perimeter of the lighthouse and had not seen a soul. "There's no one on the property. Surely, Percy wouldn't leave him unguarded. That is, unless he wanted to throw us off the scent."

"Maybe Percy thought this place so remote, we'd have no chance of finding him," suggested Patrick.

"Still. No guards at all?" Skirt asked.

"We haven't been inside yet. Percy could have positioned some captors in the stairwell," Jonathan added. "Either way, we might as well see what we got here."

They stalked cautiously, including Caroline, who had insisted on riding double with Skirt. She had spent many hours caring for wounded soldiers and thought she might be of some help if Albert had been abused. Patrick readied his lock picks to open the heavy wooden entry. The rusty hinges squeaked with his pull. The lock and chain finally disengaged and allowed the door to swing open. The dirty windows of the enclave made it hard to sort out anything but shapes. It wasn't until all eyes had adjusted to semi-darkness that they could proceed. They found nothing.

"I know he's here!" insisted Caroline. "I saw them bring him here with my own eyes."

"He's not up above," Whiskey insisted as he returned from climbing the entire stairway to the pinnacle. "And there are no guards."

"They must have moved him again," Jonathan thought aloud. "But where? And when?"

"He's here, I tell you. There must be a secret passage or hidden room. Start banging the walls. Look for any trap door, hollowed wall, anything! Just keep trying!" Caroline's insistence seemed to light a fire under the others.

"I am not giving up," proclaimed Jonathan. "This is our last chance. Our only chance. He's here somewhere."

They searched again, using candles up close, checking every wall, every door, every possible hiding place.

Suddenly, Caroline shouted, "I found something!!! Come. Hurry!" She was attempting to pull up a rug situated under a large heavy desk.

The carpet lay suspiciously askew as if it had been recently lifted and put back in a slightly different place. Each took a corner and elevated the bulky furniture while Caroline freed the rug.

They pulled on the rusty handle to raise the trap door. A steep set of stairs led to a dark, dank cellar. Each lit a torch before climbing down to look for Albert.

First to make his way down into the underbelly, Jonathan was overpowered by the unexpected odors. "It smells like death down here," Jonathan shouted up to the men behind. "Use your neckerchief to cover your face." He witnessed flashes of movement – probably rats or roaches lurking in the darkness.

"Father, are you down here?" he yelled. "We're here to take you home." He swung his torch back and forth, trying to discover anything that resembled a man. The light illuminated a moving pile of rags in the corner. Jonathan rushed over and pulled aside the coverings. "Father? Father?"

The moaning man tried to sit; his face appeared unrecognizable.

"Jonathan, is that really you?" A dry scratchy voice reached out toward his son.

"Yes, yes, Father. I'm here to take you home. No more worries." He tried to help his father stand, but he was so dehydrated and cold that he could barely move on his own volition.

Patrick arrived in support of Albert's other side. Together they reached the concrete stairs, handing him from one man to the other until he reached the first floor. Caroline gasped when she laid eyes on Albert. His condition was almost more than she could bear.

"Get him up on this table so I can look at him," she ordered. "He needs water immediately. Get me your canteens. I can use my apron to clean him."

Jonathan propped his father's head so he could sip, while Caroline dabbed away the blood on his bruised face. While Caroline was doctoring, Whiskey and Skirt found an abandoned wagon down the road and rapidly hitched up one of their horses. Bringing the conveyance around front, they were anxious for Jonathan and Patrick to settle Albert in the back with no delays. "We're burning daylight out here. Let's move!"

"We're coming!" Jonathan and Patrick lifted Albert into the back of the wagon. Jonathan took the reins while Caroline cradled Albert's head.

Albert soon relaxed into a deep, healing sleep. With his torment over, he could finally turn his thoughts to something other than surviving. The physical abuse, his advanced age, and the deprivation of food and water almost proved fatal.

Reaching a safe place, Patrick took Caroline back to the pub. Skirt and Whiskey agreed to take Albert to another camp, where he would be safe from discovery. Jonathan's father would remain there for the duration of the war to recuperate from his ordeal.

Jonathan headed back to the main camp to collect Annabelle and take her home. He risked heading into the British, who were returning from St. James Island. Hopefully, he'd stay one step ahead of his enemy. Images of his father created only a burning hatred in his heart. This fury was directed at this soulless man, who perpetrated such undeserved abuse on another. Percy needed killing, and he wanted to be the one to put a musket ball straight into his black heart.

Percy had returned from the skirmish on James Island, prepared to crush the Warrentons once and for all. Tomorrow, the major expected to see his nemesis locked up in the brig, ready to exchange his freedom for his father's. If events had gone as planned, Albert's spirit would be knocking on death's door. He couldn't wait to see the look on the young viscount's face when he learned that his life had been given up for nothing. Then, and only then would Percy be satisfied.

On reaching his destination, however, he received the shocking news that Albert was no longer captive in the lighthouse. With certainty he had been rescued, but when and by whom were unknown. Once again, Percy had been skunked by Jonathan Warrenton.

This time, Percy kept his fury tightly coiled inside. He couldn't request more soldiers because arresting Albert had been against the law. So, he had nowhere else to turn. Albert was free and Jonathan was in the wind, or worse still in the swamp. He relied on his best fifty soldiers still under his command to chase the cursed Patriot.

He had one last chance. By the end of the week, all British soldiers were being ordered to stand down and prepare to evacuate Charleston. If they were to be gone by the middle of November as planned, Percy had only three weeks to destroy the Warrentons. He would attain vengeance or die trying.

All known sightings of the Swamp Fox militia were regularly scouted throughout the bayou. Many of the Redcoats had frequented the well-traveled paths of the wetlands but not its hidden dangers. So, with great trepidation, these same soldiers carried out the major's orders while secretly wishing him good riddance.

Chapter 25

Was it only this morning that Jonathan left to rescue his father? It seemed like an eternity. She was terrified that Jonathan would not prevail. However, when the men who had joined the battle on James Island returned battered and bruised, her mind was consumed with those in need. She learned that the British reinforcements quickly outstripped the patriots. After several intense skirmishes, the patriots withdrew with several wounded and one casualty – Captain William Wilmot. Little did anyone realize this hero would be the last continental soldier to die for American freedom. It was becoming more and more obvious the war was over – the British Army's sole intent appeared to load up and return to England.

Annabelle made herself at home by becoming fast friends with Sean and Danny at the outdoor cookstove. Before helping them prepare the evening meal, she tended the injured. Now, when full darkness blanketed the sky, she was reluctant to return to the cabin. Not knowing Jonathan's whereabouts weighed on her mind. Was he able to find Albert? Or was he captured on the other side of the island? She would never find sleep with her imagination running wild.

She finally conceded to fatigue and trudged back to the cabin. She was just too tired to speculate any longer. All she wanted was to crawl under her covers and sleep for days. However, just about to snuff out the lamp, she heard someone approach the door.

The latch creaked open. "Just wanted you to know I'm back; be ready to leave at dawn." Jonathan sounded exhausted.

As he turned to leave, Annabelle stopped him. "What happened? Did you rescue Albert?"

"My father's alive. He's in bad shape, but he'll survive. Whiskey and Skirt are taking him somewhere safe." He paused and took a deep breath before continuing. "He's had quite a beating and needs peace and quiet to heal."

"I'm so sorry that Albert had to endure such abuse. Percy must be a devil. Does he know that you found your father?"

"If he doesn't, he will soon, I suspect."

"Then what?"

"Only time will tell. I'll see you in the morning. I must get some shut-eye." Jonathan returned to the pit to join his comrades and try to get some rest.

The next morning came early. Jonathan appeared at Annabelle's door just as dawn was breaking. "Time to get moving. We've got a long journey ahead."

"It's not that long. I always make it here in less than a day. What's the hurry?"

"It's safer for us to take round-about routes. The British are hiding in wait on all the familiar roads and pathways. We're going straight through the heart of the swamp. If Percy's soldiers try to chase us through that quagmire, they'll get trouble they hadn't bargained for," he explained patiently. "Gather your things and let's get started."

"You sure we won't get lost?"

He gave her a look. "Really? I've spent the last four years living in this marsh."

Annabelle did not want to leave quite yet, so she took her sweet time hoping to aggravate him. Finally, she announced. "Ready. Are you sure we must go today? I could really use another day's rest."

"Stop making excuses. I need to get to New Hope. I'm worried about Mother, alone and susceptible to anyone who might want to take advantage," he tried to explain. "Don't worry. I have everything necessary for making camp waiting for us at the fire pit."

"Making camp?" she said with great trepidation, her voice rising in pitch.

"I told you we were taking the long way through the swamp. It could take more than a day."

"I'd rather ride home alone. I'm pretty sure I can remember the path. You needn't bother with me." She retreated from the horses Jonathan had saddled.

"Are you daft?" Jonathan couldn't believe she would even contemplate being so reckless.

"Percy and his soldiers don't care about me. They have more important pressing problems."

"Nobody imagined Percy would stoop to arresting my father. Yet stoop he did, and almost killed him to catch me. If they were willing to torture and hang an innocent man, just what plans do you imagine they would have for my fiancée if they discovered you alone in the woods?" He gazed intentionally over her body.

"Stop trying to scare me. I'm as afraid of camping in the swamp as I am of Percy."

"It's obvious you've never met the man." Jonathan was at his wit's end. He brought the horses back around to where Annabelle was standing and encouraged her to mount. "It's time to get out of here. Now!"

Annabelle's mood darkened with the reality of sleeping out in the open among night crawlers. "I suppose there's no chance you'll change your mind?"

"None." Jonathan urged their horses forward.

When the sun hit its pinnacle, Jonathan finally came to a stop near the riverbank. It was an unusually warm day. Annabelle watched in horror as a sleepy alligator moved from its perch on a sandbar before sliding silently into the dark waters. "Alligator! There are alligators in this water. You lied! You told me they moved south for the season."

"It's been a warm autumn; a few must be lagging behind. If it's any conciliation, it probably means we're going to have a mild winter." He turned to help her dismount, showing absolutely no reaction to the alligator swimming ahead. "We'll stop here for a quick repast, then we're going downstream in a pirogue."

"No, no, no. You never mentioned rowing in murky water filled with vermin. I refuse!"

"Again, Belle, we have no choice. We're being followed. The only way to lose them is to be miles down the river before they find us."

"But we can't just leave the horses."

"Believe me, everything has been taken care of. The horses are trained to return to a spot where some of our men will pick them up. We also have transportation waiting at the channel's end," he explained patiently.

"But..."

"No buts. While you put together a meal, I'll ready the boat."

Annabelle shot him a stubborn look, standing aloof. That is, until she heard her stomach growl and realized she was starving. She guessed it wouldn't hurt to set out some corn pones and cheese.

Jonathan found the pirogue hidden in the underbrush exactly where he was told it would be. With oars intact, he dragged it to the shore and shoved it into the stagnant, unwelcoming lagoon. He tested it for seaworthiness from every angle. He would hate to see Annabelle's reaction if the damn boat sank. She was acting like a fly in ointment.

After a quick repast, Jonathan coaxed Annabelle into the pirogue. The watercraft was a lot stronger than it appeared and could travel effortlessly around the stumps.

"Hold onto the sides and don't try to stand."

"Believe me. I'm not moving a muscle until we're on dry land."

He glided through murky waters while listening to any unusual sounds on the embankments.

"How far do we need to travel downriver? I'm already feeling uncomfortable…"

"Shhhh! Do you hear anything behind us?" he whispered. He thought he heard men's voices.

"No, I don't think so," she said softly. "Just the waves against the banks. Wait, I do hear something – voices, and they don't sound too far away."

"Me, too, damn it. How did those bastards find us so fast? They can't be English regulars; the war is all but over. This is all Percy and his personal grudge against me. I regret that you've been caught up in his web of hatred."

"Don't worry about me. I feel sure you can beat him at his own game out here." Now Annabelle was energized. She loved a challenge. "So, what's our next move?"

Jonathan grinned at Annabelle's new attitude. "I do have a few ideas, but they include a quick detour through some snake-infested waters and quicksand."

"Let's show them who they're dealing with, shall we? They should know better than to wander into the Swamp Fox's domain."

Purposely, Jonathan took a tributary that was filled with creepy shadows and smelly bogs. The sudden flight of some seafaring birds from the surrounding marsh verified what he already knew. His enemy also had men along the shoreline. First, Jonathan would outsmart the canoes that were following him down river. Then he would make quick work of evading the land force.

"Hold on, love, we're in for a rough ride."

Anyone familiar with this part of the swamp knew to stay clear. Around the next corner were several well-known water moccasin nests. Jonathan knew the huge underwater dens filled with writhing snakes were on the right side of the upcoming turn. He paddled lightly with great care not to stir up the water. He also stayed as far left as possible. With a sigh of relief, they made it past the serpents. Once they were in the clear, Jonathan reached out and grabbed some good-sized rocks from the shoreline and pitched them into vipers' nests.

Without warning, the turbulent water rippled across to the embankment. Jonathan rushed to cover Annabelle's mouth to stifle her screams. Snakes now covered the expanse of the elbow turn along that tract of the river. There was nothing meaner than a riled-up water moccasin. The boat coming up behind them would think twice before ever entering these moccasin waters again.

Jonathan and Annabelle paddled quickly down river to another tributary where they would again lead their enemy astray. Both felt content with their accomplishment, until screams of terror transverse from behind.

"What have we done?"

"Why do you think they're following us down into the swamp? They have only one mission and that's to kill me. If they weren't ready to play dirty, they should have stayed out of my backyard."

"You're right, as unpalatable as it may be. We have no other option but to do everything in our power to stop them. So, what's next?"

"We're going to pull onto shore and make our way through a quicksand-covered peninsula."

"That does not sound like the quickest way home."

"Oh, it's not, but once we cross over, we're home free."

"How well do you know this area?"

"Like the back of my hand. When the British first occupied Charleston, we had to hide out here for days at a time with the British surrounding us. It's hard to believe, but they never found us."

"I must say, trudging through quicksand sure beats tangling with snakes." She gave a little shiver.

Before long, they crossed over to the opposite riverbank. After helping Annabelle disembark, Jonathan hid the pirogue under some bushes. Turning, he explained his plan. "You must stay directly behind me – walk in my footsteps. We'll go slowly at first, until you get the hang of it."

Clutching his waist, she carefully followed him through the treacherous sandbars that sprinkled the peninsula. It wasn't long before they heard voices closing in. They picked up speed and reached the opposite shore just as the soldiers appeared through the woods. Noticing the couple on the bank across, they rushed forward to surely apprehend them. But one by one, each of the men became bogged down in the murky mess of plough mud. Darkness was falling. It would take quite a bit of time before the whole crew could tug and pull themselves free.

Finally away, Annabelle and Jonathan moved steadily toward the rendezvous where horses would be waiting to take them out of the marshland.

"I'm exhausted. Are we ever going to take a break?" Annabelle complained.

"I'm heading for a hidden treehouse built when we first decided to make the swamp our home. It should do well enough for tonight."

"Sounds better than sleeping on the cold ground with all the insects; that's for sure."

Deep in the dense forest, Jonathan led Annabelle to a small clearing among a stand of moss-laden trees. Nestled in the trunk yet high off the ground, appeared a weathered shelter, completely secluded from below. Jonathan climbed up first, hauling all their possessions with him. Then he helped Annabelle. They worked in tandem to make the tree hut as adequate as possible. After finishing supper, they dropped back down to wash up before the night descended.

Returning, they each sat on the bedroll, while Jonathan recounted the successful rescue mission of his father. He left nothing out, letting Annabelle feel that she had played a part in freeing Albert. After the tale, both curled up exhausted, in each other's arms.

"Are you still angry with me?" Annabelle asked quietly among the crickets and night sounds.

"I'm not angry; I'm hurt. I thought you wanted to be with me. Forever. It was understood that we were to be married. And now, you're wanting to throw it all away."

"That's not true. I only said that I want you to think about it. I was thrust upon you against your will, and that's not a good feeling. I want you to want me on my own merits."

"Do you honestly think I'm the kind of man who would marry someone thrust upon him? There's a bit more to me than that. You'll have to be more specific about what you want from me because I'm utterly confused. Shall I court other women? Would that make you happy? Or do you want me to become engaged to another woman so you can be free of me?"

"No, of course not. I just want you to be sure that I'm the woman you want to spend the rest of your life with. And how can you know, if you don't meet other prospects?"

"I grew up in Charleston with all the available ladies. So, I know them quite well. Believe me when I tell you that you're the only woman I have ever considered marrying."

"Are you sure?"

"Absolutely. But, what about you? You sound like you're anxious to spread your wings – without me."

"No, not without you. I just love the sense of freedom living in America is going to bring me."

"Why can't we enjoy this magical freedom together?"

"Is it possible for me to be free and married to a viscount?" Annabelle was sounding more and more drowsy.

"If you're asking whether I'll allow you to make your own decisions, the answer is yes." He nudged closer to her to finish their conversation, but he could see her eyelids closing in the moonlight.

He leaned over and kissed her gently. Then sighing softly, he whispered in her ear, "You are my true love, and next time we'll share more than just a kiss."

Chapter 26

Annabelle awoke to the aroma of coffee brewing over an open fire. She had slept so soundly, she should have felt refreshed, but, instead, she was exhausted, still feeling the tiredness of her muscles. "Jonathan?" she called from the treehouse. "Is the coffee ready? I'm having a hard time waking up."

"Sure thing."

He nimbly climbed the tree, then sat down next to her with a steaming cup. "After all you went through yesterday, it's understandable that you're worn out. Believe me, there's nothing I'd like better than to remain here with you for the day, but our enemies are still out there, so we've got to keep moving."

"I understand, just give me time to finish my coffee. I'm really looking forward to what else you're cooking."

"Comin' right up." He descended, leaving her to rise on her own.

After a light breakfast, they packed their gear and made their way in a southeasterly direction that would bring them to a hidden path behind the manor. It wasn't long before Annabelle could see the familiar sights of the rope bridge across the lagoon and the hide-away path just beyond, as they made their way home. "I had no idea we were this close to New Hope."

Soon they began to pass through the properties of their neighbors. Some of the cabins were burned out, others were abandoned, while a few poorly maintained structures held struggling families. Of course, there were also grand mansions that escaped being billeted by the British.

Riding through an unusually dense thicket, Annabelle heard a soft cry. She thought perhaps a goat had snagged itself in this thorny undergrowth. "Do you hear that bleating? I think a small animal is stuck or lost in here somewhere. It's probably a goat."

"Now that you mention it, I do hear something. You want to check it out?"

"Yes, of course."

"We're wasting our time if it's a goat. It'll be fine; they can eat their way out of anything."

"I don't believe that."

He looked at her and smiled. "I've dealt with my share of farm animals. But if you want to look around, let's do it. It won't hurt us to walk a bit."

They went in opposite directions, searching in and under the hedges along the path. When Annabelle noticed some fabric peeking through the brushwood, she separated the branches. There sat a little girl, dressed in tattered, dirty clothes, hiding her face in her knees beneath wrapped arms.

"Sweetheart? What on earth are you doing here alone? Can you tell me your name?" The child raised her head to reveal copious tears running down her face. "My name's Sophie."

"It's nice to meet you, Sophie. I'm Lady Annabelle from New Hope Manor. Take my hand, and we'll you get you out of here."

As soon as their hands clutched, the child threw herself in Annabelle's arms.

Sophie hugged her with a terrified grip. It did not take long for the crying to recede into staggered hiccups, but her shivering was as intense as ever.

"Jonathan. Over here. I've found a child. Could you bring me a blanket? We need to keep her warm."

Within moments, Jonathan wrapped her frail shoulders and knelt face-to-face. "You must live close by. If you can show us where, we can easily take you back."

"My home ain't there no more. I was fishing down by the creek. Mama told me not to wander too far, but I didn't listen, so I didn't get home 'til after supper. When I got there, our house was gone – burnt to nothin'. The ground was smokey and hot. I looked everywhere, but I didn't see nobody. I was afeared to go any closer."

"Don't you worry, we'll find out what happened to your family. But until we do, would you mind coming home with us. You can stay until we locate your parents." Annabelle stroked her sweet head as tears welled in her own eyes.

"I'll find your ma and pa," Jonathan assured the little girl. "Do you have any brothers or sisters who live at home with you?"

"I've got two older brothers, but they're always running off. All they talk about is joining up with the Swamp Fox and fighting them red-coats."

"Were they home yesterday before you left?"

"No."

"Well, we won't worry about their whereabouts just yet."

After pulling beef jerky, bread, and apples from their pack, Annabelle laid out a blanket for the three of them. She knew Sophie must be hungry and thirsty, yet she never demanded anything. Slowly, as the girl ate and drank her fill, she stopped shaking, but you could see her giving into exhaustion. Jonathan stashed their gear and waited for Annabelle to hoist Sophie up to him after he was mounted. In front, he snuggled her to his warmth on the saddle. Before too long, he noticed her head bob and eyes close.

They were still a couple of hours away from safety.

Reaching home, Jonathan handed the child down to Annabelle. He walked their horses to the barn while looking back to see the twosome enter the house.

Amelia had heard the horses and stepped out on the veranda to greet them.

"I've been out of my mind with worry." Amelia embraced Annabelle lovingly. "My stars, what have we here?" She had just noticed the shy girl hiding behind Annabelle's legs.

"This is Sophie – one of our neighbors. She came home from the pond and found her home burnt to the ground with no family to be found. So, she'll be staying with us for the time being. Jonathan's at the stables."

"Well, of course she will."

Hearing Annabelle's voice, Berthe arrived in time to overhear Sophie's saga. She felt a kinship with the freckled redhead and vowed that she would comfort her in the same way she had been cared for by the Gainsboroughs.

"My, my, what adventures you and my son must have had," Amelia told Annabelle, sounding very curious. "I can't wait for you to share them with us at dinner tonight. In the meantime, why don't you go freshen up while Berthe takes care of our guest."

"As usual, you are a sensible woman, Amelia. Jonathan will be in shortly. I trust that Patrick O'Leary reported the success of Albert's rescue."

"Yes, he did. What a fine young man. Berthe is a lucky woman."

"I know how much you love and adore Albert, and how difficult this whole ordeal has been." She hugged the older woman with true affection. "Jonathan has many more details to share with you, but all in all it's been a happy ending for everyone."

"I'm looking forward to this evening. Now you go get some rest," Amelia insisted, pretending an aloofness that she didn't truly feel.

When Sophie reappeared at the dining room door, Amelia was a bit put out. Even though the child was clean and freshly dressed, she would not relent. "Children do not sit at this table until they are at least twelve years old and have learned their manners. Berthe, will you please take Miss Sophie to the kitchen?"

"But, Amelia, this is her first night away from her family…"

"No exceptions. Do you have any doubts about Berthe's ability to care for her properly?"

"No, of course not." Annabelle was a bit miffed.

"Then, we'll not speak of it again."

After that short altercation, Annabelle, Amelia, Miriam, and Jonathan gathered in the dining room for a lovely meal.

Jonathan regaled the ladies with his adventures, making for an interesting and entertaining evening. If only Albert had been there, it would have been perfect.

Annabelle discovered that Miriam had become more than an acquaintance to Amelia during the duration of waiting for word of Albert's situation. She observed them huddled once again after dinner, trading quips and small talk. She watched them from across the room with narrowed eyes. Suspicion filled her. She replayed the image of Miriam's attempt to kill her. Someone stooping that low did not become a paragon of virtue overnight. However, Annabelle decided to silence her tongue and remain vigilant.

Excusing herself, she left to assist Berthe in preparing Sophie for bed. When she reached the top of the stairs, she heard Sophie splashing in the claw-footed tub. "Do you need some help?" asked Annabelle.

"Not really, but I'd love your company. It feels like it's been ages since I've seen you."

"I've missed you, too. Anything unusual happen?"

"Not unless you consider Miriam and Amelia becoming best friends. Those two are inseparable. Miriam goes everywhere with her. It's the oddest thing. Since Albert's kidnapping, Miriam's proclaimed herself Amelia's guardian angel."

"Do you trust her?"

"In a pig's arse!" Berthe exclaimed. "She tried to have you run over; why on earth would I trust her?"

"I don't either, but there's not much we can do about it now; it's too late."

"Speak for yourself, I'm keeping my eyes and ears open. If she's trying to take advantage of Miss Amelia, I'll know and then I can take care of it."

"No, you can't. Miriam would have you sacked if she knew you were watching her. You mustn't, she might catch you."

"I don't give two hoots what Miss Amelia thinks. My loyalty is to you, and only you," Berthe insisted.

"What did I ever do to deserve such a precious friend as you? I do love you dearly."

Berthe gave her a large cheeky grin. "And I you, missy."

"What do you suppose Miriam's really up to?"

"She hasn't let slip what her plans are yet, but I know she has something underhanded in mind." Berthe alerted.

"How can you be so sure?"

"I've watched her around Amelia. Every move she makes is calculated. She would like Amelia to believe that you are the usurper, trying to steal her son from under her nose. I can hear the spiteful little remarks she slips unnoticed into the conversation. You are the target for all her barbs. I see right through her cleverness, but I don't think Amelia has any idea what the woman is up to," Berthe explained further.

"Just what I need right now. I mentioned to Jonathan that I thought we both needed more time before we made any decisions about our engagement, and now he thinks I don't want to marry him. I've really messed up, Berthe. And I don't know how I'm going to fix it."

"I have a feeling Amelia's not going to be helpful. But I wouldn't worry too much. I can see with me own eyes that the man loves you. It'll all work out, you'll see."

"Thanks for your vote of confidence. But I don't know how realistic it is."

Both women turned all their attention to Sophie. She took their mind off complications they rather not reflect upon.

Chapter 27

While Percy was pre-occupied with his duties for the Crown, William Brumley thought it was the perfect time to put his own plan into play. Of course, his idea was to decimate the Warrentons financially, not mortally. He had devised a plot that would allow him to legally steal a portion of their fortune – a very large portion.

He knew that If Percy learned of his proposal that he would want a cut of the profit, so he had every incentive to keep the major in the dark. He believed that if he continued to send Percy reports on his undercover work at New Hope, his tormenter would leave him alone.

The government building where Brumley was to meet Lt. Governor David Collins stood as a one-story, rectangular brick structure with a trapezoidal roof. It was strategically situated at the corner of East Broad and Bay Streets. Not wanting to be identified, William parked his carriage around the corner on West Broad.

As he approached his destination, he saw that the sliding sash frame on the front window was slightly open for all within to enjoy the fresh sea breezes. Or perhaps, his co-conspirator was just airing the room from his cigar smoke? The smoke appeared thick and odorous even with the air circulating.

As William stepped inside and scanned the room, he was pleased to see that he was the only visitor. He would have the privacy he needed to discuss his plans in full.

Lt. Governor David Collins perched behind his desk and pointed to the empty prison cells on each side. His rotund belly filled the swivel chair.

"Good to see you, David. I'm glad to see you finally returned from your travels. I have a very lucrative proposition for you." William removed his top hat and hung his coat on the rack near the door. Then he leaned over the desk to shake hands.

"I've lost my arse in this damn war," said the Lt. Governor. "I hope you have some way for me to recoup a shilling or two."

"I hope to do just that." Brumley smiled with avarice at his friend.

"We're alone. I even had the prisoners moved to the Watch House. I want no evidence of your being here."

"I appreciate your caution. Our reputations must remain pristine." William pulled out a chair and cozied himself closer to the desk. "I must say your missive arrived at the most opportune time. I was afraid all my arrangements would go to ruin. But now is the perfect time for you to authorize me to bring all my plotting to fruition."

Collins blew his tobacco smoke into the already hazy air. "I am more than happy to oblige...for a price, of course. As I mentioned before, my bank account is a bit short."

"All I need is your official seal and stamp on these papers I had drawn up to legitimize my theft of a prime piece of real estate."

"I have no use for real estate here in the colonies. My family has already returned to London. The rest of us are to leave by mid-November, so it seems you have nothing that interests me."

"Ah, you don't understand; it's not only real estate. The Warrenton family has incredibly valuable masterpieces and sculptures. I will not only take over the estate itself but all the treasure it holds. And if there is a safe, that will be emptied as well." William Brumley was almost licking his lips.

"Now that's more like it. Let's get down to business. Show me those papers of yours."

Brumley handed him the documents. "Are you familiar with the Warrenton name?"

"Yes, the Warrenton name holds a great deal of power in England. They are well thought of by the Crown."

"No longer. The duke was just arrested for treason, and his son rides with Francis Marion. I can't imagine that the king will waste his time on righting this transaction."

"Indeed." Collins opened his desk drawer and pulled out a wax seal and stamp.

"Shall I put both our names on the deed or just my own?" William asked his friend, knowing full well that he would decline.

"I'm afraid I must put my trust in you and remain a silent partner in this proposition."

"Fine with me. All we need now is for you to put your official seal on these papers. This will ensure the forfeiture of the Warrenton Estate to me for reasons of treason perpetrated by the father and sedition by the son."

Lt. Governor Collins melted the wax and applied it to the false document. They sat in silence while watching it dry before William picked it up and put it in his satchel.

"Well, it's best we conclude this meeting." Collins removed his pocket watch, and pretended he had another engagement to attend. Rising slowly, he reminded William of his obligation. "I expect a full accounting by courier – two days hence."

"And you shall have it, sir." William had just accomplished the first step in his reprehensible plans. The next step included Annabelle Gainsborough along with her abundant dowry. If he could not convince her to marry him, then he would contrive another way. But marry her he would. He had known the moment he feasted his eyes on her that she was the only woman he truly wanted. Nothing could stop him now. Nothing.

Chapter 28

With the forged document in hand, which gave him the authority to confiscate the Warrenton Estate, William Brumley headed to New Hope.

As he drove down the country roads, he scanned the spacious fields of harvested crops and noticed the scattered rows of ripe pumpkins, waiting to be loaded on wagons to nearby towns. The apple trees across the vast orchards had been picked. *All this will soon be mine,* he thought. He could imagine the money piling up in his bank account from the cash crops grown on what was soon to be his property.

Ahead of him stood the stately manor with its white columns, expansive porch, and moss-laden trees along the driveway. He salivated with daydreams of being the grand owner and hosting elaborate parties with Annabelle at his side. Her dowry would afford him many opportunities to raise his stature. Of course, as a Loyalist, that might all change once the war was over and the British were no longer welcomed in Charleston. No worry. He would just take the profits and sail back to England with his bride. Although his own manor was much smaller than the Warrenton property, it was in proximity. This would allow him to transfer valuables at his leisure. In time, William hoped to convince Annabelle to love him and be in accord with his future expectations. Surely, she would eventually forget her engagement to Jonathan and adapt to their life together.

Spirited with anticipation, William parked his carriage in the usual spot and climbed the stairs to the entry. He preened at his reflection in the door's glass panel while tapping the knocker to gain attention.

The butler met William without comment, hiding his distaste. "Do come in, Mr. Brumley. Allow me to take your top hat and justico."

William was already acting quite the lord of the manor as he sauntered through the hallway to the parlor. He loosened his cravat to gain some comfort for his fleshy neck, then made himself comfortable on the loveseat and admired the surroundings as if they were his own.

"How nice to see you, Mr. Brumley," Amelia welcomed him with forced charm.

Amelia joined him in the parlor, followed by Annabelle and Miriam. What did he really want with them, Amelia wondered. She wearied of all the manipulations and scheming that seemed to encompass her family.

William's eyes hungrily followed Annabelle as she sat opposite him in a wingback chair. But the surprise he registered when he spotted Miriam turned his thoughts elsewhere. What the hell was she doing here? Was she working another contrivance? He was familiar with her loathing for the Warrentons, so maybe, he could again use her to accomplish his ultimate objective.

"What has brought you all the way out here, Miriam? You've always disliked the country."

"Yes, I am a city girl, that's true, but the scenes around Charleston have been disturbing of late with the soldiers marching about, and Amelia was nice enough to invite me for a short visit. And, I must say I am enjoying myself very much."

"Well, as usual, I am very concerned for all your safety. You are so far from town, and more times than not, your menfolk are traipsing off somewhere, leaving you three to fend for yourselves. Where are they this time?" William took the liberty to gaze at Annabelle to see how she would answer.

"As always, Albert and Jonathan are looking after our best interests," Annabelle answered, forcing a smile.

"Yes, of course," Amelia added. "You needn't worry; we are well cared for."

"I don't believe I've seen Albert since the masquerade party, and Jonathan, well, I have yet to formally meet the man. I'm beginning to think he's a figment of Annabelle's imagination." He laughed heartily.

"I assure you he is real. It's probably best that you do not make his acquaintance. He doesn't take lightly to those who betray their country to serve the Crown. Even less would he approve of your constant visits to his home."

"Tut, tut. Surely, he knows that not everyone is quite as fervent as he about this new United States. He can't be angry at those who do not agree with him."

"Believe me, anger is too mild a word for the way Jonathan feels about spies and turncoats," Annabelle continued.

"Well, I assure you, I am neither." Brumley was becoming a bit agitated. "Do you think you might ring for tea? I must say I'm a bit parched."

"Yes, of course," Amelia answered. "Annabelle, would you help me? I believe Berthe is busy with Sophie. Together, we'll be fine. It won't take long." She and Annabelle left the room to Miriam and William.

Immediately, William took the opportunity to arrange for a tete a tete with Miriam. "Tomorrow, I want to meet you back at your townhouse about noon to discuss my plans with you."

"I have no desire to meet. I now know the truth about you from Albert."

"Just hear me out. Give me a chance to explain."

"Why should I?"

"Because obviously you're not thinking straight. Please, meet me and I'll clarify everything."

"I agree, but this is the last time."

Annabelle walked in with the tea tray and Amelia followed with an assortment of raspberry tarts and tiny Queen cakes.

"Let's just relax and enjoy ourselves, shall we?" Amelia stated, anxious to evade the topic of Jonathan and Albert.

After the refreshments and everyone comfortable, William leaned back in his chair. "I do have another reason for my visit today," he pronounced, dabbing his mouth from crumbs. "It's not a pleasant subject, and not one of my making, I assure you.

"The magistrate contacted me and asked if I would take ownership of your estate in the light of Albert being found guilty of treason, and Jonathan being charged with sedition. Both have been sentenced to death by hanging. So, you see, there is no recourse for the government to take. Your estate needs a new proprietor, and I have been appointed the receivership."

"Swine!" Annabelle confronted in fury. "You're nothing but a thief! How dare you come here under false pretenses and try to steal our home. I will not have it. Get out!"

William, too, rose to his feet. "I don't think you understand. It's a done deal. I have the documents right here that give me the right to claim the entire estate – the crops, the barns, the manor and everything in it. I'm afraid it's you who will be 'getting out' as you say. I was going to give you a week, but I've just determined that two days should be enough time for you to vacate. Just be sure to take only the clothes on your back. The rest is mine."

Amelia buried her head and wept uncontrollably. Losing their home was the last straw; she could take no more.

The entire time William Brumley was conducting this charade, Jonathan, Whiskey, and Skirt had been listening intently to every lying, deceiving word he uttered. This was exactly what Jonathan expected from this low-life swindler. He had learned enough about him to know that everything he touched was tainted in criminality with greed the driving force. And somehow, his family had landed in the middle of all his machinations. Jonathan sighed aloud with the satisfaction he was about to receive in turning the tables on this viper.

When he could remain quiet no more, Jonathan signaled his friends to stay put, and casually entered the parlor. "Who do you think you are and what are you doing in my house?" Jonathan crossed the room in front of his adversary, towering over the weaselly Brumley.

William gasped in disbelief. Percy had promised to have both Jonathan and Albert well in hand by now; that he would have no opposition in his takeover. "I-I-I-thought you were in custody."

"I know exactly what you were thinking. You came here, hoping to intimidate my mother and fiancée and steal our property."

"But—"

"I always knew you were a sorry excuse for a man, but never did I realize just how low you would stoop to satisfy your greed. Bloody hell!! You are attempting to steal another man's life's work!" Jonathan continued. "If the women were not here, I would tar and feather you, and that's only after I had crushed you like a bug. But since they are, you will survive another day. But not only will you not own this property, you will never set foot on it again!"

"I have the papers right here. This manor belongs to me!" Brumley shouted while waving them in Jonathan's face.

"Like hell!" Jonathan grabbed the man by the shoulders and shook him within an inch of his life. "Give it up. You lose. Now bloody well move your ass out of here while you're still in one piece."

"It's mine!" He scooped up the fallen papers and darted toward the front door. But Jonathan, reaching out, held Brumley's arm and jerked him backwards. Then he planted his fist smack dab in the middle of the Tory's bulbous nose.

Blood sprayed everywhere. The women started screaming. The greedy charlatan began to whine, after hearing his cartilage crunch.

Jonathan braced with a satisfied look at his handiwork. Then he seized the forged documents and quickly shredded them before they were thrown into the fireplace. "Do you understand what just happened to your precious papers?" he bellowed. "That will be your fate as well if you continue to harass my family. Now get out and never darken this door again."

With a look of pure fear, Brumley wiped his nose and left with complete surrender on his mind.

Chapter 29

The Warrenton household stood astounded as they watched a defeated Brumley stumble down the steps to his waiting buggy, all the while babbling incoherently. By the time his coach disappeared in the distance, an enormous sense of relief swept over each.

Jonathan turned and embraced Amelia. He understood how bravely she'd faced each trial confronting her. "Mama," he spoke with soothing reassurance. "It's finally over. Papa's coming home, as am I. No more tears." He looked down, then kissed her cheek.

"What a horses' ass," Skirt remarked. "Did he really think he'd get away with that idiocy?" He and Whiskey had witnessed the final altercation.

"He had all that forged paperwork," explained Whiskey. "His filthy, underhanded plan would have worked if Jonathan hadn't stopped him short. I admit I took pleasure in the look on his face when Jonathan finished. Priceless."

"My son was smashing!" Amelia chimed in. "He gave that odious creature exactly what he deserved."

"Odious doesn't' begin to describe the likes of that devil," Berthe retorted. "I knew exactly who he was the moment I'd clamped me eyes on him. It made me queasy the way he ogled Annabelle."

"I take ill just being in the same room with him," Annabelle grimaced.

"Undoubtedly, it was extreme good fortune that I was home, but even if I hadn't been here, and he succeeded in convincing you to turn over this property to him, his success would have been short-lived."

"You would have beaten him within an inch of his life," Whiskey stated definitively.

"And tossed him onto the first ship back to England," Jonathan agreed.

"He must have known you'd put a stop to his shenanigans," Skirt then questioned. "So why would he take the chance?"

"He didn't believe he was taking a chance. Obviously, he was privy to Percy's plan to hang both me and Father. No doubt, they've always been in cahoots. Brumley's visits out here were only a cover to spy on our whereabouts."

"Well, that was one reason. The other was Lady Annabelle," Miriam added.

"What if he returns when you're not here with more papers to sign?" Amelia asked, not ever wanting to feel so defenseless again.

"If Brumley knows what's good for him, he'll stay far, far away," Whiskey stated.

Annabelle wanted to see Miriam's reaction. "What about you? You know him well. Is he really as vile and greedy as he appears?"

"Don't ask me; it's obvious I'm not the best judge of character. Albert is convinced William cheated me out of my husband's estate."

"That 'stone-crow'!" Berthe exclaimed. "Is there no way to pinch that swindler?"

"Alfred promised to try but thought it doubtful."

Annabelle pleaded while looking at each one. "Why don't we have Brumley locked up? We can all testify against him before a magistrate."

"Because the magistrate's a Tory and probably Brumley's friend and willing accomplice," Jonathan explained.

"Of course, that makes perfect sense."

"Oh, I agree," a fatigued Amelia consented. "Let's not talk about today's unpleasant scene another minute. Shall we convene to the dining room. We have much to be thankful for."

As the evening ebbed, each retreated to private chambers. All, that is, except Annabelle and Jonathan who had slipped outside to enjoy some time alone. The starry night captured their attention, as they embraced warmly.

"It's getting a little chilly out here, love. Why don't we make our way up the back stairs to my private hide-out?" Jonathan suggested with a twinkle in his eye.

Annabelle laughed. "What's a hide-out?"

"It's a secret place that no one else has knowledge of – a place of refuge. I would read books, play soldier, and daydream to my heart's content."

"I had just such a place at Gainsborough Castle. I carried pillows, blankets, and my most special possessions up a winding staircase to a room high above the world, where my imagination could soar." She twirled in his embrace, pretending she was back in the turret. Then with the same twinkle she gazed up at him. "I often dreamed of finding my perfect prince."

His eyebrows raised a bit as he smiled in return. "And have your dreams come true?"

"More than I could ever have imagined. And how fortunate was I to find not one but two handsome royals. The first being an intriguing young tradesman I met onboard ship. The next was a true warrior, who fought bravely for everyone he loved, and all that he believed in."

"Which one have you fallen in love with?"

"I love them both. Now what shall I do?"

"You must choose. And soon."

"But I'm not ready. Which one will give me the time I need?"

"The one who truly loves you, of course," he replied seriously. "Just remember that if you wait too long; you risk losing both."

Their cryptic conversation ended as they crept to the top floor. To Annabelle, the area appeared to be a typical attic with old furniture, large and small trunks near the landing. She waited until Jonathan lit a candle.

"Come this way." He guided her to a hidden room that included several dormer windows overlooking the front yard.

It was the perfect place to spy on the comings and goings of visitors. A single bed rested against the attic wall, along with a pile of blankets and downy pillows. A rudimentary desk and chair with an oil lamp on top sat across the room.

"This is such a welcoming place. But where do we sit?" Hardwood planks stretched the length of the room.

"On the daybed. Pretend it's a big, comfy settee."

"But it's not. It's a bed."

"So it is, but for now, we can pretend."

While reclining, she watched Jonathan cross the room to light the lamp and snuff out the candle. A low, soft glow created a romantic ambiance. A shiver of excitement began to build as her eyes followed his every move: the tilt of his head, his clear blue eyes distinguished by skin that had been deeply tanned by the hot Carolina sun. Annabelle remembered on board how he had held her small hand in his. She had been fascinated by the look and feel of them –

strong, but gentle hands with rough, calloused palms. Recalling how those hands had touched her with desire brought roses to her cheeks.

Facing away from her, Annabelle continued to watch him as he searched the desk drawers. Without the usual layers of clothes, she observed his backside garbed in tight breeches. This was the first time she'd ever seen the curve of his buttocks and his open shirt. She found him very pleasing indeed. Jonathan abruptly turned to face her. "Found it!"

Caught unaware, she jumped and turned red with embarrassment. She felt that he could read her thoughts just by her guilty look.

"Are you all right? Your face is flushed. Are you too warm?" He had no idea what was wrong.

"No, no, I'm fine, although it is a little close in here. Would you mind opening a window?" She just knew she sounded ridiculous.

"Of course not, I'll be glad to."

"What is it you found in the desk drawer that's so exciting?"

"Just an old diary of mine when I was ten years old. It might be fun to read and find out how I became the man I am today."

"Sounds like fun. When do we start?"

"Actually, I have other plans for tonight."

"Like what?"

"You'll have to wait and see."

"Well, I'll have to wait another day," Annabelle insisted, "because it's time I returned to my chamber before anyone realizes I'm missing."

"I think we should spend the night up here, together. The entire house is already asleep. Nobody will notice if we're not tucked into our rightful beds."

"What would your mother think of me?"

"Who's going to tell? Besides, you've insisted that I give you time to discover the world and everything it has to offer. How are you going to be able to move forward alone if you're too afraid to spend one night alone with the man you're going to marry? A man who loves you."

"One has nothing to do with the other."

"Doesn't it? Do you want to stay with me tonight?"

"You know I do."

"Then what's standing in your way?"

"Just my own fears, I guess."

"Well, I've said my piece; it's up to you."

She began to pace and reason. What should she do? Of course, she wanted to stay in this special, cozy room that made her feel so close to him. What made it so difficult was the fact that she did love him, and she precisely knew the outcome of this night. She desired to remain with her whole heart, but she was worried about the aftermath. There were always consequences. Always.

After several more minutes of contemplation, Annabelle turned to face him, gazing thoughtfully out through the dormer window.

"Yes," she finally spoke.

"What does that mean?"

"Yes, I'll stay."

"You're sure."

"Sure as tomorrow's light of day."

Guiding her in his arms, his unspoken words spoke volumes. They reclined on the bed and eased into comfortable conversation. Between the laughter and stories told, they exchanged glances and held hands. As time passed, their glances lingered, and all conversation ceased. Jonathan could wait no longer. He reached over and gently kissed her. She returned his overture by opening her arms to him and welcoming his embrace. Soon they were lost in their love for one another.

"Are you sure this is what you want?" Jonathan wanted no regrets. With certainty he would have none. More than ready to acclaim her as his, he clearly understood that this would be a night filled with love and passion. But did she?

Chapter 30

William Brumley left the Warrentons' estate feeling powerless and frustrated.

"Percy failed me again," he voiced aloud. "The bloody bastard." How could he have ever trusted that fool? Now, because of Percy, his future was in grave jeopardy. He had not only lost the estate he desired but had been outed as a Tory.

He whipped the horses into a gallop, so he could arrive in Charleston soon after dark. He was determined to locate that useless blunderer, whether at British Headquarters or the Poinsettia Tavern. Having heard that he frequented the pub more often than deemed wise, he surmised Percy was drowning his failures in pints of ale.

He entered the Tory haven to a cacophony of laughter and thick tobacco smoke. How disgusting to smell the permeation on his well-tailored clothes. He stopped a barmaid to inquire of Percy's possible whereabouts, then registered him sitting in the back booth alone.

William needed answers, but this Brit was unpredictable as well as volatile. But, damn it, he needed to know what the hell happened. Grimacing with distaste, he eased into the booth and faced an intoxicated Percy.

"What happened? It's inconceivable to me how you could possibly lose both father and son."

"Maybe if you'd taken a more hands-on approach instead of standing on the sidelines, success would have been ours. But you did nothing. As it is, I don't owe you any explanations."

"I adhered to the letter of our agreement. My contribution was not to roll around in the muck with you. Damn it, I had the Warrenton estate in the palm of my hand, just to have it snatched away by Jonathan Warrenton himself. Now, it's gone forever." William pounded the table. "And all because of your bloody incompetence!"

"Get out!! Get out of my sight before I run you through, you cowardly flap-jaw." Percy stood up ready to unsheathe his sword.

"Just calm down." William Brumley held out his hands in supplication; he couldn't risk losing Percy's patronage altogether. One could never tell when he might come in handy. "I apologize for my outburst. Won't happen again."

"You're damn right it won't, not if you want to walk out of here," he growled. "It's time you admit that the Warrentons are here to stay. Find some other mark to seek your ill-gotten gains."

"I'm not giving her up."

"By her, I assume you mean the beautiful Lady Gainsborough, or perhaps the lovely Miriam Worthington."

"Both. As a matter of fact, I'm meeting Miriam tomorrow at her townhouse early afternoon to discuss my marriage to Annabelle."

"Have you really convinced yourself that Annabelle Gainsborough is going to be allowed to marry the likes of you?" Percy began to guffaw uncontrollably. "You'll need help to hogtie that wildcat."

"I'll do whatever I have to do. Don't you doubt it." William was dead serious.

Percy refrained from the sly, evil grin within. He could care less what that buffoon did with Warrenton's fiancée; his only concern was finding Miriam. He was intent on finishing what he'd started the last time they were together. Brumley had just given him the information he needed to waylay Miriam when she returned to the manor from her townhouse.

William rose bright and early the next morning with his plans for Annabelle front and center. He had started with a complete list of everything he needed for their wedding to take place. First and foremost was to convince Miriam to help him by being his eyes and ears inside the Warrenton household. He'd also need her after he gained possession of his bride-to-be. Miriam would see to Annabelle's cooperation.

Miriam was busy packing some extras when William arrived at her townhouse. She found his jolly mood a bit off-putting, since never witnessing this side of him.

"Well, it's time to get started," he said. "Are you ready?"

"I have no idea what you're talking about. I still have no reason to trust you. In the past, I've discovered you're nothing but a practiced 'flimflammer.'

171

How could you possibly believe I'd go along with another one of your noxious plans?"

They moved to the settee in the parlor.

William sidled closer to her and affectionately placed a caressing kiss on her held hands. "Because you and I are two of a kind. You are not afraid to go after what you want."

"That may be partly true," she answered after a moment or two of reflection. "But as yet, I fail to see what I'll gain out of all this intrigue."

"You want to know what's in it for you?"

"Exactly."

"Me, for one thing. You and I have always had feelings for each other." He was indelicately referring to their long-term affair after her husband had passed. "It's been a while since we've connected, but that can be easily remedied."

"Except the fact that you've been dogging Annabelle since you first laid eyes on her tells me that you are lying through your teeth."

"Don't you understand, it's not Annabelle I want. It's her dowry. Have you any idea how much money she's worth? Thousands of pounds!" he prevaricated convincingly. "You are the one I want to be my companion for life, but I need the girl to make us rich. Her money will afford us both a future we could only dream about."

"But she despises you. There is no way you are going to turn her from Jonathan toward you," Miriam insisted.

"I don't need to convince her of anything," he said slyly. "I'm going to kidnap her and hold her hostage until she relents. And believe me, if she doesn't cooperate, there will be consequences."

Miriam felt a gradual softening. "I'll do what I can, but I doubt I'll be much help." Leaning in and kissing him, she knew better than to trust or believe his feelings toward her, but she couldn't seem to help herself. She had been secretly in love with him for a long time.

He, of course, returned her affection but without much enthusiasm. "Have you decided to aid me in procuring a bride?"

"Just let me know what you need going forward. Truthfully, I never have cared for the harridan. So, who knows, this could be fun."

"Believe me," he oozed. "We're going to have a beautiful life together." He smiled at the realization that Miriam was hooked.

She stopped him as he turned to exit, "Before you leave, I need your help in carrying a trunk out to my buggy. I've packed warmer clothes to take back with me to the Warrentons' later today."

"Do you own a gun?"

"Only a small, two shot derringer. Why?"

"I've been hearing tales of brigands riding about the countryside, stealing everything they can get their hands on. You should take the derringer with you and keep it handy. Just to be on the safe side."

"By all means," she answered, pleased that he cared enough to worry. Miriam rose and removed the small gun from the desk drawer. "I'll just carry this in my dress pocket, hidden from view."

William kissed her one last time, making plans to meet in the Warrentons' barn after the kidnapping was accomplished. He'd give her more instructions then.

Miriam made sure everything at her townhouse was locked and secure before she readied her departure back to the manor. She felt at ease with her small trunks nestled in the back of the carriage and her derringer in her dress pocket. The horses whinnied with anticipation of travel until she snapped the reins. "Giddy up."

It didn't take long for Miriam to wind along the country roads toward New Hope. She breathed in the crisp, late autumn air and surveyed the fields of dry corn stalks on each side. Daydreams filled her with thoughts of her future – security, prosperity, and her paramour, William.

Lost in numerous fantasies, Miriam was unaware of a rider behind her, until the horse saddled close to her carriage. She shaded her face from the afternoon glare as she tried to decipher the identity of the uniformed soldier. Percy's husky voice immediately brought fright to her heart.

Trying to battle the fear, she realized that the major had patiently stalked her leave-taking and ideally chose this secluded stretch of road to approach. From experience, he must have known that little traffic occurred at this time of day. Even the remaining British were ordered back to the fort to await a departure time.

"Well, what have we here?"

Snapping the reins, she started the horses into a cantor to get as far away from the odious man as possible.

"You will not escape me this time!" he shouted, as he kicked his horse forward to catch her conveyance. With little difficulty he sidled alongside and grabbed the halter of the lead horse, stopping the buggy. Wasting no time, he jumped aboard and took the reins from Miriam.

"I'm getting us off the road. The way I see it, we have some unfinished business."

"Get out of my buggy!" Miriam shouted while pummeling Percy.

He turned, slapping her hard across the face. "Remember what happened when you fought back last time. It'll be more of the same if you don't stay put and shut up." He rode off the road until they were well hidden in a gathering of trees.

Stopping abruptly, he pulled the brake. Wasting no time, he immediately lunged for her. Grabbing her low-cut neckline, he yanked it down to her waist, exposing her to his view. "Now that's what I've been waiting to see." He sat back for a moment while feasting with lust.

Mortified and scared to death, she dared not move or stop him. Her body reacted as if paralyzed.

He pinned her arms down forcefully, so he could take full advantage, taking his time to fondle at his leisure. "Don't tell me you don't want this too. You've been asking for this a long time. You've always been nothing but a whore. I knew the first time I laid eyes on you. I know you want me. I want to hear you say it."

Her instinctive fear was slowly turning to rage. While he momentarily released a grip, Miriam felt the derringer in her pocket. When she saw Percy unbutton his trouser, she removed the small gun and aimed it point blank toward his heart. *POP. POP.* Two shots.

Percy's face registered shock at the sight of crimson spreading over his shirt. He clutched his chest and tried to stop the blood flow. "What have you done?" Feeling his life leaving his body forced a look of pure hatred just before he slumped over unconsciousness.

By this time, Miriam had gathered her wits and vowed to do whatever necessary to survive. Looking down, she readjusted her dress by making herself presentable again. Then, with a reloaded gun, Miriam had to make sure the bastard was dead. If he were still alive, she would be put in jail. Carefully, she reached over his body to feel for a pulse in his neck. Nothing. She shook him a little before turning his head to see if he was indeed dead.

His vacant eyes stared skyward from his lifeless form. Then, using all her strength, Miriam pushed and pulled until his body rolled off the side of the buggy. Making sure no one saw, she calmed the horses, who whinnied and stomped their hooves in agitation. She quickly reined the buggy back to the road and continued to the manor.

Reality hit her on the ride home. Her body began to shake as beads of perspiration ran down her chalky face, and nausea came in waves. Luckily, her dress was not torn nor splattered with blood, and she was able to straighten her hair pins.

In shock she may be, but Miriam did not feel one bit guilty. Percy had justly gotten what he deserved. She would tell no one about what had happened today. Not a single soul. She had to take her secret to the grave. And Percy was rotting in hell where he belonged.

Chapter 31

The following morning, Jonathan had much to reflect upon as he rode through the swamps to militia headquarters. He hadn't been satisfied with his last dealing with Annabelle. It miffed him that she appeared to be unmoved by their lovemaking the previous night. Knowing that this was her first time, he was touched by her willingness to follow his passion wherever it led. He felt transformed by a night that was incredibly tender and loving, so why was she so aloof this morning? In his eyes, she acted more reserved than usual. But before he could even begin to share his feelings, he watched her leave without a word.

With some difficulty, he pushed aside his personal issues for now until he could find out what was going on with this never-ending war. Much speculation had circulated around Charleston, so no one could exact the future.

Finally riding into camp, Jonathan was surprised to find it crowded with buzzing conversation among the soldiers.

"Hey, Smoke," Bubba greeted. He was standing near the campfire, ready to hang a big pot of beans over the fire. "Hope you're hungry."

"Have you ever known me not to be?"

"Well, laddie, now that you mention it." They both laughed.

"I'll be back as soon as I get settled." Jonathan rode down to the livery. He knew that Whiskey and Skirt were nearing their way to his estate with Albert. The compatriots should arrive there unscathed and return quickly.

"Meeting tonight at the bonfire," one of Marion's officers shared. "Lots of news. All good!"

"See you then." Smoke left the horse's stall leaving a pail of fresh water and oats. Worn-out, he walked the short distance to his cabin. Resting in solitude, Jonathan mulled over the day's events and his future. Lack of sleep the night before seemed to cloud his thoughts about family and Annabelle. At the sound of the bullhorn, he rose and rejoined the large group to hear Francis Marion's news from New York.

The militia was aware that Cornwallis had surrendered to General Washington and the Continental Army at Yorktown. So why had nothing changed? Why did this not seem like a decisive victory? Why were there British forces still stationed in and around Charleston? So many questions yet no answers. As usual, the Swamp Fox imparted all the information he himself had received from a range of sources.

"I have good news for all Patriots living and owning property in the Low Country. The British have finally decided that it is no longer profitable for them to reside among us. They will begin preparing for evacuation immediately. Ships will be readied to return the lot of them to the British Isles by the second week of December."

"What are we supposed to do in the meantime?" a young militiaman shouted.

"Accommodate them in any way you can," the Swamp Fox answered.

"I'll accommodate them, all right. With my boot on their ass!" another spit out.

"I'd like to give 'em a jab of me blade," yelled another.

"What about an eye for an eye? They burned down my cabin and killed my brother. I ain't about to accommodate them a damn bit."

"Calm down! Calm down!" Marion admonished. "What I meant to say was, stay out of their way. No shooting. No knives, no ambushes, no more stealing."

"And what exactly are the Redcoats going to be doing when we lay down our arms?"

"According to Major General Alexander Leslie, they will be withdrawing their forces from the advanced works on Charleston Peninsula, December 14 or thereabouts. Until then, we will abide by a truce signed by Washington himself."

"And you expect us to oblige those butchers? Have you not seen the damage Percy and Tarleton have done to our homes and families?"

"Tarleton is no longer here, and you'll be happy to hear that Percy has been found murdered and dumped in a wooded area on a road leading out of Charleston." Marion realized their fears were very real, but his orders were to convince them to stand down.

Jonathan pumped his fist in loud cheer when he heard Percy's fate. "About damn time!"

"Do you really think we can trust the soldiers to hold their fire and their tongues?" Whiskey and Skirt had just returned and dismounted.

"Yes, I do," answered Francis. "You don't seem to realize that most of the English soldiers want to go home even more that you want them to. They consider this a God-forsaken land. They miss their families and have nothing here to fight for. They're just young men who are compelled to take orders for good or for naught."

"Hell, it's only for a couple of weeks. Even we can act civilized for that long," Jonathan added.

"Speak for yourself," several men joked.

Everyone started laughing and talking about their coming freedom. "Do you know what path they're going to take to the sea?"

"Yes, they're to march down to the Peninsula, onto Gadsden's Wharf. Their ships will be waiting."

"And what will we be doin'?"

"We'll be respectfully watching them leave."

"Maybe just one last boot in the ass?"

"No. No boot in the ass!"

It was a time for triumph among the militia. All the young men, especially those in their teens, were fatigued and sick of living in the swamp, hiding from their enemies and planning raids. This war had taken its toll. In no mood to celebrate, Jonathan decided to spend time with Whiskey and Skirt. The three men moved away from the bonfire to find a quieter place to talk.

"How is my father's health? Did he have any trouble making the trip back home?"

"No trouble at all. We were amazed at his recovery. Still a bit banged up, of course, but his mind was clear," Whiskey explained.

"After we told him the story of his rescue, he was very appreciative of all our efforts," added Skirt.

"He also enjoyed hearing about William Brumley's failed attempts at stealing the estate. He was just sorry he couldn't have been the one to send him packing."

"Can you believe all we've been through together these last five years?" Jonathan asked in all seriousness. "I could not have asked for two finer friends and compatriots. I thank you both for your loyalty and companionship."

"My problem is that I haven't given a thought to life after the war. My family have always been landowners in Ireland. But I own no property here. I arrived penniless and have remained so," Whiskey shared.

"No problem. I have more land than I could possibly cultivate. I will gladly deed you a healthy portion," Jonathan insisted.

"I could not possibly take charity. Thanks, friend, but no."

"You can always pay me on account whatever you think it's worth. What do you say we talk again when all is settled?"

Whiskey smiled as he began to speculate that he might have a future after all. "Sounds fair. How about you, Skirt? Do you have any dreams?"

"I've always wanted to own a pub. I hear tell that the owner of the Poinsettia will be leavin' town soon so I'm hopin' to take it off his hands for a song," Skirt explained his plan with a wink. "Of course, you both might be of a mind to helping me convince him."

"Looks like we Three Bushwhackers will live to ride together again," Jonathan said.

"Just so you realize that I'm still the handsome one," Whiskey insisted.

"Fine with me," Jonathan agreed.

"I'll drink to that," added Skirt.

"Hell, you'll drink to anything!"

Chapter 32

William's plotting continued to consume him. After the plans he had made with Miriam, his mind seemed to burst with visions of grandeur. Losing the Warrenton Estate remained a humiliating defeat. But still, he would allow no setback to prevent him from his goal of marrying Annabelle Gainsborough.

Today was the beginning of preparations for that upcoming day. Now where should he begin? William had allowed himself a full day on Market Street to purchase what was needed. If only these agonizing headaches would cease. They'd been occurring more and more frequent; his only respite being the liquid Laudanum given by a Tory doctor. After taking a large swallow of the elixir, he strolled past the shoppers, tipping his hat to passersby. His pain receded just as William came to the first establishment on his list. He entered the locksmith with a confidant stride. The bell chime on the door brought the proprietor out of the back room.

"Good morning, Mr. Brumley. What can I do for you this grand day? I do hope the safe I installed last week is sufficient to your needs."

"Indeed, it was, kind sir. Hopefully, I'll soon have something worthy of its use. But today, I have another job for you, and I'll need it done immediately."

"You realize, Mr. Brumley, that it is a long drive to your property. I would lose a great deal of money being absent from my business." The owner hoped he could raise the price for his services by complaining.

"But you must! I need you to secure a lock on my bedroom door. It is most imperative. I'll make it worth your while."

"Well, if you're willing to pay a bit extra, I will be happy to drive out tomorrow morning." As they shook hands in agreement, the locksmith thought he caught a confused look in Brumley's eyes. He glanced again, but it was gone. It must have been his imagination. He just didn't want to accept a job he was going to regret.

His next stop was the jewelry store. Brumley was disappointed that the enclosed cases held fewer selections than expected. But, of course, he knew that few of the populace had the funds to spend on luxury items. His glazed eyes showed disdain at such mediocre rings. He surmised the patrons who had lost everything to the war had bartered their jewelry for money.

"What can I do for you today, Mr. Brumley?"

"I am in the market for an engagement ring. I want only to peruse your finest offerings. This ring is for a very special young woman."

"I understand completely." The jeweler removed a tray of his finest gemstone rings to display.

Looking over the five-cushion-cut sapphires, William felt another headache begin to pound. Rubbing his temples, he absently chose the largest carat and the gaudiest setting. The store owner raised his eyebrows in surprise.

"Are you sure? There are other rings here that are of better quality and suitable for a young bride."

"Did I ask for your opinion?" Brumley asked rudely. "Size the ring to five and have it ready by late tomorrow. I have another commitment in the morning."

William hurriedly exited the store, turning down the alley in seclusion. With shaking hands, he unscrewed his bottle of Laudanum and swallowed deeply. Damn, these headaches! Immediately, he began to feel relief accompanied by an overall elation. Looking around, he thought the sky looked so clear today – so blue with white fluffy clouds floating by. Why hadn't he noticed before? It must be a good omen for today's endeavors.

So, exuding a lofty air, William sauntered across the cobblestones to the front entrance of his tailor. He stepped inside and rang for his clothier.

At once, a stooped little man scurried toward him, a well-used tape measure draped around his neck. "Ah, Mr. Brumley, it's an honor to receive you. What can I do for you today?"

William reveled when merchants catered to him as if were King George. "I need formal attire for my wedding."

"Well, I have some very special fabric to show you." Without further ado, the store owner promptly gathered his finest fabrics, displaying them across the long counter area he reserved for just this purpose. "Any of these would do nicely for your nuptials."

Brumley decided on a gray waistcoat and pin-striped breeches. The price was exorbitant, but he was feeling generous and wished to outshine all the other men attending his wedding. He waited patiently as his measurements were taken, all the while preening and daydreaming about the upcoming ceremony. It had been a long time since he had felt this optimistic.

At the last minute, the tailor keenly chose to add gold lace on the formal banyan and accent the coat with gem buttons. He wanted to take advantage of Brumley's vanity. Evaluating his customers had made him a rich man, and it was a fact that Brumley had always preferred more plumage than most. Satisfied with the overall image of his elaborate attire, William was not averse to paying extra for it to be ready in such short notice. Holding the material up to himself one last time, he admired his handsome features in the full-length mirror. He could visualize a dazzling Annabelle by his side.

He hated parting with coin but realized that all this time and money were put to good use. One last look of arrogance was caught in his mirrored reflection before he turned away and bid the owner farewell. Now he was headed to his final destination.

William drove his buggy to the seedy docks where the criminal class frequented. The rotten smell of fish assailed him along with the stench of street trash. He stopped his carriage outside a ramshackle pub. There were many ruffians congregating outside, waiting for some rich bloke to come by and hire them. They were willing to do almost anything for a few extra pounds.

Although William was not unfamiliar with this area, he was not recognized as he stepped away from his conveyance to enter the dingy tavern. Focusing his sights around the dimly lit room, he knew exactly whom he was looking for. This was not the first time he had hired muscle to do his bidding. The main tap room was filled to bursting, so William had to elbow his way to the bar. Tobacco smoke lingered in the air like ghosts. Gas lamps cast an eerie glow to the secluded booths. The mixture of bodily odors engulfed him, making him a bit queasy in contrast to the bracing sea air in his carriage. Finally, William reached his objective and ordered a large jug of ale. An overflow of patrons soon filled the room with raucous consumption and eager harlots. He'd better hurry and find his muscle before they succumbed to the evening's temptations.

Across the bar from where he stood, two swill-bellies, eyed him with blatant curiosity. With a nod, he bade them to join him. The closest one rose to reveal a tall, emaciated man with dark, greasy hair. The other appeared short and stout with curly blond hair. His most impressive feature was his ears, which stuck out from his head at right angles. The perfect pair. Exactly what William had been looking for.

"What can we do for ya, guvnur? I'm Stretch and this here's Rabbit. Ya look like you might have a problem we could be helpin' ya with."

"You are correct. How would you like to earn a ten-pound note for an easy job? No rough stuff, just a quick snatch and grab."

"Make it ten apiece and you got yourself a deal."

"Agreed." Brumley refrained to shake their outstretched hands. Just the dirt under their fingernails disgusted him. He never thought he'd find himself back in a place like this.

"Just tell us what needs to be done, and we'll take care of it." They grinned at him, exposing stained, rotten teeth.

William painstakingly explained in detail exactly what he wanted done. Stretch and Rabbit never flinched at the thought of kidnapping a young girl. They hastily accepted half the money up front with greedy hands, promising to fulfill their end of the bargain as planned.

With his business dealings ended, William couldn't wait to leave. Especially, since his head began that incessant pounding again. Damn it, he needed to get out of here. Now. Away from the compounding noise and smoke.

As William stepped outside the front door, he gulped in the fresh air. He immediately felt somewhat better but knew from experience that his headache was only going to get worse. All his attention was focused on reaching his carriage. That's where he would find peace. Yanking open the door, he searched under the seat in desperation. Unmindful of his addiction, he sighed in relief when finding his treasure. Without hesitation, William swallowed the clear, syrupy liquid in the little, green bottle.

Chapter 33

Annabelle ran down the stairs from the attic as if the house were on fire. Her love for Jonathan filled her completely, so much so, that she had no idea how to put her feelings into words. So, she had run. Run from herself. She no longer doubted his devotion, but now understood that in her mind she had confused Jonathan with George. Her love for George was simple and pure with no complications. Yet she could not let his image go to give Jonathan her whole heart. It was only after last night that she had realized that Jonathan was both the wholesome, pragmatic George as well as the well-heeled aristocrat. Annabelle debated whether to race back to him and explain, but uncertainty stopped her. *Soon,* she thought, *I'll tell him soon.*

Annabelle had no time to waste on her own inner struggles, because this was Berthe's wedding day, and she was determined to concentrate solely on the upcoming nuptials. After all, Berthe was her only family, and this was her chance to show Berthe how much she meant to her by making sure all went well.

Berthe was waiting, as usual, for Annabelle to join her for breakfast at the kitchen table, both realizing that this would be their last morning together. Silent expressions spoke volumes, until Annabelle handed Berthe a surprise bouquet.

"Annabelle, did you really make this by yourself?" Berthe awed the arrangement of roses, mums and greenery with flowing white ribbons intertwined.

"Not completely, Daisy picked out the herbs. I had no idea which ones would be appropriate. Is it too much? The lemon balm and lavender give off such a lovely fragrance."

"It's perfect. Thank you."

"It was a labor of love, I assure you."

"As much as I'm going to miss you," Berthe hurried to say, "I have no regrets about leaving this house. There's someone or something amiss. I'm not sure exactly what it is; all I know is that I don't trust the people here."

"I know." Annabelle realized that Berthe was referring to Miriam. "I'll be careful, I promise."

"Just keep your eyes and ears open."

The butler entered the room, interrupting them by handing Annabelle an unusual letter. He also held an identical envelope addressed to Albert Warrenton. She put the envelope in her pocket, intending to read it when she had a free moment. All her time and energy were needed on the event.

While Annabelle and Berthe waited on the porch for their wedding conveyance to arrive, Jonathan came bounding out of the front door.

"Annabelle, there you are. I've been looking for you. I wanted to say goodbye. Berthe, I see you're ready to get on with the wedding."

"Right you are." She beamed. "Am I to presume that you two will be next?"

"I don't know." He looked at Annabelle with question in his eyes. "Are we?"

It was as if she were struck mute. She wanted to scream, 'yes' to the heavens, but her mouth was dry, and she couldn't utter a word.

Jonathan just watched her, not saying a thing. He knew something was awry, but he also knew that she had taken great pleasure the night before. So, what could be wrong?

"I guess that's a subject for another time. I'm on my way back to camp. I'll look about for Sophie's family while I'm there." And with a tip of his hat, he was gone.

Patrick had sent a carriage to pick up Annabelle and Berthe. They were ready and eager when it arrived at the Warrentons. After the footman loaded the carriage with Berthe's trunks and things, and tied Lady onto the back of the wagon, the two enjoyed their farewell ride to Goose Creek. Upon arriving at the wedding venue, Annabelle busied herself with final details. Patrick's mother had already decorated and lined the chairs near the trellis. A simple wedding cake and trays of food were displayed in the parlor.

Annabelle had only to attire Berthe for the ceremony. What a turnabout it was for her to be dressing Berthe instead of her cockney maid assisting her. She delighted fitting her friend into an embroidered white dress with a graceful empire waist of Fil de Vie. She added the layered velvet trousseau, which showcased the V-neckline and lacy balloon sleeves.

"Oh, Berthe, this is perfect. You are such a talented seamstress. I can't believe you made this entire outfit yourself."

"Thank you. Do you really think I'm talented?"

"Indeed, I do. It would be an honor for you to make my wedding gown when the time comes."

"Oh, no milady. That would be too grand for me. But I was thinking about trying my hand at sewing. I could make reasonable clothing for common folk. Mrs. O'Hearn says we could sell my work at the Mercantile. Just think, I could earn my own money." It was evident that Berthe had given much consideration about her future.

"That's a splendid idea. I envy you; I really do. You have so much to look forward to. Patrick is a wonderful man. And now you've got yourself a business as well."

"Isn't America great?" They both broke into mirthful laughter.

"Now it's time to do something with that mop on top of your head," Annabelle teased.

"Good luck."

Annabelle took her time to sweep Berthe's red ringlets upwards, styling with intertwining rose buds. The mirror reflected happiness shining through her friend's eyes.

The last touch held the homemade bouquet encased with a 'borrowed blue' ribbon. Handing it to Berthe, Annabelle felt a surge of pride and love. Alone in their thoughts, they reached the venue. Both embraced, hearing the solo violinist from the orchard. When it was almost time for the bride to make her entrance, Annabelle walked first and took her place, then turned and watched Berthe slowly make her way to a new life. She often imagined herself experiencing this same bliss, but after how she reacted this morning, she had doubts that her wedding would ever take place.

After sleepwalking through the rest of the afternoon, she hugged Berthe one last time. Promising to visit the couple soon, Annabelle mounted Lady and rode toward home. Since it was only mid-afternoon with plenty of daylight, she expected to arrive at the manor in time for dinner. Thirsty and stiff after two hours' ride, Annabelle stopped at a scenic brook near neighboring homes. She realized William Brumley lived in the vicinity, although she had never visited him. She shuddered just recalling his most recent visit to New Hope and his altercation with Jonathan.

The morning of the wedding began differently at the Brumley estate where Stretch and Rabbit were setting up their 'snatch and grab.' They waited behind the hedge that lengthened Brumley's manor. Throughout the morning waiting to sight her carriage, both needed to get a look at their prey. Neither one saw Annabelle, who was inside the conveyance, but the kidnappers took notice of the horse tied to the back. Miriam had informed William that Annabelle was to be driven to the wedding by the O'Hearn family but would be riding home on horseback.

"'Tis a fine animal she be riding. She'll be able to outdistance us any day of the week. We'll have to find a way to stop her cold on her ride home. Chasing her down could be a problem."

"And just how are we going to get her to halt for the likes of us?" Rabbit was more muscle than brains.

"I figure we'll have to set up a roadblock. Put a wagon or a tree in the middle of the road. That'll make her stop or at least slow down."

"But what about other travelers? She ain't the only one riding that road."

"It'll have to be something we can put up quick-like and take down the same way."

"I have it. What if we use one of Brumley's old wagons and pretend it's broken an axle in the middle of the road? When she slows down or stops – we grab her, tie her, and throw her in the back of the wagon. Then we hightail it back to Brumley's."

"You make it sound easy."

"Easiest money we ever made."

"I hate it when you say that," complained Rabbit. "Something bad always happens when you're so cock sure."

William soon listened to what they had seen and what they planned to do. He readily approved it; his excitement growing. He commandeered an old wagon and hitched a couple of horses to it. "Here you go. See that you bring Annabelle back in one piece. No rough stuff and no 'beard-splitting.' That is, if you want to get paid."

Stretch and Rabbit agreed to his terms but grumbled about the hands-off rule. "Damn, what's that smell? Is this a dung wagon? I ain't riding in no wagon that's been cartin' manure." Rabbit started walking away from the offensive odor.

Stretch laughed aloud. "You're one to talk, Rabbit, you don't smell no better."

"Like hell. You're the walking compost pile!"

"It don't matter how bad this wagon stinks, so stop bellyaching. It's time to find us a good spot to set up our ambush."

Annabelle had started out at a trot but had slowed down to enjoy the beautiful scenery along the way. She was completely oblivious to any impending danger. All her thoughts were of the previous evening, and how she was going to repair the damage she had done to her relationship with Jonathan. She had just rounded a curve when she almost ran into a broken-down old wagon sitting in the center of the road. Two raggedy farmers appeared to be trying to fix an axle on one of the wheels. As she tried to pass by skirting the wreckage, the two surrounded her and grabbed Lady's reins.

"All right, missy. Time for you to get off that there horse and come with us."

In her loftiest manner, she looked straight at them. "My name is not 'missy.' It's Lady Annabelle Gainsborough, and you are in my way. Kindly return my reins so I may continue."

"Well, Miss 'Snooty-Tooty'," Stretch continued. "From now on, you ain't going nowhere but where we takes you."

He roughly pulled her from the horse. Then he pinned her hands behind while Rabbit secured them tightly.

"You're hurting me. Why are you doing this?"

"Money, ma'am. Pure and simple."

Using one of the filthy grain bags left in the back of the wagon, they maneuvered it over her head and tied it snugly around her neck. Then, after lifting her like a sack of potatoes, they bound her kicking feet as well.

Overwhelmed by the horrendous smell, she would have vomited if she weren't concentrating so intently on her bindings. She could feel the pain and bruising from the bouncing, as the cart hit every rut in the road. She could barely think. Who would do this to her? If anyone believed they could convince her father to pay a ransom, they would be gravely disappointed. She began to shriek at the top of her lungs.

"Shut up, or I'll gag ya!" Stretch yelled. He didn't want anyone to wonder about what they were carrying.

Annabelle finally lay back in exhaustion. She felt a change in the dirt road, like they were rolling over a cobbled driveway. Soon the horses halted, and the two men lifted her out of the back of the wagon. They carried her like a gunny sack up some stairs and into a large foyer. Carefully laying her on the hardwood floor, she was relieved when they took off the bag and untied her hands and feet.

She could barely stand after the beating her body had taken. "Where am I? And why did you kidnap me?"

The two kidnappers did not answer, only loomed over her, until a voice from behind closed doors summoned the three inside. Helping her walk, they ushered her into the adjoining room and then waited.

The mastermind behind the abduction sat smugly on a loveseat while sipping a celebrated cognac.

"William!" Annabelle shrieked. "Why would you do this? I thought we were neighbors and friends." She had always known there was something off about him, but never did she think he was capable of this evil. After sighting the crazed look in his eyes, she realized he was a madman, and she must deal with him accordingly.

Draining his glass, William rose and sauntered over to stand in front of Annabelle. "I don't know why you're so surprised, my dear. You've always known I wanted you."

"You also knew that I was engaged to Jonathan. I love him, and we are to be married. You can't change that."

"We'll see about that." Grabbing and pulling her close, William laughed. "I've got you now, and you'll do as I say." His eyes blazed with mania, his voice exuding superiority. "Besides, who would look for you here? Nobody. They'll think you ran off."

"My family won't believe that. They'll come looking for me."

She turned and darted toward the closed doors, in hopes of escaping his evil grasp. But the hired ruffians on the other side blocked her exit.

"Highly doubtful." An evil, guttural laugh escaped across the room as he watched Annabelle desperately push. "Tsk, tsk. Don't fight it...darling, not when I have such grand plans for the two of us."

"Leave me out of your plans." She glared sideways at him suspiciously.

William firmly held her chin, painfully twisting her neck to look at his face. "You don't seem to understand. You are going to be mine forever. And I am going to demonstrate my love in ways you could never imagine."

She jerked her head out of his hands. "No. No. No!"

"Oh, yes...darling. As a matter of fact, you'll soon be Mrs. William Brumley." He strutted like a peacock.

"Over my dead body!"

"If need be, but I hope it won't come to that. For the time being, you'll be locked upstairs in my bedroom." A wicked sneer now replaced the ugly chuckle.

"Like a caged animal? Someone will find me. I know they will!"

"Maybe so. But by then it will be too late, my dear. You will already be mine."

Chapter 34

Smiling to herself, Miriam gazed out the window of her expansive guest chamber at the Warrenton Manor. She gloated at successfully pulling the wool over this entire family. All except for Berthe, who had continually given her the evil eye. Thank goodness, that low-class little snoop was out of the house for good.

At first, she had tried, really tried to make amends. Everyone acted so kind, especially Amelia. But that foolish old woman made her deception so easy; she just couldn't help herself. Devoting all that time to William had taught her how to scheme and lie with impunity. And now she had found the ideal pushovers to help her get exactly what she wanted.

Miriam had always understood William Brumley's character. After her husband's death, she soon learned how he had deceived her spouse. At the beginning, she had planned to cheat him in return, but then, over time, she had fallen for the ruthless charlatan. And now, she was in dire need. Her heart ached for him in such a way that nothing, and no one, could stand in her way.

She had encountered William only once since the kidnapping, five long days ago. Her part in their scheme was to convince the Warrenton family that Annabelle had run away of her own accord. Miriam could not believe her success. It amused her that Amelia seemed secretly pleased with Annabelle's absence. Apparently, the Duchess hoped that her son would find a more appropriate partner. Albert appeared a bit more skeptical, but still, the old duke fell for her lies as well. Jonathan, on the other hand, could ruin everything. Each day, Miriam offered more detailed excuses for Annabelle's absence. But time was running out. Today, she would meet William at the barn to finalize his irrational plan. Afterwards, she would depart from the Warrentons' and join him at his manor. Of course, she was expected to assist him in arranging his sham wedding.

Oblivious to Miriam's hatred of Annabelle, Brumley had no idea that she was plotting Annabelle's imminent demise. But, in truth, soon after the wedding, Annabelle was to meet with a tragic accident. Then, there would be only she, William, and Annabelle's money.

Quite adept at keeping secrets, Miriam's newest discovery revealed a letter to Albert from the Earl of Trent's solicitor. Snooping through Albert's study, she had found it detailed that whomever Annabelle wed would receive a dowry of 100,000 pounds. This tidbit was worth keeping to herself for now. Perhaps, she would find a way to gain access to it. It seemed a good possibility that she just might find the money a bit more alluring than William Brumley.

After spending the last five days with Francis Marion as one of his several lieutenants, Jonathan was ready to take his leave. He had never considered all the paperwork and final orders the Swamp Fox had to deal with as their commander. This being their last assignment, the band of brothers was officially discharged from the military.

The Swamp Fox reminded them that their effort in the creation of this new nation was not fought in vain but would live in perpetuity. Following his speech, all heads were bowed as Marion offered a short prayer of thanksgiving before dismissing each man with the knowledge that his unit would honorably escort the British Soldiers safely out of Charleston.

It was early afternoon when Jonathan arrived home. Too late for lunch, but too early for tea, he handed off his horse to a footman before running up two steps at a time to the front door.

"Anybody home?"

First to reach him was Albert. He bear-hugged his son. "Good to see you. Are you here to stay?"

"That I am. The war's over. I'm a civilian now. Where's Annabelle?"

"Darling!" Amelia raced to the foyer, embracing him tightly. Tears of happiness filled her eyes. "Do I dare believe that you are home? Really home?"

"Yes, Mother. I'm not going anywhere. Where's Annabelle?"

"Annabelle?"

"Yes, where is she?"

"Well, son," Albert sounded distressed. "We're not exactly sure."

"When do you expect her?"

"We don't," Amelia sounded defensive. "Annabelle departed with Berthe to the wedding and hasn't been heard of since."

"But that was five days ago. Are you saying that you haven't heard from her in five days?"

"Exactly," repeated his mother, miffed. "It's just so rude of her."

"Father, why didn't you contact me the first moment you knew she was missing? Surely, you at least contacted Patrick to see if she was staying with them?"

"Well, yes, I did do that. Apparently, she rode toward home as soon as the reception was over. Then..." Albert shrugged. "Nobody knows."

"Again, why didn't you get word to me?"

"We know how important your work is and didn't want to bother you for no reason." Amelia tried to justify her lack of concern.

"You think Annabelle's disappearance isn't reason enough?"

"Miriam had been told by friends that Annabelle had moved to Charleston."

"If that were true, wouldn't Annabelle have told you? You both know that she wouldn't want to worry you."

Amelia sniffed distastefully. "Well, Miriam says Annabelle's losing interest in you and wanted to make a clean break."

"Oh, she did, did she. Exactly what else did Miriam tell you?"

"Well, she also insinuated that Annabelle has a secret fondness for William Brumley," offered Albert.

"Yes, and now that Annabelle has her dowery back, she is flush," Amelia added knowingly. "Obviously, she doesn't need us anymore."

Jonathan's fury was evident in every word. "Explain to me how a woman as ruthless as you know Miriam to be convinced you to believe such blatant and obvious lies?" He stared straight at his mother. "You must have wanted to believe her. You wanted to do nothing."

"I wanted no such thing," mewed Amelia. "But she was so credible."

"No, Mother, she wasn't. You wanted every lie that Miriam told to be true," he chastised. "Didn't you realize that Annabelle could have been thrown by her horse and lay dying in a ditch or kidnapped by British soldiers?"

"We never meant..." Albert stuttered. "It never occurred to us. Not after Miriam's explanations."

"If she is hurt in any way, I will never forgive you! You both turned your backs on her, and after all she has done for you."

Jonathan continued, "Father, do you know who rode blindly into the swamp, surrounded by British soldiers, to let me know that you had been kidnapped?" He pointed a finger at Albert.

"Annabelle?"

"Right. Belle risked her life to save yours without a thought for her own safety."

"And, Mother, who rode through those same swamps at night to find me and warn there was an arrest warrant waiting for me if I showed my face?"

"Your fiancée, of course." Amelia was finally beginning to see the errors of her ways.

"So, what the hell was wrong with you? How could you both abandon the love of my life? She could be lost to us forever." Jonathan still couldn't believe that his parents could have been so callous.

"Son, I am so sorry. Miriam just seemed to know. She was so sure that Annabelle was fine and doing exactly what she pleased."

"It boggles the mind that you two would believe anything that woman says." He paced. "Father, did you forget it was Miriam who helped plan your capture and almost got you killed?"

"I'm so ashamed."

"And, Mother, you knew that she was in cahoots with Percy and Brumley to have me hanged."

"I remember, but we thought she had changed." Amelia cried. How easily she and Albert had been deceived.

He was thoroughly bushed. "Enough!" Needing to be alone to reason things out, he walked onto the porch and cleared his head in an attempt to figure his next step.

He could sense his father's presence behind him. "Where is this prolific purveyor of lies?"

"She took one of the horses out for a ride around the property," Albert answered. "She'll be back soon."

Jonathan turned to face his father. "From this point on, we are going to work together as a family, and we are going to find my fiancée. Now, do you have any ideas?"

"Well, if something nefarious were to have happened to her, it would have taken place between here and the Mercantile. Don't you think?"

"Yes, I'm going to change clothes and eat quickly; then I'll follow her tracks from Goose Creek," Jonathan asserted.

"And I'll send out messengers to all our neighbors to be on the look-out for anything suspicious."

Amelia joined in the effort. "I'll go through her room to see if there is any sign of packing or reason to believe she left purposefully."

"Nothing matters now but finding Annabelle," Amelia and Albert said in tandem.

"Let's get started," Jonathan agreed.

Chapter 35

Surreptitiously, William Brumley arrived at the Warrenton estate. Although familiar with all its comings and goings, he kept a darting eye on his surroundings. Waves of paranoia had been disturbing his concentration lately, and only the curative tonic in his little green bottle seemed to soothe his mind. After a quick swig, he hunkered down to wait for Miriam's arrival. To pass the time, he pondered his future. He could not have come this far without her. After all, it had taken a great deal of cunning for Miriam to pull off the ruse. He could only imagine how she had been able to keep the dogs from his door. Although fond of her, it was Annabelle that he truly desired. But for the time being, it would be necessary to keep Miriam on a tight leash. However, her role in this scam should be rewarded. Perhaps, he would share Annabelle's fortune with her – a small share, of course.

As of today, William's bank account registered nil. He had accrued a great deal of debt in coordinating his upcoming wedding, and his vouchers would soon be coming due. Of course, he could always board a ship back to England to avoid prosecution, but that would be such a waste. When he succeeded in making Annabelle his wife, he envisioned himself as an envied businessman to be reckoned with.

Annabelle herself remained the biggest obstacle. William cringed every time he encountered the she-cat in his locked suite. Growing weary and frustrated with her incessant screaming, he had to fend off her kicks and fist-pummeling. He would not long stand for it nor would he be humiliated at his own wedding. So, how could he convince her to cooperate? Before overthinking turned to paranoia, he again opened his bottled cure and swallowed.

Looking out from his hidden position, he watched as Miriam made her way to the barn's open double doors. He observed her peruse the area with caution before handing out carrots and apples to the livestock.

By the time she had finished, William crept up beside her. Enfolding her arm while kissing her cheek, he led her to a quiet place directly below the hayloft. William brushed off the straw on two nearby rickety chairs.

"Did you have any trouble slipping away?" William sat down, turning to face her.

"No, none. I always go for a ride about this time."

"After today, you won't have to worry about prying eyes any longer. Remember, tonight you're coming to the manor to stay. Annabelle is more difficult than I anticipated, and I need you to convince her to be more cooperative."

"I'm sorry, but I don't think she'll listen to me. Have you forgotten? There's no love lost between us."

"Maybe you can chip away at her defenses. In time, I know you'll prevail, but for the moment, there is something urgent you must take care of. Annabelle will not allow anyone near her with a tape measure, so I need you to meet with the dressmaker. You're close enough in size." He continued, "I'd like you to be fitted for the wedding gown. When it is complete, the laces and bows, plus finishing touches can be applied."

"Making adjustments sounds like fun, but convincing Annabelle to wear it could be a bit dicey."

"Don't worry, by that time, I'll have convinced her to behave." He kept thoughts of possible forceful means to himself.

"Whatever you say. But I suggest you stop mollycoddling her."

"Stop giving advice; we'll both get what we want in the end." His tone was ominous.

"I believe you, William, you always did have a remarkable imagination when it came to getting what you want," she responded lightly, as she leaned over and kissed him meaningfully.

Her overt gesture broke his concentration. He pulled away and quickly changed the subject.

"Most of the invitations have been returned. The majority have accepted. I've had to hire extras to clean and prepare my manor for the wedding. The staff have been given instructions to decorate both the parlor and the adjoining room. And my favorite part – an elegant carriage, covered with flowers and ribbons will be awaiting our honeymoon departure."

"Sounds magnificent. I see you left no stone unturned. I'm sure it will be one of Charleston's most memorable events."

"Then why am I anxious all the time?" he puzzled. "My headaches are becoming worse. I'm hoping when this is over and all has gone well, I'll finally find peace."

"Well, just remember, I'll be by your side all the way. So, you can stop obsessing. You know I'm more than capable to take care of everything," she emphasized. "There's nothing we can't accomplish together."

"I feel relief just knowing that you're on my side." He retrieved his bottle, then took Miriam in his arms kissing her like a lover.

She cooed. "I've missed this. I can't wait for us to be a couple again."

"You've taken a great load off my shoulders. I'll do anything to make you happy," he lied.

She smiled seductively, as she pulled him closer. "This is a good place to start."

William and Miriam had no idea that Sophie was lying on a pile of sweet hay high above them in the loft. The little girl had fallen asleep while playing with her pet hamster in her favorite hidey-hole. She was awakened from her slumber by the unwelcome voices of that hateful man who tried to steal the manor and mean Miriam. She held an instinctive distrust of both.

For that reason, Sophie remained quiet as a barn mouse. The ten-year-old almost broke the silence when the words 'kidnap' and 'Annabelle' drifted upwards. But she was able to stifle her gasp and listen more intently. Sophie discerned that the Englishman had kidnapped Annabelle with Miriam's help. It took every bit of willpower to remain undetected until they left.

Not far behind Miriam, Sophie ran toward the manor. Making sure the woman didn't see her, she lagged behind until Miriam had entered the back stairs. Then she began to run as fast as her little legs would carry her to the front door.

"Uncle Albert! Aunt Amelia! I know where to find Annabelle! I know where she is!"

At the sound of her plea, Jonathan stepped outside to meet her at the steps. The moment she reached him, he swung her into his arms.

"Oh, Mr. Jonathan, I know where milady is. I heard every word. It's that horrid Mr. Brumley and Miss Miriam. They're in cahoots. They talked about kidnapping her. I think she's locked in a room at his manor. They kept talking about a wedding. I'm thinking he's going to force milady to marry him. You must save her, you must."

"What a brave girl you are." Tamping down his fury, Jonathan gave Sophie a quick hug before putting her down. "Where's Miriam now?"

"She's in the house. I saw her go in the back door when I was running from the barn."

"Sophie, because of you, I'll be able to find Annabelle and bring her home," he spoke reassuringly. "I wish I had time to spend with you, but for now, you must run into the kitchen with Daisy and have a bit of early tea. But, when I return with Annabelle, you'll be the first one she'll want to see. She'll want to thank you, too."

"I am a little hungry." She appeared completely at ease by Jonathan's words, before scampering off.

Jonathan angrily took two steps at a time to confront Miriam. He reached her door with pounding raps.

Her handmaiden opened the door and explained that her lady was unable to receive now and immediately tried to close the door on Jonathan.

He stopped her by slamming the door wider. "Leave. Now."

In shock, her eyes almost bulged out of her head. "But…"

"Now!" He bellowed.

She ran past him without a backward glance.

Jonathan walked confidently into the room, finding Miriam settled in a corner chair with a book. "Where is she? And don't waste my time pretending you're innocent. I'm not leaving this room until you spill out the entire outrageous scheme you and Brumley cooked up." He was on the warpath. "So, unless you want to find yourself in prison for kidnapping and murder, start talking. If you lie to me even once, I will make sure you spend the rest of your life in prison."

His uncompromising tone made Miriam shiver with fear. "Murder? I never killed anyone."

"I know your secret," he stated nonchalantly. "Francis Marion received a copy of the magistrate's report on Percy's death. On the way home, I passed the spot where his body was found so I took a closer look. Imagine my surprise when I saw the crooked wagon tracks of that old hay wagon you drive to town. And we both know you're the only one who owns a derringer."

"That crazy bastard attacked me!"

"I believe you, but I doubt the magistrate will care."

"I'll cooperate if you promise to leave me out of it."

"Nope. You made your bed."

Her fear showed he was getting his point across. "You've depleted my goodwill with all your lies and dirty schemes. My parents will never be the same, knowing how easily you made fools of them. Damn, woman, you just keep sinking lower and lower."

"It seems I'm out of options, so let's get this over with." Miriam gritted her teeth. She could feel her future darken into oblivion.

"Start at the beginning and leave nothing out."

For the next fifteen minutes, Jonathan listened to all the details of Brumley's unseemly ploy. The longer she talked, the more infuriated he became. It enflamed him to hear how proud and eager she seemed. This destructive deception had all been just a game to her.

But it was the forced wedding that sickened Jonathan the most. More than anything, he wanted to find his friends and trounce everyone involved in this criminal debacle. Yet, if he did that, it might destroy Annabelle's reputation. No one would believe that she innocently spent days in Brumley's bedroom – alone. He must find a way to save both her person and her standing in the community. No one could know the details of her kidnapping. The populace would believe the worst, and her good name would lay in tatters.

After absorbing everything Miriam had to say, Jonathan reflected on the entire situation, hoping to find a practical option. A smile crossed his face as inspiration bloomed into a perfect solution. He believed that although subtle, his ingenuous plan would punish Brumley more than a good thrashing ever could.

"Do you think he will be able to convince Annabelle to actually go through with this marriage?" he asked Miriam.

"I'm not sure; she's pretty stubborn. But I do know that he will stop at nothing to get his way."

"Well, then, you're to go back to his house, as planned, and continue to assist him in this farce of a marriage, as though nothing has changed." Jonathan was thinking aloud while his notion rumbled around in his head. He just needed a few more facts to make sure it worked.

"You trust me not to spill the beans?"

"Not entirely, but when I explain my plan, I think you'll realize it is to everyone's benefit."

"You sound pretty sure of yourself."

"First and foremost, I want you tell Annabelle everything you and I will have discussed. This will ease her mind and prepare her for what is to come."

"What is to come?"

"Our ground-plan."

"What are you talking about?" Miriam was puzzled.

"Listen closely; I think you'll find it right in your wheelhouse."

Chapter 36

At first, Miriam's confrontation with Jonathan had left her shaken and worried. After digesting his proposal in detail for Annabelle's release, she had to admit that it was doable. His ingenious plan would allow William's comeuppance and safeguard Annabelle's reputation. Better yet, she, herself, would be spared the shame and humiliation she so justly deserved. So, with no choice but to adhere, she grudgingly returned to William's manor as planned.

On her arrival, Miriam quickly pleaded fatigue and isolated herself from William. With no prying eyes, she paid a visit to Annabelle, intending to keep her promise to Jonathan. She was surprised to see a guard posted at Annabelle's door. Ignoring his inquisitive gaze, she knocked softly. "Annabelle, it's Miriam. Open the door; we need to talk."

In moments, the door opened a crack. Miriam slipped in before Annabelle could voice opposition. "I have news from Jonathan. He just returned from Marion's camp this afternoon. And he went berserk when he heard you were missing, and he had not been notified."

"I thought he knew and just didn't care," Annabelle whispered, her throat raw from all the screaming and protests.

"Nothing could be further from the truth. Now please, sit down. Allow me to inform you of what you can expect on your wedding day."

"There is nothing on this earth that could make me marry that odious man!"

"Jonathan would never let that happen. He loves you too much." Miriam took hold of Annabelle's hands and explained her fiancé's plan in detail.

Relieved and no longer suspicious, Annabelle assessed herself and the wedding. The full-length mirror reflecting her image by candlelight showed a haggard woman ready for change. "I'm such a mess. Would you arrange to have some hot water drawn for my bath?"

"Of course," Miriam was relieved that Annabelle was cooperative to the very last detail. "I'll have someone up here immediately."

Leaning back in the claw-footed tub, Annabelle felt her energy and courage returning. Her despair and hopelessness had been replaced by Miriam's words of hope and trust. She was looking forward to tomorrow's festivities, because at the end of the day, Jonathan would be hers. That is, if God forbid, nothing went awry.

The next morning, William wakened, feeling confident that the day ahead would be everything he had dreamed and planned. It delighted him to hear that Annabelle had ordered a honeymoon bath. In his delusion, he just knew that she was finally compliant and obliged to walk down the aisle into his arms. After taking another swig of his special tonic, he grew more self-assured. Lining up the staff in the foyer like Percy would have, he barked out orders with explicit instructions. Each vision of pomposity was met by his pointed finger, and every grandiose detail was not left to chance. With that taken care of, William and Miriam met for breakfast in the dining room to discuss the day's events.

"As you can see, I don't really need you to help with any preparations. I want you to concentrate on Annabelle. Make sure she stays calm and is prepared to grace the stairway when the music starts. Do you think you can accomplish that?"

"I convinced her to bathe, didn't I?"

"You are a treasure, Miriam. Indeed, you are."

"I told you not to worry. That I'd take care of everything."

"I never doubted you. And I don't want to lose you. After we receive the dowry, we can decide our future. Please tell me you'll stay."

"I think I can make that happen." She looked at William with a lover's smile. "Is there anything else I can do for you before you tie the knot?" Her hand touched his.

Leaning forward, he pulled her closer with a greedy kiss. Then standing, William cupped Miriam's hand, leading her to a small downstairs bedroom that he had been using since Annabelle's arrival. Without guilt or pause, they both entered and proceeded to consummate their future relationship.

Mid-afternoon arrived when Jonathan tied his horse to a tree on the back side of William's property. Unobtrusively, he made his way around Brumley's manor to observe the actions and movement of the staff. The whole scene made him nauseous. What torment Annabelle must have endured, thinking that she was to spend the rest of her life with a man she detested.

While the staff were busy making last-minute preparations on the front veranda, Jonathan remained undetected behind some evergreen bushes – all the while checking a row of upstairs windows. He recognized the rose trellis beneath the second-floor window next to William's suite, that Miriam had already told him about. This was where Annabelle resided, and luckily, a wrought-iron balcony positioned above it would allow him to climb and enter through the outside doors.

As she agreed, Miriam was with Annabelle in William's suite. She took her time styling the young bride-to-be's raven ringlets with white ribbons and gemstone hair pins. Miriam envied all the extravagant preparations and special touches arranged for what should have been her wedding. Taking a breather, Miriam walked outside to view the entry gates adorned with roses and ribbons. Even the sconces and white columns on the front porch were decorated with the same elaborate décor.

She imagined the guests being escorted by two butlers through the foyer with rose petals on the floor, leading the way. Lit candelabras glowing on each entry table enhanced the ambience toward the small ballroom. Rows of covered fabric chairs were lined with bows, attached on the backs. Tears fell from her eyes as she visualized William standing with the magistrate, waiting for his bride to join him. Opposite the ballroom was the parlor, where the serving maids had begun to cover the reception tables with trays of sweetmeats, oysters and gumballs. At one end stood the groom's cake – a fruitcake with icing. The other showcased the bride's white Bundt cake, decorated with charms holding two ribbons baked inside. Miriam didn't think she could stand to see Annabelle and William pull the ribbon in the cake for good luck. When would she have her special moment?

Fortunately, Jonathan found that the trellis beneath Annabelle's window held his weight. He scaled it and hoisted himself over the balcony. The louvered doors opened easily, so he slipped inside to an empty bedroom chamber. Hearing murmurs and hushed tones in the room next door, he knocked softly on the connecting door before entering the adjoining chamber.

Annabelle had been looking out the window for ages, hoping for a glimpse of his arrival. Upon hearing a quiet knock, she turned, almost collapsing with the sight of him. Tears coursed down her face in relief, as his outstretched arms beckoned her. She ran into his welcoming embrace. Jonathan stroked her head while placing gentle kisses on her forehead and face. He dried her tears with his kisses before meeting her mouth with his. Even though Annabelle had prepared herself for Jonathan's entrance, it still made her heart swell uncontrollably.

"I can't believe you're really here!" Annabelle sobbed. "I thought I'd never see you again. That you'd never find me."

"You should know that I would search for you until the end of time."

"I didn't. I thought I had lost my chance. There was so much I wanted to tell you, especially how much I love you. Really, really love you. Our last night together was magical; I just couldn't bring myself to tell you."

"I knew you felt embarrassed and shy. It's all my fault for not being more understanding and leaving so abruptly."

Suddenly, Annabelle was filled with hope. Embraced in the arms of the man she loved, she asked playfully. "How about we recreate our last evening together? With practice perhaps, you'll be able to make all my insecurities disappear." She smiled at him sweetly.

"No doubt." He smiled in return. "It's said practice makes perfect."

"Imagine that. I do believe we're in accord." She reached to put her arms around his neck.

He, in turn, pulled her close. "I believe I'll begin at the top of your head and continue to the tips of your toes." She blushed.

Impatiently, he began to kiss her with renewed passion.

Knock, knock. Miriam opened the door and walked in briskly. "No time to waste. This show's about to begin. Time to get dressed." She stopped short as she caught the two lovers jump apart. "Sorry," she continued. "But we have a wedding to attend and little time to prepare. Jonathan, you'll need to leave us. We'll see you after the ceremony."

"But there shouldn't be any ceremony," Annabelle shrieked in horror.

"Didn't I caution you to trust me?" Holding her tightly, Jonathan reiterated. "Yes."

"Annabelle, we need to dress," Miriam insisted. "Remember what I told you? Just stick to the plan."

Annabelle inhaled deeply. "Let's do it. I'm ready."

Jonathan kissed Annabelle's cheek and squeezed her hand before leaving. Miriam crossed the room and laid Annabelle's wedding dress over the canopy bed. She picked up the hairbrush from the vanity and arranged the hair pins next to the bridal hat with veil. Then she reopened the door and relayed to a passing girl. "Tell Mr. Brumley that his bride will be ready."

Annabelle concurred. "The bride will be ready, indeed." She began to tremble, hoping for everything to go as planned.

Chapter 37

Jonathan was able to ascertain that most of the guests were already seated in their assigned chairs, as he descended the staircase toward the small ballroom. He could hear the pre-nuptial songs being performed by a harpist accompanied by two violinists.

Remaining unobtrusive, he glanced around the corner through the branches of the topiaries to observe the filled room. He noticed rows of wealthy, titled ladies and gentlemen patiently waiting for the ceremony to begin. The question in everyone's mind was, 'Who is this elusive bride?' William had never mentioned her identity. It was odd, to be sure, but undeniably intriguing as well. A quiet buzz and exchanged glances revealed a curiosity and eagerness. Jonathan turned his attention to the front of the aisle, where the magistrate and William stood. He watched as the groom faced the guests like a preening peacock, standing proudly in his formal banyan of frills and ruffles. *What a jackass,* thought Jonathan.

William stood at the altar feeling almost euphoric. Perhaps he had consumed more of his precious Laudanum than was prudent, or maybe he was genuinely elated now that all his dreams were about to come true. Whatever the cause, he couldn't be more pleased. He felt like a king amongst his subjects, as all eyes riveted on him. Finally, he would be respected by his peers. The hallway clock chimed six o'clock, signaling the wedding march song to begin. A staff member adjusted the wedding gown train behind the bride, after securing the hair pins to hold the veil tightly in place over her face.

Excitement grew as the bride glided down the hallway stairs. Her dress was magnificent, fit for the Queen of England. The high-collared Victorian style ensemble with the long, puffy sleeves was exquisite. Gathered silk covered the petticoat skirt in lacy layers of decorative bows, attached from the waist down. Matching tiny bows over the fastening buttons were on the back of the dress. Even the silk hat with thick veiling had been sewn around the entire brim.

The bride rounded the corner to process down the aisle, as the guests rose one by one. She could hear their oohs and aahs over her extravagant wedding dress. She nervously looked ahead at William and wondered if Jonathan was nearby.

William fixated on his bride gliding up the aisle. The nearby bright candelabras began causing double vision and dizziness. With unsteadiness, he realized that he had over imbibed his serum but dared not lean on the magistrate. He had to gain control quickly or he would ruin everything. After taking several deep breaths, he regained his equilibrium and focus.

He cupped the bride's hand in his shaking one. His need for Laudanum overshadowed the repeated vows. It took every bit of willpower and concentration to finish.

He heard as if from a distance. "I now pronounce you man and wife. You may kiss the bride."

William's glassy eyes beamed in anticipation to finally 'have and to hold' the woman of his dreams! How long he had waited. Trembling, sweaty hands raised the veil as he leaned in to kiss his beloved.

He froze. Why was Miriam standing here as his bride? His foggy mind couldn't register the switch; his throat was too constricted to object.

Miriam quickly kissed him to subdue his stunned expression. To avoid his escape, she grasped his arm and hung on tightly. Whispering in his ear, "Unless you want a scandal you will never live down, you will pretend all is well. No one will suspect differently."

"No. No. NO," he began.

Miriam tugged at his sleeve. "We will greet our guests as the perfect couple. Otherwise, I will throw you to the wolves, and you will pay for all your crimes." She enunciated with a fake smile in case the guests were watching.

He exhaled a deep sigh, looking at Miriam like a lost puppy. Then he kissed her cheek, and proceeded docilely, hand in hand to the reception area.

While Miriam and William were faltering at the altar, Annabelle had joined Jonathan to watch the final scene of the wedding saga unfold.

"Now, that's a match made in heaven." Annabelle teased, as she gazed up at a face filled with love and happiness. "Or hell… I just hope that marriage to Miriam will turn out to be a crueler punishment than anything I could have imagined."

"I hate to rush you, but what are we waiting around here for? I'm ready to get out of this prison!" Annabelle exclaimed, as she pulled him toward the front door.

"Don't you want to congratulate the happy couple?" Jonathan asked dryly.

"The only happy couple I'm worried about is us!" she insisted. "Now come on."

"At your service, *mademoiselle*."

"Should we abscond with their wedding carriage?" Annabelle laughed in a teasing fashion.

"That is entirely your choice."

"I've never needed pomp and circumstance. Do you have a better idea?"

"As a matter of fact, I do." He tugged her toward his stallion.

"Are we getting married now?"

"No."

"We'll be married soon?" Annabelle asked.

"As soon as you want."

"No big wedding."

"Lord, no, not after that abomination we just witnessed."

"So, it's honeymoon first?"

"Our honeymoon began the first night we spent together. Now we begin our life as one. Close your eyes and remember the moment we just knew."

She closed her eyes, thinking back in time. A blissful smile beamed like a starry night. "I recall a magical treehouse. It surrounded us like a heavenly cloud, where we were the only two people on earth."

"I remember it well." He grinned, before mounting his stallion, and nestling her in front of him. "Imagine recalling the story to our children of how we fell in love. Do you think they'll ever believe that romance could grow out of the swampy lowlands among the vipers, alligators, and quicksand?"

"Of course, especially if we build our real home next to our storybook dwelling." First teasing, but then, she realized that she belonged here, here in the Low Country of South Carolina, and this was exactly where she wanted to spend the rest of her days.

CPSIA information can be obtained
at www.ICGtesting.com
Printed in the USA
BVHW071020030223
657822BV00009B/128